THE FOREIGNER

THE

PICADOR · NEW YORK

FOREIGNER

FRANCIE LIN

www.picadorusa.com

Picador® is a U.S. registered trademark and is used by St. Martin's Press under license
from Pan Book Limited.

For information on Picador Reading Group Guides, please contact Picador.
E-mail: readinggroupguides@picadorusa.com

Designed by Jonathan Bennett

Excerpt from "The Hollow Men" in *Collected Poems 1909–1962* by T. S. Eliot,
copyright 1936 by Harcourt, Inc., and renewed 1964 by T. S. Eliot. Reprinted by
permission of the publisher.

ISBN-13: 978-0-312-36404-5
ISBN-10: 0-312-36404-0

First Edition: June 2008

10 9 8 7 6 5 4 3 2 1

FOR MY PARENTS

The Duke of She said to Confucius: Where I live, there is an upright man named Gong. When his father stole a sheep, the son spoke out against him.

To which Confucius replied: In my state, the son would protect his father, and the father would protect the son. That is what *we* call righteousness.

—FROM CONFUCIUS, *The Analects,* 13:18

PART 1

CHAPTER 1

IT WAS MY BIRTHDAY, my fortieth year. I am not a sentimental man, and my birthdays have always passed quietly, with a minimum of anguish and fuss, but for some reason, this year, a sense of dejection hung in my chest like a fog as I drove eastbound across the Bay Bridge to meet my mother for dinner. Rain lashed the windshield. A truck had overturned just past the 880 exit, encircled by flares. Farther on, a dog had been run over, the mangled carcass pulled off to the side and left with its golden fur matted and damp. All these things—melancholy, rain, a little accident, a little blood—all of them are, in hindsight, nothing: souvenirs of a happier time. But back then they seemed to me portentous. Maybe they were.

The Jade Pavilion reservation was for 8:00, and the dashboard clock said 7:52. The traffic budged forward. "Come on. Come *on*." My mother hated to be kept waiting; tardiness was the unforgivable sin. I hadn't been late for dinner more than three or four times—respectable, considering that we had had dinner every Friday for fifteen years, with few exceptions. Dinner, usually followed by an overnight stay in my old childhood room, with a Hershey's bar and a nip of whiskey to settle my dreams. I am being unnecessarily poetic here, for my dreams don't need settling. When I was younger, I used to dream of palaces and kingships, and the sight of an enemy flotilla from the turret of a well-defended fort, but now, more often, I dream that I get up, have my breakfast, and take the Powell-Mason streetcar to my office downtown. My dreams and my reality are more or less the same, and I like the regularity and implied balance.

I was bothered, then, when I arrived at the restaurant late and breathless, and found the place nearly empty, my mother nowhere to be seen.

"You want to sit down?" asked the hostess, snapping her gum. Full-blown orange peonies bloomed in her dark hair.

"No, I'll wait outside." I tried not to stare at her. The flowers reminded me of the sweet, tangled sleep I used to have, full of a woman and damp sheets and sunset light spilling all over the floor. The starched white collar of her uniform framed a tender little hollow in her throat, where she fingered a string of milky glass beads.

"I'll . . . I'll wait outside."

The restaurant was tucked into an elbow of a huge strip mall. Out in the mall concourse, I called my mother several times, but only got the reservations service. She owned a motel, the Remada Inn, where she had raised both my brother, Little P, and me. The name "Remada" was an inspired bit of trickery on her part, as people tended to mistake ours for the Ramada Inn, yet the misspelling protected us from charges of fraud. Not that the motel had too much business in any case; it was not convenient to the airport, and the customers were mostly long-term tenants stuck in various states of financial or emotional decline.

My mother despised them all. She had arrived in the United States from Taiwan about forty-five years ago, but in that time she hadn't assimilated so much as grown a prickly, protective shell. Some immigrants were confused or frightened by their dislocation in America, but she tended to see her difference as a mark of the elect. "Americans!" she would say darkly when she heard reports of some social aberration like divorce or pedophilia. She prided herself on speaking very correct English without any slang, but her grasp of detailed grammar and connotations was slippery. In her private grammar, *American* was an epithet with dark, obscure associations, like bottom-feeders glimpsed in the depths of a dirty lake. "Those Americans." "That American." *Those* and *that* deployed like tiny bombs, her scorn and contempt decimating the weak, the dreamy, the lazy, the undecided and naïve—everything she associated with America, with Americans. Divorce, alcoholism, teen pregnancy, unemployment: these, she thought, were the provenance of weak American standards, of a long compromise between comfort and immortality.

Eight-fifteen, eight-twenty. I dialed my mother again: no answer. She had been determined that Little P and I should not be absorbed into the general culture, and accordingly, our childhoods had been strictly regimented, full of paranoia and dour regulations that seemed arbitrary to me now, though at the time I believed that there was some kind of system beneath her injunctions. We were not, for instance, allowed to wear shorts, jean jackets, baseball caps, or thin leather ties, nor were we allowed to stand on outdoor benches or decorative rocks, or the retaining walls of gardens in the park. Soda had to be sipped through a straw and could not be drunk while standing or walking. No girls. Certainly no boys. She had been obsessive about hygiene also, and well into our teens we had to submit to a full inspection of our nethers, back to front. On restless, unhappy nights I can still see the thinning part of her hair as I stand naked on the motel toilet lid, looking down at her probing my dickson clinically with a cotton swab dipped in alcohol.

Eight-twenty-five, eight-thirty. A small, mouse-haired Chinese woman with enormous glasses sat opposite me, finger-dipping into her change purse. She wore a shapeless gray skirt, and her pale, moon-shaped face was framed by thin, wistful plaits. About my age. A nice girl. An accountant, probably. Eight-thirty-five, eight-forty. I crossed my arms and tried to imagine taking her to the Metronome. Under dimmed lights, on the wide parquet, with the broad strokes of a waltz sweeping through the hall, perhaps I could love a woman like this. She didn't look coordinated, but she might be good at the cha-cha at least. Coins spilled from her pocketbook onto the floor; she got down awkwardly on all fours to retrieve them. Perhaps just a waltz then.

The tip of an umbrella planted itself near my foot.

"Hello, Mother."

She had come steaming up the concourse looking fierce, draped in an old blue silk dress and wielding her umbrella like a majorette's baton. I was touched to see that she had put on makeup for the occasion, although her mouth was like a hard little knot in her face, her eyebrows sketched on at an angle of permanent displeasure.

"Hair!" she said, pointing the umbrella at my head.

"I didn't have time to comb it."

She took a tiny brush from her purse.

"Mother!" I ducked, backing away. "Nobody is even looking at me."

"Doesn't matter." The brush hovered and jabbed. "Don't you want to look nice for yourself?"

"Mother—"

We regarded each other silently for a moment, with the old, familiar suspicion and appraisal, so deep and habitual that they were, for us, a kind of love. Up close, the makeup made her look rather hollow and aged. I was wearing the shoes she'd given me as a birthday present, an expensive pair of soft suede Ferragamos, and their rich, understated luster stood in sad distinction to her frayed silk and battered handbag. Defeated, I bent my head and allowed her to groom me with quick, fastidious little licks of the brush, a bit of spit wetting down the hairs.

"Was there a problem at the motel?"

"Police!" she said with relish. "Raid! That guy, that Room 210, he is *parolee* from the north. Oregon. They track him down, they come to take him away. You know I like fairness, so at first I say no way! Are you kidding? You cannot just take my customer away like that! But then I check my book." Her mouth crimped down in a little caret. "He have already paid up front for a week in cash. So take him, I say! Room 210. Here is the key. Not my affair." She gave a little moo of satisfaction and clicked her tongue, making a sound like faint applause.

The mousy woman had brightened when my mother appeared, sitting up straighter and adjusting her plastic frames attentively, and my mother now hailed her.

"Mei Hua! I am glad you could come." She held out her hand to the girl.

"Mother—"

"Just a friend, Emerson," she said casually, as she commandeered Mei Hua and steered her toward the restaurant. "I invite her at the last minute. What is a birthday without friends?"

"But I only made a reservation for two."

She gave me a restrained but significant look. My mother wanted me to get married. This desire had consumed her for so long that it had ceased to be meaningful and was nurtured now with franticness, like a tire spinning uselessly in the snow. Over the years, she had presented me, humiliatingly, to a range of women she found appropriate—all Chinese or Chinese-American, though with variants: tall, fat, myopic, depressed—who appraised me with gimlet hardness behind their demure, almondlike eyes; you could hear pension and interest calculations being totted up in their heads. My mother herself had entered marriage purely as a matter of ritual and practicality. "Love!" she would say dismissively.

"Mother," I repeated.

She gave me a dazzling smile full of teeth and breezed into the Jade Pavilion.

We clustered ourselves at one end of the huge round table, my mother sitting between the woman and me as if to broker the peace. In stony silence the three of us studied the menu, though this was only a formality, since my mother always did the ordering. She summoned the waitress with an impatient snap of the fingers, as one would call a dog, and when she had finished ordering and had wiped all the dinnerware pointedly with her napkin—she thought the Cantonese were dirty—she pinched me under the table.

"Talk," she mouthed, her brows melting a little with the force of disapproval. I looked over at the woman. The plaits, the dull, round face. Eyes magnified alarmingly by the glasses. She had a weak, tremulous smile, and I saw that she had worn what was probably her nicest blouse. The obvious care she had taken with her appearance made me sad, and also enraged: I would have to be kind.

"And what do you do, Mei Hua?" It came out rather strangled. Mei Hua blinked at me.

"I am the accountant." Blink, blink. Her English was not quite native in its propriety; she spoke as if reading from a primer. "And yourself?"

"Myself?"

Again, she blinked worriedly. "What is your professional job?"

"Oh . . ." Looking down, I licked my finger and rubbed at a dash of rollerball ink on my cuff. "I work in finance. Corporate finance." The ink smudged, making blots. "It's not very interesting."

"He is only modest," my mother said lightly, suddenly reaching over and dabbing at the ink with her wetted napkin. "He is the *financial analyst*."

The title, or perhaps just the hushed way my mother said it, must have rung a bell, for Mei Hua lit up like a signboard and regarded me with more confidence. This was irritating.

"You can call it whatever you want." I tugged my sleeve away. "It's still a boring job. A job for peons and drones."

"Modesty," my mother affirmed, giving Mei Hua a knowing glance.

"And a little immoral."

"Emerson!"

"I think it must be very interesting," said Mei Hua.

"Sure. I look for ways to cut costs at mismanaged companies." I popped a shrimp chip in my mouth. "Basically a nice way of saying that I cut jobs, and put honest people out of work so the board members can have their multimillion-dollar condos in Vail and spend their Christmas holiday dogsledding in the Arctic. Nothing more interesting than that!"

"But you are compensated, of course?" asked Mei Hua.

"Of course, of course. Well compensated. I mean, what's a few thousand jobs here or there as long as I get some good scratch out of it? Dental and one annual eye exam too."

"You see?" said my mother, apologetic, as if I were not there. The food was arriving, and she began plying both Mei Hua and me with generous servings of rice and braised tendon and pea greens, almost purring in the warmth of her own benevolence. "His heart is so tender, always caring about the others! Even strangers! And even though his work gives him the moral pain, he sacrifices his principle to support me, to support his family. A good man. A good head of household."

"I can see," said Mei Hua, blinking her gigantic eyes.

"He has always been the good boy."

"Oh, pshaw." I made a self-deprecating moue, but she took me at face value.

"The modesty again." An exchange of looks.

"Listen to her." I chuckled, feeling a little crazed. "Someone once said, 'Mothers are the best lovers.' I guess that's true, if by 'best' they meant 'blind.' Who else would refer to me as a 'boy'? It's my fortieth birthday. Obviously."

"Means nothing," my mother snapped. Then, regaining herself, she smoothed her hair and poured Mei Hua some more tea. "A son is always the little boy to the mother," she explained, filling her own teacup. She filled mine last. "Especially when the little boy is still not married."

"I am sure he will find the right woman *soon,*" said Mei Hua. She had a very flat voice; it sounded like a threat. My mother clutched Mei Hua's arm as if she were drowning.

"You say so, but how?" she said fervently. "He has no interest in seeing the girls! Every day he just work, work, work, and then on Friday, all he want is to have dinner with Mother."

"*What?*" The tea burned my lip. "Hang on, this is for *your* benefit too, you know."

"So it is *my* fault you do not have a wife, is what you are saying." My mother's lip quivered.

"Oh, Mother, please."

"No!" she cried. "Let us be honest with each other! Just say it, say it straight out! You think I am the bad mother."

"I didn't *say* that."

"It is not the words but what they *mean*." She pressed her napkin to her lips. "And it is true! I am the failure. I have failed." Tears rolled down her cheeks like rainwater, a sudden midsummer squall. Crocodile tears, I knew, for she never cried except to extract promises or confessions; when she was truly upset, she was dry as a bone, and dangerously still. Of course Mei Hua didn't know that. She put an awkward arm around my mother's shoulders.

I sighed. "Mother . . ."

"To have failed after all my effort," she went on, lamenting. "Everything I have done, all my life, has been for him. His father and I, we come to this country, we have nothing! We know nothing. But we come here for him to have the better life. I work the business. I buy the clothes. I buy the car. I send him to college. And for what?" Her lips narrowed. "Forty years old today, and no wife. No family. What will he do when I am gone, I ask you?" A fresh burst of tears.

Mei Hua murmured something comforting in Chinese. Both of them looked at me, distant and hostile—me, callous, thick-skinned, the author of their misery.

What kept me from storming out of the restaurant at that moment, though, was the old, undeniable truth that trumped any complaints about injustice: she had sacrificed everything for me, and I had never repaid her. She had given up her relatives, her home, the direct line to her memories; a whole history had been lost, a huge rift in time had been made. How could I ever make that up to her? The question was always there. It had no answer.

Guilt turned quickly to resentment. I was tired of being the torchbearer of the Changs, tired of the low-hanging ghost that never lifted. I watched Mei Hua pour my mother more tea, my mother absorbed in this silly girl the way you pretend interest in your shoe when you are trying to avoid a confrontation.

"What about Little P?" I said.

Instantly, my mother's tears dried up. "What about him?" She swallowed visibly.

"I suppose you think *he's* done his duty by you. Why don't you set up girls for *him*? Why don't you needle him about marrying a Chinese girl, or carrying on the family blood? Maybe because he hasn't been home in almost a decade? Maybe because he never calls or writes? If you think I'm the ingrate . . ."

But then I caught sight of her expression and trailed off. The shock on her face was painful to me, for it seemed to indicate how deeply she still missed him—even after his abandonment, even after all these years. Little P is my mother's favorite. He came into her life so late that she considered him a gift, and I have never had the heart to dispute that claim. Even now I felt a sharp regret for having dredged up his name and wished I'd kept quiet.

Her mouth wobbled without sound as she fumbled with her chopsticks. In her confusion, she looked suddenly very old, and her arm shook a little, setting her rice bowl chittering against the edge of her plate. Mei Hua drew back, alarmed. Blindly, my mother reached out for her teacup. The hand was brown and disfigured by the heat and pain of arthritis. I put the cup in her hand for her and watched her lift it jerkily, slopping tea in her bowl.

"I'm sorry, Mother." I touched her elbow.

She shrugged me off. I said nothing.

She turned to Mei Hua. "How many years do you have?"

Mei Hua frowned. "I am thirty-one."

"Thirty-one." She sniffed. "At your age, I have one son already. A husband. A *family*. Tell me, what do you have?"

"I?" Mei Hua looked stunned.

"You young people," she went on harshly. "You think my life is a joke. You look down on me, you pity me. You think the tradition, the marriage is a burden only. You are the little American child all your life, the little Peter Pan, never to grow up. No obligation. No loyalty. No sense of the future."

Mei Hua blinked. "I—"

"I am not feeling well," my mother interrupted. She put a hand to her bony chest abruptly. "I want to go home."

"Mother—"

But there was no stopping her. Holding her purse under one arm, she walked unevenly toward the door, trailing pride and hurt behind her like a veil. After a few paces, she turned.

"I have never like this place," she said with passion.

"Mother." I tried not to shout. "We've been eating here for years. Come back and sit down."

She shook her head violently, wiping her nose with a tissue. "Too dark in here. Too salty. A disappointment," she said, voice breaking. "Every single time."

She left.

The check arrived at this juncture, on a scratched plastic tray. Mei Hua went to the ladies' room while I paid the bill. The restaurant was nearly empty. All the other patrons had gone home, and the waitstaff had slipped into the insular, chatty world of stagehands, joking, shouting, confessing to one another as they swept the floor and stacked the chairs upside down on the tables. All of them were recent immigrants, and as I sat and waited for my receipt, I had a brief spasm of envy. They weren't rich, but they knew where their pleasures and loyalties lay. They had memories of a damp summer in Guangdong, repeated over many years; the smell of a Chinese street; the look of a Chinese sun descending over a Chinese shop. All of these things, taken together, defined something true, something uncompromised about them.

My mother hadn't waited for her fortune cookie. With a dull, familiar feeling of anomie, I cracked both cookies open and pulled out the little slips. The first one said: LOVE IS LIKE THE SPRING RAIN, TO AWAKEN ON THE UNPRODUCTIVE GROUND. The other said: YOU ARE THE GREATEST PERSON IN THE WORLD.

CHAPTER 2

I DROVE MEI HUA HOME AND WALKED her to her door, where she grabbed me by the shoulders and tongued me with some savageness.

"For your birthday," she said, her breath ragged as she pulled back.

"Oh," I said, dabbing the corner of my mouth discreetly with a thumb. "Thank you. Sorry about all that. You know, at dinner. With my mother."

"But she is *right*," said Mei Hua. "We are so selfish, the young people. We are wanting the dedication to everlasting family. We must start *now*." She hauled me in for another long kiss.

"*Yes,*" I gasped, breaking away. "Certainly very selfish. No dedication. Good-bye."

"Will call you!" Her voice echoed down the little alley of condos as I hurried to the car.

I debated driving back to the city, but the force of habit was too strong, and instead I went to the Remada for my usual overnight in my old room. When I reached the lot, the lights in the motel office were still on. I knew I should find my mother, should apologize, but I was too tired just then to summon up energy for the wheedling, the coaxing, the thousand little tricks that reconciliation would require.

I dragged my carryall up to balcony level, let myself in, poured a nip of Jack Daniel's. Nothing dispelled the day's melancholy, not the blue light from the TV nor the glow of the bedside sconces. Mei Hua's strong, bitter licorice taste lingered in my mouth; even the whiskey didn't chase it. She was annoying, and rapacious, and I felt nothing like love for her. But my body claimed otherwise, and continued to claim otherwise as I unwrapped my Hershey's bar and sat down on the bed.

My mother pervaded the room. She was in the stiff curtains and dark ruched bedspread, the caustic smell of ammonia; you breathed her in wherever you went. I could have been married years ago, if my mother hadn't interfered. J, the love of my life, twenty years older, sex and mystery embodied in her languorous, full form. That *American* girl, my mother called her.

I took another sip of whiskey. In time, I might have made J love me—though my mother would never believe it. The old argument between us had never been laid to rest; it ran like groundwater under every word and gesture. You can have American friends, my mother would say, and American neighbors, and American boss, but when it counts, for the family, you marry a Chinese. What does the foreigner know about love? she would ask. What means love to them? What means marriage? No amount of reason would shake her faith in the unbridgeable distance between the ways of loving. If I argued that, at least, the Americans were happy, her response was always one of great scorn: *"Happiness! If all you want is happiness! If you want to settle for happiness!"*

But what else was there? I fumbled for the whiskey, knocking over my glass.

The answer came tiredly, inevitably, from the history of our long dispute: *an idea,* she would say—just *an idea,* and nothing more, as if this should explain everything, should counter all loneliness and longing.

"Bullshit," I muttered. "I can't live on an idea." I got down on my hands and knees and found the highball under the bed. "What do you *want* from me? I gave up my life to be with you. Friday night dinner. Half your health care premium."

I remembered J in the dim parking lot, the luminous white curve of her shoulder showing in the dark, the feel of her fingers brushing up against mine in secret. I had worshiped her, my first—my only—love.

Still, given time, I might have gotten over her, if not for the other treachery. My mother. I took another swig of whiskey. It had been years before my mother had confessed to me what she had done with the letters J sent me after I left: how she had secretly removed them from the mail and sent them back, marked PERSON UNKNOWN. By the time I discovered this, J had moved, seemingly disappeared, and I couldn't find her. Too late to ask now what she'd wanted to say to me. The possibilities sometimes tormented me at night: she loved me; she was lonely; she thought of me constantly.

Or maybe it had been bad news: she was in love with someone else; she was getting married—some other man, more worldly, less timid, less weak.

But it didn't matter anymore. The chance was gone, and that uncertainty, that idea of an alternate life, would always be with me. I'd never said a word to my mother about her betrayal. Useless to be angry, I had thought, when all that was so long ago—but somehow I couldn't let it go, not quite. I hated, suddenly, my old bedroom, its hybrid look of anonymity and home: the individually wrapped cups by the sink, the water-stained carpet, the old crack running down the wall. The crack used to resemble a map, the shape of Brazil, or Africa, or some far-flung river. Now it was just a crack in the plaster, in the room I had never left.

"Such a disappointment," I repeated. "Such a disappointment."

I tossed the whiskey bottle away, grabbed my trousers, and flung open the door. Some kind of conviction or decision had taken root, so deep that even I didn't know what it was. But it would begin with an accounting; it would begin with a confrontation of facts.

I stormed down the stairs to the parking lot and unlocked the front office, slamming the door behind me.

"Mother!"

Somehow, the night had passed into early morning, and the lucent predawn light showed weakly at the blinds. The back room was dark and studded about with glass jars full of her medicinal herbs. On the far windowsill, a large, warty piece of galangal hung suspended in its matrix like an embryo, while a ceramic *plat* on the sideboard labored under ten tiers of lucky bamboo. The wooden sofa, the carpets, the love seat—she had draped everything in plastic; she had covered the floor with protective vinyl sheets.

Raggedly, I ripped the plastic sheeting off the armchair and struggled to tear it to bits, knocking into the bamboo and stumbling over the coffee table. A jar of dried rose hips fell and shattered on the floor. Panting, I drew up short and wrenched open the connecting door to her apartment. "Mother!"

The narrow hallway was clean but dark, and the garlanded portraits of her parents hung at the end, stern, impassive, the candles on the shelf beneath them blown out.

"Mother!"

In the kitchen, a plate of sliced apple sprinkled with salt browned on the counter. The bathroom was freshly scrubbed, and her false teeth kept silent counsel in a dish of mineral water. She had mended and washed a pair of panty hose and hung them to drip-dry on a makeshift line across the tub.

In the bedroom, a hand—bluish, cold, fingers curled toward the baseboard. She had been putting a handful of fake flowers in a vase, the stems now scattered violently across the floor.

"Mother?"

I walked over to her, stooping down to gather up the broken bouquet. Carefully I placed it back in her hand and closed the fingers around it.

Sirens approached. The noise grew louder and louder, until it seemed to be right inside my head. On and on it went, the snarling, the horns, the high-pitched wailing, and then, just at the point of pain, it passed. Perspiration ran like tears down my face. I got up and found the phone in the front office.

"Nine-one-one," said the dispatcher. A pause. "This is 911. Hello? Hello? Can you hear me?"

I opened my mouth to give her the address of the Remada Inn. But instead I heard a flat voice issuing a strange, fragmentary bulletin.

"My mother is dead," it said. "My mother is dead."

CHAPTER 3

O F COURSE SHE WAS NOT DEAD, not exactly, or—rather—
not yet. The paramedics arrived in a welter of lights and
noise that drew all our customers out of their rooms; they milled
around the parking lot in varying states of undress. As they
watched, the attendants wrapped her up, lifting her into the
ambulance with a professional efficiency that stunned me, for it
seemed to make light of the pale transformation lying silent on the
gurney. One paramedic even hummed as we sped to the hospital.

The diagnosis was heart failure, a stopping of the heart that left
her comatose, her body curled into a faint fetal position in the
hospital bed. I stayed with her, dozing on the couch, watching the
brisk rotation of nurses come through.

At work, the annual reports swam before my eyes. A week, two
weeks passed, and she didn't wake up, although sometimes she
spoke, a broken Chinese word here or there that I couldn't understand. I checked in on the motel, where her rooms and mine

remained exactly as we had left them: the scattered flowers on her floor, my empty whiskey bottle and unmade bed.

This white period of waiting might have gone on forever, except one evening the doctor came in and closed the door deliberately behind him. I had just arrived at the hospital after a long, hazy day of meetings and could not quite register what the man was saying as he put a piece of X-ray film in my hands.

"What's this?" I asked.

Again he spoke, urgent, directing the film toward the overhead light and moving a pencil across it. The image was indecipherable to me, tissues of white on black, like galaxies.

"Her pelvic bone," said the doctor. "Eaten away. There. And there."

I stared, could not make sense of it. "And?"

"'And?'" The doctor withdrew the film, blew out a breath. "Mr. Chang, why hasn't she come in before? With a cancer this advanced, we don't know where to start."

"I didn't know," I whispered. "She never said a word."

"No pain?" He sounded skeptical. "No fatigue?"

"She wouldn't have said." I thought of her trembling hand around the teacup the night of my birthday dinner. "She was taking herbs. Chinese medicines. I suppose she was treating herself."

"Herbs?" He looked like he was going to kill me.

His pager went off. He glanced down at it briefly, moved toward the door. Then relented, slightly. "I'm very sorry, Mr. Chang. I'll be in tomorrow morning to go over her course of treatment with you."

"Wait!"

He paused, half out in the corridor.

"You said . . . Is she . . . in pain?" I asked. The idea had bothered me since the night she had been admitted.

"Maybe," he said. Then, reluctant: "Well, yes. Probably." He ran a hand over his thinning hair, came forward, patted my arm reassuringly with a big paw. "But she's too far along to know it."

When he was gone, I drew my chair up to the bedside and took her hand. The nurses came and went, their footsteps sharp and echoing in the halls.

I don't know how long I sat there. At dusk, I thought I felt her stir a little. She made a small sound in the back of her throat.

"Mother?"

But it was nothing, only a catch of her breath. She lay there, sleeping deeply in her bed, beneath the surface of consciousness, like a person floating just below the waterline in a river. I felt, suddenly and very surely, that I could wake her up if I wanted to; I could call her up out of that subterranean world of dreams. But then whatever pain she was suffering would become real to her, reclaimed along with her motel and her account books and her pride and sorrows. Already, perhaps, she had suffered for months without saying so.

The room had gotten colder; shadows drew close around me. In retrospect it seems that a hand other than mine had grasped the tubing and loosed the clamp enough to allow the morphine drip to accelerate—1.00, 1.50, 1.75 milliliters. The evening sky had darkened the room enough that objects appeared gray and impersonal. I have no recollection of intent. I remember carefully removing my shoes and then lying down on the bed next to my mother, trying to warm her thin, curled body.

And when, in the morning, I awoke, she was staring at me, head fallen to one side, looking into my face with uncharacteristic fondness, a soft, cloudy expression. Her lips were parted as if to speak, but whatever she meant to say to me I would never know. Years ago, in the motel parking lot, I'd come across an injured gypsy moth, hand-size; ants had swarmed around it, industriously breaking down the feathered body and fins while the great laboring creature flexed its wings mightily, like the slow blink of an eye, or the beat of a heart, failing. Each day there was a little less of it. Like the death of an emperor, or the slow passing of a legend into nothing— a thready skeleton, its splendor now gone.

"EMERSON CHANG?"

The receptionist looked up crossly from her desk, a cigarette in hand.

"Yes?"

She puffed at me. "You can go in. Mr. Carcinet is ready for you."

I was at the lawyer's, a week or two after the memorial service. My mother had named Pierre Carcinet the executor of her will. The man had been a friend of my father's when my father was alive, and although my mother had never liked Mr. Carcinet personally, I suppose she had named him executor because he was a lawyer, and she had always liked the propriety of doing things through official channels. I had met him at the service. A tall, cadaverous man with a voice that rasped like a twig. The receptionist directed me toward an inner door.

Mr. Carcinet sat behind a massive ebony desk, smoothing his tie as if it were a pet. He was long and sallow and angular, bald as a skull, with something fastidious about his ashy-looking mouth.

"Ah, Mr. Chang." He stood up and indicated a chair, moving an enormous pile of papers to one side of his desk in order to look more directly at me. As I sat down, he put his fingertips together and regarded me silently over their tented peaks, once in a while putting the tip of a gray tongue to his top lip, as if perplexed. His huge bony elbows jutted out on the arms of his chair as he rocked back and forth minutely.

"Well," he said at last. "I'd like to say I'm sorry once again for your loss. I understand that you and your mother were quite close, and this must be very hard for you."

"I suppose so," I said, resenting the sympathy. His vast, shiny black desk was out of proportion to the tiny airless room. I could see my face distorted and reflected in the glossy finish. I hadn't shaved since the service—had not been out of my apartment at all, in fact. A sparse, erratic beard stuck out in strands from my chin, and my suit was rumpled; my hair was too long and matted like a thatch.

"As it involves the motel," Pierre Carcinet was saying. "The"— a shuffling of papers—"the . . . Remada? Inn? The will must be probated in order for any transfer of property to take place. This can take a while, I warn you, so the sooner we get the process started, the better, yes?"

He paused for a moment. Then for some reason he lowered his voice.

"You have a brother, correct, Mr. Chang? But I understand he hasn't been, shall we say, very *close* in some time?"

"I haven't seen my brother in almost ten years."

I felt suddenly cold at the mention of Little P. It had been so long since I'd discussed him with anybody that, without quite knowing it, I had come to feel proprietary about his existence. It had never occurred to me that my mother would discuss him with anyone else. I saw his dark face fleetingly, almost Russian in its long proportions. The memory gave me an unexpected wrench.

". . . tied up in property," Pierre Carcinet pronounced, looking at me expectantly. When I didn't say anything, he put his hands on the desk and leaned forward.

"This *means*," he said, enunciating, "that you and your brother have quite a responsibility on your shoulders. If you should decide to sell the motel, I hope you will confer with me from time to time in order to make sure there are no complications."

"I haven't thought about selling the motel at all," I said, offended. "It's the family home."

Mr. Carcinet gave me a long, penetrating look and rubbed his chin reflectively for a while.

"Well, this brings me to the, shall we say, unpleasantness," he said at last. "I don't mean to be blunt, Emerson, but I'm afraid the decision about the motel will not be yours to make."

His thin face behind the desk wavered a little, then stabilized.

"What do you mean?"

"I mean," he said steadily, "that in her will, your mother left the Remada Inn to your brother, Peter Chang. You will receive some of her stock holdings and a smaller property she owns in Taiwan, but the motel goes to Peter."

Mr. Carcinet seemed to be fading into the distance; each time I looked up, he appeared farther and farther away, sad and puzzled across an expanding lake of glossy desktop. He stood up and bent toward me.

"Are you all right?" came his voice distantly. "Emerson? Water," he said, conferring with someone else, and then a buzz of voices like bees on a screen door.

Slowly he came back into view, along with a flowered Dixie cup full of tepid water.

"I'm all right," I said, straightening up. The water tasted like chlorophyll, and I choked a little as I drank it.

Mr. Carcinet put his hands in his pockets and sat down again. "I'm sorry, Emerson," he said. "I'm sure this is a shock." He sighed. "It might console you somewhat to know that the property in Taiwan is already in your name, at least. Your mother was a detail-minded soul. If you like, I can check into the value of your equity. I'm sure it's—you could say—substantial."

I shook my head, mute. "It's not the *money,*" I managed to say, inadequately. And it really wasn't the money. It was driving my mother to the grocery store each week; to the bank every other week; repairing her sinks; preparing her tea; presiding over her monthly mah-jongg game; washing her hair in the kitchen sink every third Friday. Vacations spent squiring her around Niagara Falls, New York City, Yosemite. The Statue of Liberty. The pale veined parchment of her arm against the hospital bed, trailing clear tubes.

Mr. Carcinet offered me a hard fruit candy from a tin, but I wasn't hungry. He picked one out himself with his long, flat fingertips.

"Now part of the reason I called you in here, Emerson, is to ask if you have any idea where your brother is. I sent him a letter a couple of weeks ago at the Taipei address your, ah, mother provided, but

I have not received a reply, and there is no phone number or e-mail."

"I don't know where he is," I said dully. "I got a postcard from him last Christmas, but there wasn't a return address. I think he's still in Taipei. The address my mother gave you should be current. I don't have a number for him."

"And there is no other way of contacting him? Relatives? Friends?"

I thought about this. There was my mother's brother, of course, whom I had never met. After my mother died, I had called him at the number in her address book, but my Chinese was so poor that the person on the other end had hung up on me. I didn't know any of Little P's friends.

An idea, only half-articulate, took shape in the dull recess of my mind.

"I could go," I said.

Mr. Carcinet rolled the candy from one cheek to another.

"Go where?"

"To Taipei. I can arrange time off from work next month. I'll track him down. Maybe I can get him to come back with me. At least long enough to settle the estate."

He tented his hands again. "That may be unnecessary. If you can get a valid address for him, most of this can be accomplished through the mail."

"Of course it's necessary!" I shouted, startling him. I retreated and composed myself.

"It is," I said bitterly, calmly, "necessary. My mother suffered over his absence. I suffered over it. All the relatives and friends we've asked to help him for our sake have suffered over him. Why shouldn't he be inconvenienced, just once, even if it is too late to make amends?"

Mr. Carcinet's eyebrows went up in a gesture that I couldn't interpret. He placed his fingers on either side of his bony nose and smiled, his lips parting in a brief, startling glimpse of red.

"You're anticipating me, Emerson. This brings us to the other part of the will. Your mother requested that her ashes be repatriated to Taipei, with your father's to be disinterred and brought over at a later date. If you were to go to Taipei to find Peter, you could discharge your, ah, responsibility to her at the same time."

My mother had been cremated. I had been keeping her in a wooden box on the living room console.

"All right," I said, faltering. "I'll take her with me."

Tears welled up in my eyes as I considered the prospect of being left behind. I was reminded of the day we had taken my father to Daly City, to be cremated. The cemetery had had a vast acreage of tombstones and crypts and mausoleums, all lined up in neat rows divided by paved avenues with signs, Avenues A, B, C, like a lost city in a book. The columbarium itself was a glassed-in summerhouse with heavy drawers of ashes laddered up the walls, and a fountain covered in plastic flowers in the center of the room that bubbled with the alacrity and shallow sentiment of artificial tears. I had gone there with my mother alone. The sun had shone through a fretwork of tree branches outside the high windows, and the atrium of the dead was perfectly peaceful, perfectly still.

When I finally got home, the light in my apartment was dim and wintry. I shut the door softly behind me. Wind ruffled the pages of a magazine in the living room. I wandered over to shut the window, then sat down, still holding my keys.

The box of ashes faced me, its wooden grain dark, stern, oddly reproachful.

"Mother?" I said tentatively. The sudden transformation from flesh to dust had been too quick; I still saw her in the restaurant, in her old blue dress, saying, "Such a disappointment"; on the floor of her bedroom, the panty hose drip-drying in the bathroom. What had she seen in those moments before her head hit the floor? What had she dreamt as she lay dying in her peace-white bed, far from home? Guilt and anger suffocated each other in me; I wished her back to life again, resurrected just for a moment, so that I could accuse, deny, shout, and beg for her forgiveness and her love, one last time.

The phone rang suddenly, breaking the dry silence. When I picked up the receiver, the line was dead.

CHAPTER 4

Iᴛ ᴡᴀs ʀᴀɪɴɪɴɢ ᴡʜᴇɴ ᴡᴇ ᴀʀʀɪᴠᴇᴅ at Chiang Kai-shek International, the tarmac glinting dully in the half-light as the plane taxied to the gate. Once through the crush of immigration, I hefted the box of ashes in its bag and went outside. The sky was colorless and the air warm, palpable, smelling of burnt rubber. A man in flip-flops sidled up to me and said something out of the corner of his mouth. I was in thrall to a very strange sensation, for the words he spoke sounded so familiar and so personal, and yet the meaning remained just beyond my grasp. It was like trying to name the face of someone I had once known, someone important but forgotten. The conviction that somewhere within me I harbored the key to perfect comprehension was irresistible. With some difficulty I recognized the word *bus*.

"I need to go to the Johnson." I showed him the reservation printout. "Johnson."

He nodded rapidly and herded me toward a large tour bus idling by the curb.

"I don't want a tour. Just hotel. Hotel. *Luguan*."

He nodded impatiently and chucked my carryall into the luggage compartment before rushing off to hustle another customer. I was hobbled by my mother, who seemed to be growing heavier, as if her ashes possessed the old cumbersome spirit, characteristically asserted now at the moment of maximum inconvenience. She had always hated buses.

"Not now," I said crossly, heaving her higher up on my shoulder. At least she was easier to manage in her new form.

I climbed into the coach. After some delay, the driver leaped aboard, and we lumbered onto the highway. The interior of the bus was oddly plush and decorated like a small parlor, white doilies laid across the headrests and the large windows framed by curtains tied with grosgrain bows. A television screen flickered silently, a bootleg version of an old Schwarzenegger flick that skipped and restarted wearily each time we hit a bump. The rain began again, a warm steady downpour that seemed, in my anxious state, like a sad truth of nature. Hills loomed in the nightscape. Through a gap in the trees, a huge white stone Buddha gleamed on the crest of a hill, one gigantic finger pointed toward the lowering sky.

The city began to appear, a grim, unassuming landscape of concrete and loose wiring, grayness and metal, with massive, burnt-out apartment structures, hundreds of units cramped together like the cells of a honeycomb, encased with metal grilles along the balconies, façades covered in dirty tile or darkened by exhaust and mold. Laundry flapped like threadbare flags on the covered balconies. Whatever I had been expecting, it was not this mishmash of concrete and palm trees, billboards and 7-Elevens, a huge three-story Starbucks gleaming like a beacon. An old man pedaled a rusty bike through the storm. A sleek fashion boutique lit by dreamy incandescent lamps stood out among the derelict garages and broken sidewalks.

To my relief, the bus route ended right in front of the Johnson. The hotel was a four-star, the kind where they sold leather handbags in glass cases in the lobby. The rate was beyond my means, but I'd splurged, thinking of it as a homecoming for my mother. She would have liked the show of wealth: the room service; the crisp, mono-grammed sheets; the soft lights; the marbleized floors. Riding up in the glass elevator, I felt a pang as I looked down over the broad foyer: surely my mother had deserved this in her lifetime? Raised in a poor family, she'd guarded the furnishings of the Remada with a jealousy that bordered on obsession.

My mother: she had never trafficked in empty affection, or in tenderness and kisses. Love—real love, she said—was measured out by the sacrifices one made to the future: money, history, time.

But she had left the motel to Little P.

The door opened with a smooth electronic tick, and the lights came on automatically in a soft display of rose and gold. A plate of fresh apples and oranges had been arranged on the dresser. The Remada could never compete with such amenities.

I put down my carryall and pulled the curtains open. The rain glazed the window, breaking up my faint reflection in the glass as I looked out onto the wide boulevard below. In the eatery across the street, a woman with a dish towel thrown over her shoulder stood watching traffic from her doorway, backlit by a greenish fluores-cent light. All up and down the road, harsh illuminated signs full of ciphers scrabbled and gibbered for attention. A mild sense of vertigo seized me, and I stepped away from the view. My only comfort was the ashes, and the thought that somewhere out there, among the strange crowds, my brother was waiting to be found.

THE ADDRESS was off Tongan Jie, a narrow, unassuming street that led to the river, flanked on either side by low, mildewed apartment buildings and shacks roofed with corrugated tin. It seemed unlikely that Little P would still be at his old apartment, but I had nowhere else to start.

The cabbie dropped me off at the mouth of the street. White heat shimmered like gauze over the asphalt. The neighborhood seemed hushed and waiting, and the air had a sweet, sluggish quality to it that I recognized, after a moment, as incense. The sound of a television murmured in the darkening street (it would rain again), and in the window of a bakery, a tired-looking woman sat and smoked, the skeleton furnishings within just visible: a few folding tables, plastic stools. The fluted roof of a temple rose from the gray. Inside, red lights in the smoke, and a dim golden Buddha glinting like foil in the cavernous gloom.

I found the building in a little dead-end alley. Black grilles covered the windows; tiles had fallen off the façade in patches, giving it a piebald look, and there was a kind of red graffito spray-painted on the metal door. I studied the entrance for some minutes; the Chinese characters had a look of angry incoherence about them that disturbed me. I fingered the buzzer hesitantly but did not ring it. Blood rushed in my ears. I found myself, suddenly, afraid. When he was a little boy, Little P used to marshal his toy boats together in the bath and then lift them one by one out of the water, giving each a resounding kiss, brow furrowed with the intensity of his love. Easy enough to deal with him then, when I had assumed the role of uncertain protector.

Rain began to fall, a few tentative spots, then a hard downpour, as if a faucet had been turned. I clenched my fists and went in.

The stairwell was damp. Fingers of mold stained the walls. Gloomily, I felt that I was breathing in spores. I was less afraid of death than of its corollaries—diminishment, illness, being alone. Was that why, despite the fear, my heart lifted as I climbed toward my brother's door?

A dirty light filtered in through a frosted window. Somewhere in the building, a couple fought, the woman's voice high and complaining, the man gruff. A shriek, a crash; the wailing of a child. As I rounded the landing to Little P's door, I lost my footing and grabbed at the handrail. When I'd righted myself, I looked down. Water was seeping from the walls and collecting on the floor in a black pool, cascading down the lip of the stairs in a steady *drip-drip,* like the ticking of a clock.

Timidly, I knocked on Little P's door. No answer. I knocked again.

"Little P!" I called. "Little P!"

Behind me on the stairs, a man in black, tensed and lean, eased himself around the curve of the banister. A raggy bandage covered his left cheek, the eye above it hidden in a blackened welt. The red scrawl on the door downstairs suddenly flashed into my mind: inchoate, wild, full of rage. Fear wiped my thoughts blank.

"I . . . we . . ." I whispered and took faltering steps toward the stairs, my back to the wall. He kept his raw face to me. A knife flashed in his hand, the blue point aimed at my heart.

As I circled him, he suddenly lunged forward, swinging the knife with dreadful precision. I dodged; the blade struck the concrete wall with a thin, singing quiver. I clattered down the stairs. But the floor was still wet, and halfway down I slipped, hit my chin on the railing, sprawled down the remaining steps, my leg wrenched beneath me as I hit the landing. Pain shot through my knee, up my back. I clutched at the banisters and pulled myself half up, draped helplessly over the handrail as if peering into a fenced-off pit. But it was too late. The dark, chiseled shape pressed close behind me, trapping me against the rail. One hand came up from underneath and grasped my jaw like a baseball, fingers smothering my mouth. He jerked my head back, and I felt the blade at my throat.

"Mlease," I said, muffled, shaking. He had not said a word. His one good eye gleamed like a bird's, hard and incurious. "Mlease. *Mlease.*"

But the blade didn't cut. I looked up.

After a moment, the man said, "Emerson?"

WE REGARDED each other sadly in the jaundiced stairwell.

"Emerson, you goddamned double-cunt." Swearwords in Chinese, at least, I understood. "What the hell are you doing here?"

He was very thin, lean, wolfish. Up close, his injuries were a fleshy patchwork, slashes and tears sewn up with metal thread. A line of coarse stitches ran across his forehead; his upper lip had been ripped open, held together with a kind of plaster. The sides of his mouth twitched now and then in an uncontrolled tic, and his nose was skewed from an older injury. All this gave him the look of a crude drawing, raw, brutal, only half-done—but I saw that the lines of the old Little P were still clear. Among the new scars was the old one on his cheek, a thin white slash from falling off his bike onto a broken bottle in the Remada parking lot. I had picked out the glass shards with a tweezers sterilized in whiskey and fire—like the cowboys, I'd told him, which had earned me a rare smile.

I followed him back up to the landing, my knee sending out little shoots of pain.

"I wrote to you," I said, faltering a little; it was not the reunion I had imagined. "And the lawyer wrote you. Didn't you get the letter?"

"What letter?"

"About the will. About the memorial."

"What are you talking about?"

"Mother. Mother's dead, Little P."

He'd been jimmying the door lock, impatient, but now his hand stilled briefly. Water dripped.

"Dead?" he said at last. "Dead? When?"

"In July. You didn't get the letters?"

"No," he said. "I was . . . I don't get much mail."

An irrelevance, but he seemed dazed, speaking in a monotone. His brow furrowed faintly—shades of the little boy who had named his toy boats *Tiny, Princess,* and *Cannibal George.*

He winced suddenly, touching a hand to his stitches, and opened the door. "I guess you should come in."

He did not turn on any lights. The room remained cold and colorless in the rain-light from the window. There was not much to see, in any case. His apartment had a temporary feel: a cot along one wall, a sink in the corner, a broken accordion door dividing the toilet from the rest of the room. A carton of Long Life cigarettes stood on end beneath the window, which looked out onto a concrete wall. Old magazines and newspapers lay in piles on the floor; a messy thatch of chewed betel nut stained the kitchenette counter.

My knee throbbed. I was waiting for Little P to offer me a chair or something, but he went immediately to the sink and took off his bandage, hissing a little as he picked it away from the wound.

"Doctors here," he said with disgust, "are total meats." He chucked the bandage on the floor, looked closely in the mirror, probing his stitches carefully with a finger. "You know how bad that's going to heal? Like fucking Frankenstein."

"What happened?" I asked.

"Aaanh . . ." He waved an arm, dismissive. "Couple of guys get a little unhappy, maybe they got a few friends . . . You know how it goes."

"Friends with switchblades," I said.

"Sure. We all went to a double matinee."

"Are you okay?" I hobbled over and laid a hand on his shoulder.

He shuddered and jerked away, his revulsion like a reflex.

"You want something to drink?" he asked after a moment. "There's nothing in the house, but the 7-Eleven's on the corner." He tossed a couple of crumpled bills on the counter. "Anything you want." He pushed past me to the kitchenette and began rummaging through a drawer.

One of the bills fluttered to the ground. As I bent over, something else, half-hidden by the slew of papers and junk, caught my eye. A length of what appeared to be hair, human hair, was caught on the edge of the linoleum. I pushed aside the newspapers and touched it. Small clots of dried blood clung to the ends.

"A pack of Marlboros too, if they have them," Little P was saying.

"What?" I straightened up.

"Cigarettes. I'm almost out of smokes. If you're going downstairs." He was speaking with difficulty through the distraction of pain, it seemed, for his lips were white, and his face had a dull veneer of sweat. He found a bottle at the back of the drawer and shook out a couple of pills, holding his head under the tap to wash them down.

"Are you *sure* you're okay?"

"Look, you want something or not?" he snapped. He wiped his mouth on his shoulder and indicated the money.

"Not thirsty."

"Fine," he said, and pocketed the bills again, though taking the money back seemed to piss him off. He was not used to offering anyone anything, I saw, and even less accustomed to having his offers refused. He found a cigarette in his pocket, leaned against the kitchenette counter. A silence fell.

"So you came just to tell me," he said.

"No, I came to see how—"

His cell phone rang. He answered; a short muttered conversation in Chinese followed, punctuated by some curses, some seeming threats. I could pick out only a few broken words: *bring, tomorrow, evening, late, tomorrow, no no no no*. He spoke fluidly, impatiently, switching from Chinese to Hokkien without effort. A tiny

THE FOREIGNER ▪ 41

jealousy warmed my blood. If Little P had been present in the hospital, perhaps he would have understood the bits of Chinese that dropped from my mother's lips as she traveled further and further away from me.

"I came to see you," I said, when he had hung up. He put out his smoke and began moving urgently around the apartment, gathering his knife, a bag, some clothes. "It's been almost ten years. Little P?"

No response. He riffled through some papers. His pain was lifting, apparently; his thoughts were elsewhere.

"Little P?"

"Listen. Emerson." He paused, motioned at his cigarettes. I passed the pack to him. "Sufficient unto the day, okay? I'm glad to see you. Sorry under such lousy conditions. But don't get too soft and psychotherapy on me. I got my thing; you got yours. I'll send you a card at Christmas." He checked his watch. "Right now I gotta go."

"Now? But Little P . . ."

"Sorry, brother. Maybe if I'd known you were coming."

"I'm in town for a couple more days," I said. "Have dinner with me, at least."

"Can't, brother. Sorry." He blew smoke out through his teeth. "I gotta work. Deadlines."

"'Deadlines'?"

He worked for our mother's brother, who ran some kind of business. I tried to remember: a restaurant. No, a nightclub—a karaoke den. "What, like a . . . karaoke deadline?"

He raised his uninjured eyebrow. "You got your message to me, all right? My condolences. Hey, for both of us. But she's gone. She's gone. I'm not gonna tear my sleeve for her."

The edge of his knife gleamed on the countertop.

But as he pulled on a raincoat, I said, "Cancer."

"What?"

"She died of cancer." I was not lying to Little P, only telling him what he needed to know. "She never went to the doctor. By the time she collapsed, it was too late. They didn't know where to begin. They couldn't even say what kind of cancer it was, it spread so far."

He'd been jerking at the stuck zipper on his raincoat without result.

"Fucking piece of *shit*." He tore the thing off and threw it to the ground. The tic had returned, a quick spasm at the sides of his mouth.

"I gotta go," he said doggedly. He motioned me toward the door and took out his keys. "Sorry, brother."

He locked the door behind us, stood back, fingered the ash off his fag onto the floor. His trousers were perfectly knife-creased. His starched black shirt and suit seemed suddenly odd, given the shabby surroundings. A pause.

"You need money for a cab?" he asked.

I shook my head.

"Okay then." A kind of bleakness in the silence between us. "Sorry about Mother." He hoisted his bag on his shoulder. "You keep in touch."

"Wait!" I cried, as he started down the stairs. He didn't turn around. I wanted to keep him here, for a few last minutes, but I couldn't think of anything to say. Then—"What about the will?"

His step slowed. "What about it?"

"Mother," I said. "The Remada. She left it to you."

I couldn't see his face, but the air around him suddenly pricked. Outside, dark shadows of rain moved behind the frosted glass.

"The motel," he said at last. "Mine?"

"I know. Maybe she thought it would bring you home again," I said, but the rebuke didn't take; he was too preoccupied with this new idea. He stopped dead in the stairwell. I approached him tentatively.

At length he looked up at me.

"How much," he said, in an odd, hungry voice. "How much do you think it would sell for? A hundred thousand? Two hundred?"

I gripped him by the arm. "For God's sake. Mother's dead, Little P."

Immediately he backed off. "You're right, you're right. Sorry. Inappropriate." He looked away. "Just a shock, you know."

"The inheritance?"

"The *death*," he said. "Of course Mother's death. Son of a cunt, Emerson, what do you think I am?"

I didn't answer. In the small silence, his cell phone rang again. He switched it off irritably.

"Okay," he said at last. "Okay. You're right. I know you're right. It's been, what? Five years?"

"Almost ten."

"Almost ten years. Dinner. I can move a few things around." He managed a tight smile. "How about tomorrow? You free tomorrow?"

"What about your deadline?"

"Fuck the deadline. That Eight Treasures cocklover never broke his back for me. I'll work it out. So—tomorrow?"

"Here?"

"At Uncle's house. Seven o'clock." He wrote down the address. I took it, feeling oddly guilty. I could have handed over the Remada right then and there, for the legal papers were tucked into my jacket pocket. But I kept this fact to myself.

CHAPTER 5

T HE NEXT NIGHT I ARRIVED at Uncle's apartment building
with the ashes as well as a bottle of plum wine and two catties
of mangosteens. A fluorescent tube hummed above me as the elevator doors slid open. I found Uncle's apartment: Number 5R, a
dented steel door with a faded banner above it, a remnant of the
long-gone new year.

At first there was no response to my knock. Then, after some
time, the door opened reluctantly, and a suspicious, wizened old
face peeped at me in the greenish light of the entryway. It made
a hoarse, creaking noise like a hinge. I consulted the address.

"*Xiao P zai ma?*" I asked faintly. There was more creaking. "Um.
Bu dong. Wo tingbudong."

Finally, with a grunt and an exasperated motion, the old woman
let me in. More creaking; she seemed to be berating me. Then
abruptly she left, shuffling off into a shadowy back hall.

I knew that Uncle had once been prosperous; the apartment

had a quality of both stateliness and neglect, the floor not tile but a battered mahogany, the furniture a mix of magnificent old carved cabinets, junky sofas, a massage chair. Someone had cleared the coffee table and sideboard, pushing the ashtrays and betel nut–stained paper scraps aside to make room for what looked like a kind of party. Little bowls of wasabi peas had been laid out; rice crackers; dried fruit; a six-pack of Taiwan beer. In the background, a huge flat-screen TV flickered soundlessly. A bird in a wooden cage hung in the window, spilling seed with a soft flutter of wings.

The bird screamed and knocked against its perch. I spun around as Little P came in from the entryway.

"Who left the dead bolt off?" he said by way of greeting.

"I don't know. The old woman."

"Fuck me. I've told her again and again." He closed the door behind him and bolted it, looking out the peephole briefly before he turned to me.

"You want something to drink?" He put down the 7-Eleven bag and unpacked it: some beef jerky, sake, Oreos, fruit.

"What's all this?"

"I figured, you know. Might be a while before I see you again. Why not make it a party. The cousins are coming." He fetched a plastic bowl and shook the Oreos into it haphazardly. "Drink? We got beer, wine."

"Anything harder?"

He looked irritated. "I just *bought* this." He checked himself. "But yeah, we got some whiskey."

"Okay."

"Homemade stuff. Pure poison."

"Fine."

He found two dirty-looking tumblers in the sideboard, wiping one with his finger before pouring out a large shot. His black eye was starting to turn a sickly shade, and his stitches rose up in a welt, an angry red worm.

"Listen." I fingered my glass timidly. The liquor was as bad as he had said, sharp and toxic, like rubbing alcohol. "I want to talk to you."

Instantly his guard was up; I could see it in the way he poured himself another shot, though he kept his voice light.

"About?"

"About the motel."

He downed his drink, silent.

"Don't sell it, Little P. And don't pretend that's not your plan. I heard you yesterday."

"More?" He got up, found another bottle in the sideboard.

"I'm not saying you shouldn't sell at all. But don't put it on the market. Sell it to me."

"To *you*?" He turned around, incredulous. "What kind of money do you have?"

"Not much." I looked down into my glass. "I can give you four thousand as a down payment, and fifteen hundred a month from then on." Even I thought it sounded meager. "And you'll have some rental income after expenses. Maybe I can take out a loan. But it's all I have right now."

He emptied the packet of beef jerky onto a tray and put it on the sideboard, not speaking.

"I just need some time," I said. "If not for me, then do it for her."

I tapped the box of ash softly.

"What's that?" asked Little P, looking suddenly wary.

"This——?" I remembered: I hadn't told him about the ashes yet. "It's . . . She asked to be interred in Taiwan. It was part of her will. I thought you could help."

"She's in *there*?"

I nodded.

"Son of a double golden cunt." He retreated to the opposite side of the room and regarded me with dark distrust, almost panic. "What the hell's wrong with you?"

"With *me*?"

"You should have told me. There's no excuse, meat lover." He was white, his breath shallow.

I put my mother aside. "Just calm down. Settle down."

"Okay." He gasped. "Everything's okay."

"We'll put her in another room for the evening, all right? Is there another room?"

He gestured to a little closet. I put the ashes inside, covered them carefully with my jacket, closed the door.

Little P, reaching for his cigarettes, fumbled them.

"Here." I handed the pack to him.

He lit a smoke, the tip trembling perceptibly in his mouth.

I waited.

"So you'll at least consider my offer?"

"What?"

"For Mother's sake. The motel was her home. Her life's work."

"Yeah," said Little P. "Her life's work." His voice was returning to its normal tenor, his pale face touched with color again. He picked up a blunt knife for the fruit. "That cunt-ass motel with the pedophiles and scumbags dealing coke behind the Dumpster. And the prosties. And the junkies. While she sat there with her plastic flowers and Princess Di photos, preaching morality and pretending everything was beneath her. Instead of just getting out."

"Diana, Princess of Wales," I corrected him, shocked. "I don't know what you're talking about."

"Yeah? And I bet you thought putting fresh flowers and mints in the bathrooms wasn't some fucking delusion, either. Just Mother practicing her good business sense, huh?" He was cutting the fruit clumsily on the sideboard, chunking the uneven pieces into a plastic colander. I thought of his knife on the stairs the day before, the keen blue steel against my throat. "That place never gave her shit for her trouble. She was a slave to scum. I shouldn't sell it, I should burn it down," he said. "Burn the whole thing down."

He nicked his finger. "Fuck." He put the tool down and drew a forced breath.

"Look," he said, lightness with a darkened edge. "This is supposed to be a party. I want you to *enjoy* yourself. We'll talk later. Have an Oreo." He pushed the bowl at me. "Have a beer."

A thump came from the head of the narrow stairs off the living room, a low, thick cough.

Little P wiped his brow. *"Gai si le,"* he muttered. "Sit tight. Try that guava."

He put down the colander and disappeared upstairs. More scuffling and thumping ensued, some muffled Chinese.

"Lai, lai, lai."

A heavy, uneven tread sounded on the stairs, and Little P reappeared, supporting the weight of a ponderously fat old man in a tracksuit and house slippers.

Slowly they descended, halting, labored, the old man clutching at the banister with a clumsy hand that jerked and felt its way along.

"Emerson, Uncle. Uncle, *jiushi* Emerson."

The man turned his half-lidded eyes to me, thick brows drawn, seeming not to register. One side of his face was slightly paralyzed—body too, which accounted for the shuffling. His little pinkish mouth opened in a yawn, showing darkened gums. He groaned.

"Is he . . . what's wrong?" I asked.

"Stroke," said Little P. He settled Uncle on the sofa and pulled a blanket up over his knees. "Treat him like normal. You don't know him. He was a real hellion before all this happened." He clucked solicitously at Uncle. *"Lai, he cha ba."* He went to the kitchen to make Uncle some tea.

Uncle and I regarded each other silently. He did not look much like my mother, though there was something eerily reminiscent of her in his face—a ghost of her about the mouth. His eyes seemed to brood, hooded and sunken, and his flat hands picked at the coverlet. I hoped my distaste didn't show. It wasn't his illness that put me off; it was something else that hung about him.

The bird screamed and spilled its feed again as the door opened and a couple of other men came in. They were in the midst of some kind of argument, one high, complaining voice and a corresponding bass, but they stopped abruptly when they saw me and Uncle sitting together on the plastic sofa. Little P, coming in from the kitchen, nodded in my direction without a word; clearly they had discussed me.

The skinnier of the two pushed forward, wet eyes shining with peculiar intensity. I had an impression of hunger there, some kind of envy or hatred.

"H-hello," I said, forgetting my Chinese in bewilderment.

"Am Poison," he said, a small ratlike man with a deep baritone. "English name. I study two year, two year," with a kind of taunt in his voice. He wore plastic flip-flops and a T-shirt that said CEN-TURY 21 DORITOS, and was chewing a wad of betel nut, which he shifted around rapidly as he spoke. His close-set eyes took me in with sly, darting glances as he gestured toward his soft, fat companion. "My brother, Da Yi. English say Big . . . One. We are the cousin to you. Son of Uncle."

Big One shook my hand damply, his silk shirt with flamboyant dragons printed down the placket billowing about his thighs.

"*Hui jiang guoyu ma?*" he asked. Do you speak Chinese?

I blushed. "*Yi . . . yi dian-dian.*"

He grinned unpleasantly, top lip curling away from a row of tiny teeth. " '*Yi dian-dian,*' " he repeated. "*Shuo 'yi dian-dian,' da jia dou tingdechulai ni zhen bushi Zhongguoren.*"

Poison punched him. Big One looked hurt.

"Do you understan'?" Poison asked curiously.

"Understand what?"

"What he say."

"Something about . . . Chinese people?"

"Ah." Poison laughed. After a moment, Big One laughed also, and the two of them herded me toward the sideboard of snacks and offered me one of Little P's beers.

Meanwhile, other people had trickled in, about five or six men. They seemed to know one another already, and fanned out across the sofa and chairs unceremoniously, eating the fruit and jerky and turning up the volume on the TV so that the news blared. They did not speak to or even look at me, and I was aware therefore that they must somehow know who I was. One of them yawned, spreading his bare, ashy knees, and scratched. An air of reluctance seemed to hang over them, like workers at an office party. Maybe Uncle had demanded their attendance.

I studied the old man again from across the room. Little P hovered over him, wiping his mouth as he dribbled tea down his chin. He was not capable of feeding himself, it seemed, let alone ordering a group of men around. Why, then, did I distrust him? My mind circled, closing in on some elusive detail, but Poison kept distracting me with a long, broken story about cars and New York, how he had gone there once and thought it was nothing, a lot of noise and money.

"*Chi fan ba.*" Little P, having seated Uncle at the long makeshift folding table, began bringing out take-out containers from the kitchen: pig knuckle, tomato scrambled with egg, cabbage and ham, soup boiled with ginger and tiny clams that Little P dipped out of a plastic bag. A huge tureen of rice was handed around, tea was poured, and the men ate, raising their bowls to their mouths and shoveling rice in, still watching the television.

Poison, seated next to me, seized the fabric of my suit between his thumb and forefinger. "This very nice, very nice," he said. "Armani, no? Dolce and Gab'na?" He rubbed my sleeve between his fingers like paper bills. "I know. I have the expensive eye. Very expensive, very nice."

I shrugged away. Actually, it was a Perry Ellis suit my mother had bought me on clearance at Dillard's, but I could not convince him, for the other men were scruffy in their undershirts and shorts and flip-flops. Under the stark fluorescence, I surveyed the table discreetly, looking longer at my cousins and my brother, my family, a floating panorama of gestures and faces in whom the units of genetic material should have clicked and yearned toward each other, like little magnetic filings, binding us.

The man on my left stood out in a quiet way. Older, more reserved, he sat at the table but seemed somehow disconnected from the others, appearing to listen with great attention to all the muttered conversation without being invited to take part. If he was insulted, he did not show it; he ate neatly and sipped a glass of warmed sake with evident enjoyment, studying his tiny glass from all angles.

"Rrrice." He crooked his finger slightly at the tureen in front of me and said, "Rrrice, please." He smiled at me, conspiratorial, as I passed him the bowl.

"I had lived for twenty years in New York," he explained. "As a professor of engineering. My name is Li An-Qing. Atticus in English."

He removed a piece of bone from his mouth and placed it on the rim of his plate, then wiped the tips of his fingers carefully on a napkin and studied me. "So you are Xiao P's brother?"

"Yes, older brother."

He sipped his sake, the sharp corner of his tongue darting out to catch a stray drop. "*Intéressant*. Xiao P does not talk about you very much. In fact, yesterday is the first time he has mentioned you in a long time."

I looked over at Little P. He was bent solicitously over Uncle, his head inclined toward the old man in an attitude of deep attention.

"I'm a lot older," I said, though that hardly seemed to explain. "We don't talk much. We don't talk at all."

"Oh? Then this must be an occasion. It was very good of you to come so far." He patted my hand. "The reason is unfortunate— your mother—but I am very glad you have come. I have wanted to meet you for many years."

"*Me?* Why?"

He laughed. "It is not so surprising. Xiao P is with us for eight, ten years. You are always curious to know where your compatriots have come from. Tell me." He hesitated. "Do you find much . . . similarity in your brother?"

"Similarity to me?"

"Similarity to before, I am talking about."

I remembered my encounter in the stairwell yesterday—the hard, narrow face; the slashing knife.

"I don't know. . . . I guess not," I said, half-resentful. "Why?"

He looked down the table toward Little P, who caught his eye and held it for a long, veiled moment before returning to an argument with Big One. Atticus stopped chewing. Then resumed, more slowly.

"*Rien d'important*," he said. He finished off his sake abruptly, in a large mouthful. "I only wish to have a better insight." He looked toward Little P again and lowered his voice urgently. "You must know that Xiao P is quite *different*."

My scalp pricked. "You say 'different' like you mean something else."

Atticus shook his head violently. "No, no, no! *Pas du tout*. I have no wish to slander your brother. You must not tell him I said such a thing. I mean only that he is quite driven."

"In work, you mean."

"Work, life." He was evasive, distracted. "In a way, I admire your brother. He has his own . . . rectitude."

"Rectitude."

"Principle. Xiao P has his principles. You could say he is the most principled man you will ever meet," he said, and laughed suddenly, surveying the table with dry amusement.

He was even older than Uncle, but despite the peppered hair and shrunken bones, his face was smooth, unlined, he himself timeless in a formal gray mandarin shirt and buttoned vest. Where did he belong among this tattered, disjointed crew? He seemed to know much more about my brother than I did. Did he know about the angry red graffito on his doors? The hair with its clots of blood? The quick, terrible economy with which he handled a blade? Atticus's fingers fluttered at his throat as he coughed a little, then resumed his eating.

"Are you," I asked carefully, "a friend of Uncle's?"

He grinned. "*Friend* is a nice word. I work for Zhou Jian-Ping— Uncle, as you call him. I manage the finance for the karaoke and some of his other business. Those two"—he indicated Big One and

Poison with a lift of his chin—"probably like to have someone else for the accountant, but the family have obligation to me."

"Obligation?" Somehow it was hard to imagine my raw-looking cousins feeling obligation to anyone, let alone this slight, courtly old man. "You mean financial obligations?"

He frowned. "How to explain. Uncle and I, we are neighbors in our youth. His father—your grandfather, you probably know—was an interpreter for the Japanese."

"I didn't know he worked for the Japanese."

"Everyone here worked for the Japanese in the 1930s. You know your history? This is World War Two. Japan is in Manchuria, Taiwan is the Japanese colony. Japan needs translators on the mainland but cannot use a mainland Chinese. Too risky. So they send your grandfather and others instead—loyal subjects of the Emperor," he said, a little derisive.

"I didn't know," I repeated. The sudden brush of my own blood with the faceless bulk of history sent a tremor through my limbs, like a drumbeat felt from far away.

"The army says one year, two years only. But five years pass, and still your grandfather is not allowed home. Your grandmother was sick then, and cannot manage your mother and Uncle both, so my father took Uncle and raise him along with me and my sister. Only temporary, of course. Your grandfather come back eventually, but very, very late—not until after Hiroshima. Uncle was about twelve, I think. He barely know his father at all. But he was always very grateful to my family. Grateful, and angry."

I glanced down at the end of the table, where Uncle was painfully feeding himself a spoonful of soup.

"I expect he does not remember enough for it to be important now," said Atticus.

After dinner, Poison and the others immediately got down to their intended business, setting up a few tables of mah-jongg, the click of the tiles like glass rolled by the sea, accompanied by a lot of cigarette smoke and cursing. Poison tried to engage me as a fourth at his table, but I didn't want to play. My flight home was tomorrow, and there was still the business of my mother's ashes to take care of; the will; the sudden yearning to talk to my brother, the hundreds of things I had to tell him, to ask.

The room seemed suddenly too crowded, and I wanted to get my brother alone for a while, though he himself appeared to have no need of a tête-à-tête. He stood on the other side of the card tables, opposite me, not playing, watching their games as he smoked. I had the idea that he was using the men as a kind of live barrier, a defense against me. I had accustomed myself to his face, with its stitches and bruises, but as I looked at him across the room now, it blinked once more into anonymity.

"Emerson?" Atticus, who had been sitting next to Uncle, got up to leave. "Will you help me?" He pulled a handful of plastic bags out of his raincoat pocket.

I followed him to the entry. He sat down with some difficulty on an overturned crate near the door and tied a bag around his left foot, then one around his right to keep the rain off his shoes.

"I am sorry you are leaving so soon," he said. "But if you come back, I invite you to look me up." He handed me his card. "It was a vigorous conversation."

"Yes, it was." I knotted the bags securely around his ankles and sat back, uncertain.

"What did you mean about Little P, about his having . . . rectitude?"

Atticus suddenly appeared very interested in his shoes and adjusted the knot around his right ankle.

"I think this will hold." He held out a hand, and I pulled him up. He tied the belt of his raincoat, stamping his feet experimentally a couple of times. He seemed not to have heard my question, offering me his hand instead. "Good-bye, Emerson. I wish you good luck."

But as he opened the door, he cast a furtive glance over my shoulder at Uncle and the others. He paused, then drew me out into the entryway, closing the door behind us.

"*Écoutez-moi*, Xiao Chang," he said quietly. "I asked before if you noticed some change in your brother. Why did you not answer me?"

I bit my lip. "Because I don't know."

"Wrong," he said. "You are afraid to acknowledge what changes you see. Well, and perhaps you are right," he said, with a small sigh. "Maybe it is right to be afraid."

"Has Little P"—I couldn't quite form a question to fit my apprehension—"done something?"

He shook his head. "I must go," he said, making a movement toward the elevators.

I caught his arm. "But you said he was principled. The most principled man I would ever meet."

"Yes, of course. *Buguo,* many kinds of people have principle. Mao Zedong, you know, was also a man of great rectitude."

"I don't understand."

The door opened, and one of the men came out, muttering: he had not won his pot. Before the door closed, I caught a glimpse of Little P and Uncle conferring. Atticus saw them too. He shook out his rain hat with an air of resolution.

"Have you notice the *maid*?" he asked softly. Then he stuffed his hat on his head and left.

Uncle's gaze followed me as I went back inside. Little P was pushing some poker chips around on the sideboard, running them through his fingers like gold coins.

"Dinner good? You like it?" he asked.

"Dinner was fine."

"Just 'fine'? That's the best fucking roast duck in Taipei. That place is famous."

"The duck was good. Listen. We need to finish talking." I made a vague gesture toward the closet where I'd stashed my mother.

He put out his cigarette in a bowl of ashes meant for incense.

"I have to go to work," he said. "These cocklovers"—indicating the cousins—"they won't move until their game is done."

"I'll go with you."

He sighed, impatient. "Emerson." Then he seemed to check himself. "Okay. Fine, come with me."

I went upstairs to use the bathroom. It was a tremendous relief to close the door and be alone for a moment. I washed my hands in the rusty water and tried to think over what Atticus had just said. Now that he was gone, my conversation with him seemed only to raise more questions. I splashed water on my face, thinking of the ashes in the downstairs closet, the dark, squat box that had come to stand in for my mother. And now I would have to give her up to Little P for burial. The thought stretched bleakly before me.

On my way back down the upstairs hall, a door flapped in a sudden draft. I paused, glancing in. A lamp shone in the far corner of the small room, among the mildewed storage boxes and old furniture. Along the rim of murky half-glow where the lamplight petered out, someone was moving.

"Hello?" I whispered, pushing open the door.

A woman, an older girl, huddled on a thin cot against the wall, half-hidden by a pillar of boxes. She drew back when she saw me in the doorway, clutching the front of a new, ill-fitting dress to her chest. Her feet were bare, her skin scrubbed clean and raw. A notch broke the line of her upper lip, an old deformity, clumsily repaired to leave a scar. She scrunched farther into her corner as I approached, and her gaze flickered anxiously around the room.

"It's all right," I whispered. "Are you . . . a friend of Little P's?"

No answer. She watched me, apprehensive.

"What's your name?" The wild vacancy in her eyes was shocking; I just wanted to hear her say something, anything. "I'm Emerson."

"Hey!" Little P's voice came faintly up the stairwell.

"Coming!"

The girl jumped at my shout, and her jagged lip trembled. But as I backed out of the room, she suddenly spoke in a voice husky with disuse, murmuring low and unfathomably before subsiding into a ragged sob like the end of a prayer.

CHAPTER 6

IN THE NARROW, mildewed back hall of the Sing Palace, Little P unlocked a door and flicked on the light.

"Voilà," he said—a dry joke, because the office was grim, with concrete walls and a ceiling that showed rusty metal beams, all lit by a greenish fluorescence. Discarded computer equipment littered the floor, along with empty boxes and half-packed crates of salt fish, jug wine; a clatch of mosquitoes whined in a damp corner. The shabbiness contrasted sharply with the Palace's lobby, which had the slick veneer of put-on class, the walls gilded and the reception counter polished black, manned by a sleepy young man stuffed into a black-and-white tuxedo.

Little P threw his jacket over a group of black banquettes, which had been torn out of the walls and stood like sheep in a slaughterhouse. The room was cold; I noticed that my brother was shivering.

"Are you lonely, Little P?" I asked him suddenly.

He was rummaging around on the desk with papers. His hands paused, then continued, resolute.

"I have people around from the time I get up to piss to my last smoke at night. No, I'm not lonely," he said. "Not lonely *enough*."

I shook my head. "I don't mean physically alone. It's something else. The way you live? The people you're surrounded by . . ."trailing off, because I couldn't nail down what was bothering me so much.

"What about them?" Defensive now. He had always been sensitive to criticism.

"I don't know. Uncle, Poison . . . I just can't believe they would really get you."

"And who would?" An edge of bitterness to his voice, just below the light teasing note. "You?"

I lowered my eyes and didn't say anything. After some time he realized his mistake.

"Shit, Emerson." He rubbed his stitches fretfully. "You've been riding my ass ever since you showed up. What do you *want* from me? What do you want me to say? Ten years. What would you understand about me after that long?"

"But that's just it," I said. "I know nothing about you. I understand nothing. I won't pretend I do. But I *want* to know—something, anything. You're all I have left now."

The sentimentality of it made him nervous. He jumped up from his desk and shifted restlessly among the junk in the room. He paused beside the long window. It was dark outside, and raining again; the glass reflected the office, the disorder, the thin, baleful figure he cut in the grainy light.

"There isn't anything to know," he said, after a while. "You've seen it all right here. I'm just a two-bit manager of a lousy KTV."

He drew the window shade.

"Mother's ashes," he said, turning back to me.

I had almost forgotten them; the charge of sudden intimacy sparked by his not-quite-confession had sent her out of mind. But the dry knowledge of loss renewed itself as I took the box out of the bag and held it out to him.

"She's in there," said Little P, hesitant, not a question but a dazed statement to himself. Slowly, he reached forward and took the box, staring down at it as if looking into a well that held an image in its deep, dark water.

"Have you thought any more about my offer for the motel?" I asked.

He frowned and set the box down.

"I'm only asking you to consider," I said, following him as he walked back to the desk and leaned against the edge. "The family home, Little P."

He lit a smoke, cupping his hand around the tip, and studied the lines of his palm.

"You talk to the lawyer and get me the papers first," he said abruptly. "Then I'll consider it."

The papers, rightfully his, were back in my hotel room. Should I have brought them? The hardened look in Little P's eye said no. I'd keep them to myself a little while longer. Still, conscience dictated that I compensate him somehow, some way, however inadequately. He was my brother; I couldn't just leave him with nothing.

I took out my checkbook and filled in the amounts.

"Here"—holding it out to him.

"What for?"

"What do you mean? For you."

"Why?" He searched my face, suspicious.

"No reason." No reason but guilt. The box of ashes seemed to darken and glower: *I give your brother the motel! You cannot just ignore my wish.* "A present."

Part of me hoped that he wouldn't take it, that some kind of pride or principle would prevent him from accepting a handout. Instead, he took the slip from my hand, glanced at the amount briefly, tucked it in his pocket.

"Thanks."

I wanted to ask him again about his face, what had happened; about Atticus; about Uncle, the knife, the girl, the red ciphers on the door. But somehow the opportunity for confidences had passed. Too much had happened, there was no way to begin. A little good-luck totem sat on a shelf above his head, a golden cat with its jointed paw weaving up and down, *tick-tock,* like the second hand of a clock.

"Well." I looked at my watch. "I have to get going."

He stood up. "I'll take care of the ashes. Don't worry."

"She wanted a temple burial," I said. A suffocating grief swept over me as I gestured inadequately toward my mother. "It's all up to you."

"You'll talk to the lawyer, right?"

"Good-bye, Little P." I put a hand on his shoulder. "I'll be in touch."

As I left, he was dialing someone on the office phone. He had taken my check out, his thumb marking the amount.

"Wei?" I heard him say, and then a low, urgent rumbling of Chinese. I turned at the doorway. His back was to me, the ashes forgotten, balanced precariously on a shaky stack of crates. I gritted my teeth and made myself continue out the door.

THE LITTLE cantina in the basement of the airport was quiet when I arrived for my flight. It was very early; the lights had not even been turned on except for a few above the bar, but there was a smell of coffee and hot oil. Small heaps of eggs and sausages sat patiently in warming pans laid out along the counter while a woman in a hairnet planted thermometers in them like flags. I surveyed the unappetizing counter, took a watery instant coffee with two sugars, and carried it to an empty table.

A few other travelers were scattered around the darkened tables, looking hollow-eyed and dazed. A man in a wheelchair approached, selling pens, toys, packages of smoky incense. I shook my head at him. Adamant, he wheeled closer, laid a selection of pens stiffly on my table. I shook my head. After a few moments he moved on, but the incense lingered, insistent, dark, smelling of death and its little gods. Yesterday, just before Little P and I had left for the Palace, Uncle had searched me out, breathing laboriously with intent, and pushed three sticks of incense into my hand, nudging me toward a little shrine set up in a back corner of the room. Two framed portraits hung over a shelf laid carefully with a plate of guava and a bowl of sand in which sticks of incense burned down to filaments: my grandparents, the same pictures my mother had had in her front hall. I had never met them, but the photos were as familiar to me as my own face. How strange, and somehow terrible, to come upon them in an alien place so far from home—like a nightmare in which you come upon strangers who have your face.

"Our grandparents." Little P had translated for Uncle. "He wants you to pay your respects. Hold the sticks up with both hands. Not like that, lower. Now: bow. Three times. Repeat after him: *Wo shi Zhou Lili de erzi . . .*"

Fumblingly, I repeated the sounds, which I guessed were a kind of prayer, and shook the joss sticks as directed. Everyone else watched me, as if the ritual were a test. Unpleasant, being observed so closely, but the ritual itself had moved me: a link, a missive, like telepathy between the living and the dead. Was it possible, through incense and prayer, to open up a channel to minds that had loved, planned, then died? The Australian girls at the next table laughed. By now the cantina had filled up with early travelers: couples; a group of monks; families weighed down by luggage and cherished grievances, bound together in close, unspoken colloquy. I was suddenly aware of how alone I was. No companion, no lover to see me off; no one to meet me at the other end.

The handicapped vendor made another slow sweep of the room. This time I stopped him and bought a package of joss sticks. A bit of incense, burned at the altar of a shrine: would it bring me back into some living connection with that old, dead love? J, with her dark promise of sex and experience; the touch of her lips on my neck, the scent of smoke and wine. My mother had deplored her because she wasn't Chinese, but the real trouble had been more timeless than that: age, and knowledge. I remembered her lovely Nordic face, its pale, moonlit coloring—how it had looked suddenly lined and weary as she made her jaded pronouncement in the darkened bedroom: "That's all it is, Emerson. That's all love is." Over the years, I had replayed those memories of J so often that they had been sucked dry of comfort, like marrow from a bone. I finished my coffee quickly and got up to find my gate.

The air of exhausted holiday mingled with sweat and heat at the gate. In the crush of boarding passengers, a couple of Americans nattered on behind me, talking about their Bali vacation, the English loud as a shout in the murmurous Chinese. The familiarity jolted me as we shuffled onto the plane. For the first time since leaving the United States, I thought of my empty walk-up in San Francisco. Every meal would be eaten alone now, over the kitchen sink or in front of the TV; no visits to the motel, no weekly devotion to mark the time from here till death. Meanwhile my mother walked her dark island of the afterlife, alone. Her ashes at the Palace slid inexorably toward scattering, defilement, oblivion. Her light, tuneless humming through all the walls of the motel; her exhausted face in the flicker of the television at night as she slept, fitful over money, how to make it all work. *What means love?* The ashes tilted precariously at the edge. Little P would never catch them, never give them their proper due.

I stopped abruptly in the aisle.

"Sir? Sir?" The flight attendant's querulous voice carried through the cabin. They were coming on, the other passengers, trapping me dumbly, without knowledge or mercy.

"Sir!"

Already the boarding ramp was being retracted, but the galley door was still open, the path clear. Faces loomed out at me as

I lunged my way toward the back, swinging my carryall blindly like a bludgeon, pursued by the flight attendant's shout: "Sir! Sir!"

The air burned above the distant runway as I spilled down the metal service stairs and knelt, dizzy, heaving. Gasoline, heat. Cries of alarm sounded above me, but then the great engines of the plane began to churn, drowning them out, faster and faster, until the blades blurred in a high, thin scream.

I must have blacked out, because when I opened my eyes, I was lying cramped on the tarmac, in perfect stillness. A couple of baggage handlers hovered over me with mute concern, but the plane was gone, my ticket home gone. I sat up.

"Taxi?" I asked faintly. "Bus?"

The workers exchanged puzzled glances and echoed: "Teksi? Ba-as?"

"Right. Never mind." I struggled to my feet and looked about the airfield, alien, desolate in its flat, parched plain. I was truly on my own now. My mother's final fate hung in my hands. I would save her, and save the Remada as well.

PART 2

CHAPTER 7

LITTLE P'S CELL PHONE WAS OUT OF SERVICE when I dialed him from a pay phone. Cursing, I hung up the receiver and looked around. I had gotten out of the cab at random and did not know where I was. I had tried to direct the cabbie to the Sing Palace, but my sense of direction has never been very good, and we had ended up in this ancient part of town, on a narrow, dark street that was almost a crevasse. Was it only a paranoid fantasy, or did the faces here seem different—more hostile somehow, or suspicious? I had walked a full block along the narrow, gray sidewalk looking for a phone. A man had been dozing in the alcove of what looked to be a dingy apothecary, huge pieces of galangal dried in jars lined up on the counter. His wife watched me from the doorway, fanning herself with a magazine.

"*You dianhua ma?*" I asked, desperate. The magazine stopped. She looked me up and down uncertainly before turning to her husband.

"*Nali you dianhua?*" she asked. "For the foreigner."

The man shrugged. The woman turned back to me and pointed down the road. As I walked off, I could see her in the shadow of an overhanging sign, peering curiously in my direction.

It was noon; the smell of salt and meat and frying oil came from the little stalls up and down the street, and my stomach pinched. I took out a fistful of change and bills. I had carefully changed all my currency back to U.S. dollars before getting on the plane; George Washington eyed me disapprovingly from the back of a crumpled bill.

A vat of dark beef broth roiled over an oil drum on the sidewalk, sending out clouds of anise-smelling steam.

"U.S. dollar?" I asked the woman tending the fire, holding up my bill. She wiped her shiny face and frowned at the money.

"*Sanshi kuai,*" she said stubbornly.

"But I only have U.S. dollar. No *kuai.*"

"*San-shi,*" she repeated, louder, more slowly, and huffed with frustration.

"*Laoban niang.*" A woman—more like a girl—sitting at one of the makeshift tables inside the dingy eatery spoke up. "*Ta meiyou taibi. Wo bang ta fu haobuhao?*"

Then she turned to me. "Whaddya want?" she asked me. "One bowl? With noodles or just soup?"

"You speak English," I said, dazed, as the girl fished some coins out of her rucksack.

"New Hampshire born and bred." She wore big, shapeless cargo pants and black combat boots, one of which she propped smartly on the stool beside her as I sat down. The proprietress brought over the bowl of soup, which was thick with beef and tomato. I felt I hadn't eaten in years.

"Well," I said, through a mouthful of stew beef. "Thank you for rescuing me."

The girl cocked her head like a bright, squat little bird. She was small and compact, with dark, intelligent eyes and a square chin, which she raised inquiringly as she fixed her glasses more firmly on her nose.

"No wife?" she asked.

"What?"

"Sorry. That was rude." She frowned. "No offense, but aren't you kind of old?"

"For . . . ?"

"I don't know. Travel. Don't get offended," she said quickly. "It's just, most of the *hua qiao* I see around here, they're college age, high school age. Root-seeking, you know?" She spoke with rapid-fire delivery, rat-a-tat-tat.

"I know. I'm not a root seeker," I said. The term had an unpleasantly swinelike ring.

"So then . . ." She spread her hands frankly. "What're you doing here? Work?"

I felt hoary, aged, my carryall balanced on a stool like a monument to folly.

"It's complicated," I said vaguely. "How about you? Where'd you learn your Chinese?"

"Oh . . ." Surprisingly, she blushed. She hadn't seemed shy. "I've always spoken. My dad sent me to weekend Chinese school. I used to hate it. Like, what's the point? But it got me this job, that's something at least. I'm doing this travel series? For Pennywise Pilgrim? I go around and sample all the local food and festivals."

She looked at me defiantly, as if she expected a fight. "It's not like *Pulitzer Prize*–winning work, you know? But I do get paid."

"I'm sure it's a very good job."

I must have sounded insincere, for she suddenly looked down at the tabletop and twisted a scrap of napkin in her hands.

"And when you do win the Pulitzer Prize," I hastened to add, "I'll be able to say I was once saved in the middle of wherever it is we are, by you, Ms. . . . ?"

"Angel. Angel Sheng-Sheng Guo," she said, brightening. Her nose crinkled as she handed me her card ("Angel Sheng-Sheng Guo, Writer"), and she had a pretty smile—not so masculine after all, despite her clothes.

Out in the street, she asked, "Where you going now?"

"Well—" I coughed and gagged. The air was full of strange ashy particles, gritty, gray snowflakes that melted and burned on my skin.

"Goddamned ghost money," said Angel, coughing. "It always makes my asthma worse."

"What's ghost money?"

"For ghost month."

"What's ghost month?"

"*Ghost month!*"—louder, as if this would illuminate. She looked at me narrowly. "You don't know? The gates of the underworld and yada yada yada?"

I shook my head.

"It's a religious festival. Like, the gates of hell or whatever open once a year, the dead come out and roam the earth for thirty days, bitching and moaning. So you have to appease them while they're wandering and hungry. You have to buy good luck for next year by showing them some respect. So that old man there?" She indicated an old couple crouched on the sidewalk, tending a fire in a red metal canister. "He's burning paper money. For his ancestors. You'll see it all around. Businesses'll do it too—they put out tables with fruit and incense and soda and stuff.

"Superstitious crapola!" she bellowed suddenly, swinging her rucksack like a weapon. "Opium for the conscience! Narcotic for the soul! And shit for the environment too, you know? Down with tradition!" She shook her fist at the old couple, who regarded her mildly, unconcerned, before turning back to their fire. "Up with the earth!"

But I didn't think it was superstitious. When she was gone, I walked back up to the main road. As I passed by the couple, the old woman accidentally knocked the money burner over, spilling ash into the gutter—the gray saltpeter of communion. Some of the cinders rolled into my path. I stepped over them carefully. Ash, too, could live.

IN THE end, it was Atticus who finally came and got me, on his silver Vespa.

"Climb up, please," he said, placing one elegantly shod foot on the curb. I stared, for he looked different in his riding gear: less gentle, more taut. His helmet was black with a mirrored visor, which he did not lift, and there was something unnerving about it, a kind of menace, or void, that erased Atticus completely, though his lilting voice still came softly from behind this facelessness: "Climb up, Emerson."

He lived in a rather swanky part of the city, in the northern district, in a large, airy, two-level apartment with stone floors that felt cool and dry after the noonday heat. Woodcuts of dragons and other animals hung in a row above a low couch, and a moody, patterned light fell on a single orchid blooming near the windows. Long shelves of English and Chinese volumes were carefully arrayed along the walls; even the bathroom had a bookshelf: Dickens, Tolstoy, an anthology of Chekhov plays. A collection of helmets brooded on a long console—not motorcycle helmets but old combat helmets, German-style and Japanese, even a kind of medieval armored piece with a feather and rusting slots. A kabuto helmet with its masked mouthpiece snarled up at me, ringed about by a few black smooth rocks.

"You look very tired, no?" Atticus asked, removing his helmet and stashing it precisely on a rack behind the door. "Through there"—he nodded toward a small door below the stairs—"is a bedroom. No, no," he said, holding up a hand as I tried to protest. "Is no use arguing. I cannot talk to a man who has not slept well. When you get up, you can tell me everything, but for now, you will sleep." It was a command.

So I carried my bag into the room and lay down on the clean sheets and slept, fitfully at first, then more deeply, sinking into a little cocooned space where the confusion of the day was walled off by anonymity and strangeness. Not my mother, not even my worries about Little P could find me here. A moonscape opened out, stars shooting across the horizon. Weightlessness and moon rock. A figure spiraling off into darkness, lonely and remote.

When I awoke, a gray light had settled over everything. There was a strange quiet in the apartment, like a high-pitched hum. I sat up, mouth tasting of dirt and anxiety. There had been a girl somewhere in my sleep, but I could not remember her, and it seemed, confusingly, that the forgetting was the source of my sorrow. I reached for my suit jacket.

Atticus was standing at the console cabinet when I came out.

"Sorry, Atticus. How long have I been asleep?"

He didn't respond. His back was to me, his head bent intently over something, so that I was nearly behind him when he finally noticed.

"Emerson!" Swiftly, he dropped something in the console drawer and closed up the cabinet with a smooth, decisive click.

"Oh, now." He chuckled at my expression. "Don't be alarm, just an old man getting a good cry over old photographs. Excuse me if I am a little embarrass; I am so used to being alone, and you startle me." He patted my shoulder and checked his watch. "Now, let me wash up and then we will go and have some dinner, no? You have slept all afternoon. Good!"

His fingers were smeared with some kind of grease.

Shower water ran in the bathroom. *It's none of your business,* I told myself. *He's the only friend you have here.* But Atticus had been a little too smooth, a little too rapid in his excuse.

The water ran. Quietly, ear cocked toward the bathroom, I opened the cabinet and pulled out the narrow drawer.

Inside, a pistol lay on a tray of blue felt, like an offering, its snub nose gleaming and velvety with oil. Bullets had been lined up in a corked test tube and tucked into a fold of felt, half-hidden by a blackened chamois; he must have been polishing the gun when I came up behind him. I touched the barrel, briefly—cold, mechanical, with no human report. I remembered Little P's knife, and my scalp tightened. It was nothing, I thought. Perhaps Atticus was a collector.

The water in the bathroom stopped. Hastily, I pushed the drawer back in and shut the cabinet.

Atticus reappeared some minutes later, looking refreshed and cheerful in a clean shirt and vest.

"In your honor, tonight," he said, "we will have a little seafood dinner. My treat, if you will."

"That's not necessary, Atticus."

"Of course it is not necessary! That is precisely what makes it a treat." He purred a little at his own joke, fussing around with his keys and pocketing his wallet. Then he became serious. "But you must not do only what is necessary in life, Emerson. You must have your extravagance too. It is the only way to stay alive. Otherwise, there is nothing but eating and shitting, no?"

He laughed and went downstairs to pull the scooter around, tossing me the key so that I could turn out the lights and lock up. He seemed so happy, and so calm.

ATTICUS, I was to discover later, had a serious political life that occupied him whenever his work at the Palace did not. During the few nights I spent on his couch, he did not come home until quite late, and when he did, he looked simultaneously beatific and spent, his face shining in a rare display of enthusiasm as he said good night and went to bed, humming. On that first evening, he stopped to peer in the windows of the Géant store, where dozens of white flat-screen televisions illuminated the sleek interior with pictures of a protest outside the Presidential Building: banners and crowds, tears and shouting.

"These are exciting times," Atticus said, observing the video feed. "Very exciting times. You do not know much about the history of this island, do you, Xiao Chang?"

"No."

"A shame." He glowed. "We are a democracy, you know. It does not mean so much to you, I understand, but for us, for us it was forty years with the martial law, and before that a few centuries with the foreign occupation. You understand what that means, Xiao Chang? No independence." He lifted a finger pensively. "No identity. Or a double identity: one for the rulers, the other hidden away. A half-life. A non-life. A killing of the soul. It goes on still, you know; we have not liberate ourselves entirely. But we have done some things, no? In just seventeen years we have made ourselves a democracy. No bloodshed," he said proudly. "No guns. Only reason." He clenched both hands. *"Il faut tenir."*

I only vaguely understood what he was talking about. The television news, incomprehensible to me, saturated the city—the noodle shops, the auto shops, the convenience stores, even some of the taxis—but it seemed not to implicate me in its grainy, discolored events. Perhaps I felt the way my mother had felt when watching *Doctor Zhivago*: that these tragedies were present but unaffecting, because they were happening to foreigners—Caucasians in her case, Chinese in mine.

The restaurant was a small cheerful mom-and-pop on Xinsheng Road, with tiny bare bulbs strung around the entrance and tanks of pomfret by the street where one could pick out a fish and have it prepared three ways: meat, head, and soup made from the bones after the rest had been eaten. The waitress seated us at an upstairs table by the open window and left us with a jug of Taiwan Sheng.

"Now," said Atticus, pouring out two glasses of beer. "You have come back."

It wasn't a question, but the statement was offered up like the beginning of a story, which I was compelled to end.

"It has to do with Little P, I suppose. Or my mother. Or both. I don't know."

"You play the role of the good brother in your family, am I correct, Xiao Chang? The dutiful son?"

" 'Role' is right," I said, with a note of bitterness.

Atticus raised his eyebrows. "I do not understand. You are not genuine in your feeling toward Xiao P?"

"I am, of course I am." A fly buzzed along the invisible boundary of the window, struggled, lay still. "But it's not so simple. I can't say if I came back for him, or for myself." I looked at Atticus. "I miss my mother. It's like . . . the world has fallen apart since she died. Those dreams you have, when your parents have died, and you wake up and realize that they're still alive—now it's like the logic of all that has been reversed. I dream she's living. And then I wake up into the nightmare that she's gone. I have no family, no place to anchor anymore. I rent my furniture," I explained lamely. "I have no pictures on the walls. Little P is my only other point of connection in the world now. I can't just let him go again."

Atticus sipped his beer. "So you are hoping for a—what? Armistice? Rapprochement?"

"Something," I said. "I don't know if *armistice* is the word—we never really fought."

"And what form do you think this rapprochement will take?" said Atticus gently. "You expect you will become the best of friends?"

"No. Nothing like that. I just want . . . I want . . ."

Atticus didn't prod me.

"Mi Mama Caminitas," I said after a moment. "Do you know Mi Mama Caminitas? It was a brand of Mexican toothpaste we used a lot when we were little. My mother shopped at a grocery outlet because the brands were cheaper, and they dumped a lot of Mi Mama Caminitas there. You've never heard of it?"

Atticus shook his head.

"You see?" I looked down at the dregs of my beer. "All these things, all these memories are disappearing now that my mother is gone. Little P is the only one who would understand. Not that I want to sit around discussing the past with him all the time, but I just want a sign, I guess, that he remembers. He's the only one who can . . . justify my memories. Make them true." I blinked, feeling naked. "I need some kind of witness. The problem is . . ."

The waitress set down a platter of steamed fish and doled out rice, soup.

"The problem is?" Atticus prompted.

Something had occurred to me, half-formed, nonverbal—a feeling of uneasiness that found its way into words.

"Who is that woman?" I asked.

"That woman?"

"That girl. The one you called the maid. I saw her upstairs at Uncle's, after you left."

"Oh yes?" A kind of shadow passed over his face, a darkness I could not interpret. All at once he seemed nervous behind the placid exterior.

"Who is she?"

He looked out the window. The street below was coming alive with evening commuters, the dusk deepening in the park across the way.

"One of Xiao P's 'principles,'" he said, forgetting me in a blind moment of derision, upper lip curled in contempt. "You wonder why he has not come home in so long, why he does not call? Ha. Principle is a good reason. Principle has its shame!" His mouth wobbled with outrage.

Then, as if coming out of a trance, he seemed to see me, and the outrage was replaced by fear.

"Emerson." For once there was no gentle good humor radiating from him. He looked straight at me, clear, urgent. "You will not mind me being so blunt, I hope, but as your friend, I must say it. Get out. Get out now, and go home."

"But why?" I asked, taken aback.

He shook his head with some agitation. "It is not for me to tell you. I am bound by certain obligation."

"What obligation? To Uncle?" I thought of Uncle's stroke-damaged face. What was it about him that I could not nail down? The missing clue seemed all at once the key to everything, to the girl, the knife on the stairs, my own brother.

"It does not matter to whom. My job, shall we say, depends on discretion. There is no obligation to keep an old man on at a job for which he is not qualified, especially now that my father has been dead for some years. One can only push one's luck so far. So forgive me my obscurantness, Emerson. I only thought I would point out the woman to you; perhaps that too was a wrong idea. But as regards Xiao P—" He stopped and frowned. "Stay away from him. The knife cuts deeper than the blood."

"But he's my *brother*."

He waved this away with a small hand. "Life is short," he said, indifferent. He tucked a bit of fish in his mouth. "You care for such things more when you are younger. Your mother, she trained you as a good Confucian son. Myself, I have never liked the Confucian tradition too much. Loyalty to a tribe—*unconditional* loyalty—is dangerous. As bad as religion, I would say. Why should we treat a blood relation differently than we treat others? Are they more valuable than other people somehow? More important?"

He wiped his mouth fastidiously. "If you must stay, I can help you find your way around. But you will think about my warning, no?"

"The knife," I said. "You said something about his knife."

"A figure of speech only." He shrugged. "The manner of weapon is unimportant. A gun, a knife, a poison to the ear. Death is death, do you see what I mean, Xiao Chang?" He wiped his mouth again, as if the conversation were distasteful to him. "Once you are dead, your good intentions die with you. Better to leave it alone."

CHAPTER 8

ESPITE ATTICUS'S MISGIVINGS, I HAILED A CAB and went directly to the Palace after dinner in search of Little P. Someone there would have an idea of where he was, at least, and I was determined to see him again before I lost my nerve. But I could not shake the sense of foreboding that Atticus had stirred up. It was dark; the bright backlit signboards cast a dystopic light on the streets, and the battalions of scooters—people muffled up in their motorcycle helmets—seemed menacing too. I felt for the documents, which I had folded and stashed in my jacket pocket. They belonged to Little P; the motel was his. The sting would not go away. Let tonight be the night I would divest myself of my lie. I would give the papers to Little P and live quietly with the loss, like a monk, or a priest, or some other holy man. The cabbie farted richly and yawned.

It was Friday, which should have been good for business, but there was nobody in the lobby of the Palace except a faintly mustachioed clerk at the front desk. He eyed me lazily when I asked for Little P and said he didn't know where my brother was.

"Well, can I at least leave a message? Message. Message. Uh . . . *liu* . . . "—I consulted my pocket dictionary—*"yan."*

He shook his head, irritable. He had been watching some kind of soap opera on a mini-TV behind the counter. Upstairs, a hollow bass beat boomed like cannons, shaking the walls; a little plaster powder fell down on his head. He had a punkish pageboy cut, very ragged and fey, and he kept sweeping greasy strands of hair back from his forehead, glaring at me.

"Poison?" I said suddenly. "Poison *zai ma?*"

Again the lazy look, this time slightly animated by doubt. He didn't have to agonize too long, because at that moment a door flew open off the foyer and Poison himself came out, shouting and guffawing with someone in the room behind him. When he saw me, he stopped dead.

"Hello," I said.

"You!" He pointed. "You hear about the game? Come back to take it in the balls, *shibushi?* A little risky-risky?"

"I need to talk to Little P," I said.

"Oh?" A glance over his shoulder, vaguely, as if Little P might be standing there. Then he crooked his finger at me. "You come."

I followed him into the room. There had been a methodical sound of clacking up and down the corridor, like stones or marbles being rolled around, and I saw now that Big One was presiding over a session of mah-jongg, pushing the carved tiles to the center of an open table as a crowd looked on. The clacking stopped when I came in.

"The Xiao P, he busy," said Poison. He was wearing a poker visor, which made his sallow face look even thinner and more rodent-like.

"Busy with what? It's Friday night."

He shrugged and sat down at the table.

"Xiao P have big plan," he said scornfully. "Too big for tell us. You ask Shu-Shu"—meaning his father, Uncle—"he tell you what Xiao P do. Xiao P tell Shu-Shu every-ting, *shibushi, Da Yi?* Like little baby." He laughed and slapped the table in front of Big One, who merely grunted and adjusted his wall of tiles minutely, not looking at me. Poison tapped his cigarette into a cut-glass dish. He had a slim silver case for his smokes, a fine affectation, and his black linen shirt showed expensive stitching on the pocket and hems. If he resented Little P's closeness with Uncle, he also seemed to live high off the proceeds of my brother's labor. His little rat nose twitched. I hated his skinny swagger, and the way he spoke of my brother as if Little P were nothing—Uncle's lapdog.

"You now want play?" Poison inclined his head toward the table.

"Fine," I said. I took off my jacket. "I'm in."

There was a half-beat of silence in the room as Poison looked up, surprised. Then he grinned unpleasantly and jerked his chin at the man sitting across from him. The man got up and moved to the sidelines. Poison placed four tiles in the center of the table, and we drew: East Wind, North Wind, South, West. Some reshuffling of the seats, a throw of the dice, and then the game began.

Thick, stale cigarette smoke hung over the table like a storm front, tempering the white light with a dirty yellow cast. My hand was scattered: a mixing of winds and dragons, with a head of bamboo ones and a few copper tiles, several shy of a short straight. I wasn't a novice; my mother had taught me how to play so that I could fill in on afternoons when she and her two friends from the local commerce association had their game. In the past, my strategy had always been to play my hand purely, as if in isolation, without too much attention to what the others were doing. It had been easy enough to guess the old ladies' hands from the way they licked their lips when they were nervous, and anyway, we played for Luden's honey lemon cough drops. This was not the same. No talk, no pleasantry, only a hard, diamondlike concentration broken at intervals by a tense *"Peng!"* Tiles were thrown down recklessly, no time to think or plot: nine of bamboo, North Wind, a run of coppers broken and mismatched on the green baize. White Dragon, green. Big One discarded a South Wind.

"Kong." I snatched his tile and displayed my set. Poison scowled, deprived of his turn. A lucky draw gave me a three of coppers; Big One threw out an eight of coppers.

"Chi!" I knocked back my straight.

Gradually I felt the attention in the room turn toward me, and a sweet, heady fire filled my veins. A ready hand, wanting only a two of coppers, a White or Red Dragon. I put down a South Wind.

"Peng," called Poison, grabbing it. Big One was studying his tiles without interest, his heavy eyes dull and unblinking like those of a limp, bloated fish, but I caught him exchanging a look with Poison, a bright, enigmatic look almost of joy. Red Dragon on the green baize.

"Peng!" I shouted, reaching for it, but I didn't have the pair anymore, I'd broken it up and not remembered the play: penalty.

Afterward, I could never remember at what point the reality of my position dawned upon me. It might have been after Poison's third *peng* off my discards; or when I looked over at Big One and saw sweat shining on his beetled brow. A pair of eight bamboo, double birds, mixed straights. Big One took the first round. Dice were thrown; the game began again. Time shrouded itself in a feverish haze. Each time I looked up at Poison, he seemed to be getting farther and farther away. And then suddenly he would loom up in my sight, his gray-capped teeth bared, jeering. The others pressed up like phantoms around us, soundless and intent.

"*Mah-jongg!*" Tiles were knocked back on the felt: three *pengs* of North, South, West; a head of East, a trio of birds in stark simplicity.

"I thank you," said Poison, gloating. The thin metallic taste of blood glazed my lip. I looked at his hand wonderingly as the others murmured, low and distorted, stretching and lighting their cigarettes: he had won off a tile I had discarded. There would be penalties against me for that play. Poison's face shone as Big One totted up the score, and in it I saw naked appetite.

"Eight-oh-oh-oh," said Poison comfortably. He and Big One whooped wildly.

"Eight-oh-oh-oh what?" I felt suddenly cold and bewildered. "What does that mean?"

"You-ess dollar," said Big One, his English suddenly very loud and clear.

"I don't have it," I said. My cousins only laughed. Big One stretched luxuriously as he got up, the smile of a fat, satisfied cat widening his face. They had not understood.

"*Zhende, zhende,*" I said. Truly, truly. "*Wo bu neng fuqian.*"

They stopped laughing rather quickly.

"*Shenma yisi?*" asked Poison—rhetorically, I hoped.

"I mean I don't have that money. No one explained . . ." I trailed off; it was plain that no one understood.

Poison took a step forward. "What mean? You have money," he stated, as if it were a fact. "Of course you have."

"I don't."

He straightened his visor. The air in the room had changed. The others surveyed us with great attention.

"You *have*," repeated Poison.

"I just said I don't. *Wo meiyou.*"

"Means, you not have money *here*."

The others gathered closer, forming a tight enclave, and I suddenly understood that they were not disinterested parties.

"You not have money here," repeated Poison. He rubbed his sharp, ferretlike chin and smiled disingenuously. "It okay." He patted me on the shoulder. "We wait for you to bring."

"And if I don't?"

A shadow passed briefly by the open door: Little P, who did not look in but continued down the corridor to the main office. Poison's glance followed mine.

"Your *didi*, he . . . to my father, very important," said Poison. "Like son. Better than son. He think."

He popped a Life Saver in his mouth and crunched it slowly, circling the game table. Big One looked on, impatient, wishing, I supposed, that he had paid more attention during his English classes. Cherry-flavored breath filled the room.

Poison circled once, twice, then stopped and leaned in close.

"If Xiao P go," he said softly, "is too bad, *shibushi*?"

"Go where? Where would he go?"

Poison shrugged. "Taipei very expensive city. He need at least eight-oh-oh-oh you-ess dollar, I think. Cost of living very expensive. Cost of—how do you call it? *Baoxian*. Insurity."

"Insurance."

"*Henh.*" He inclined his head in mock gravity. "Taipei look safe, *shibushi*? But it not safe. You trust my word, *didi*. Accident happen. Man disappear. You find him later, maybe. In the river, on the shore. You maybe not know him at first, he is so—*zenma shuo?*— change. Water no good for the beauty. Make the skin rot. Make it peel away. Finger"—he seized my wrist—"and toe."

Softly, ever so softly, he bent my forefinger back. I tried to yank out of his grip, but he held on, his stringy little hand like iron wire around mine.

"*Yige yige de,*" he murmured, tracing an imagined cut across my first knuckle, second, third. "One by one. Before the karaoke, I work at market, do you know? *Zai shichang—shichang,* you know this word? Kill the chicken, kill the pig. I know where to cut the finger, how to skin." He let go of my wrist and smiled, gray rat teeth like fangs over his underlip. "Xiao P no more better than pig," he said. "More easier, may-be. Less noise."

A cold hand closed around my heart.

"But I am the nice guy," Poison continued. "I give two week. Two week, you come here. You bring the dollar." He motioned his cronies toward the door with his head. Everyone got up, began filing out; the air seemed to leak out of the room along with them. Lazily, Poison turned to go.

"You won't see a single cent," I said, voice high and shaking. "This is a travesty. You're my own cousin. A travesty."

Poison turned and slugged me solidly in the jaw. I sprawled back against the card table.

Black spots slowly tinged my vision. Through them, I could sense Poison standing over me, small, shabby, murderous.

"I study English two year," he said. "Needs no American to come say they better."

I FOUND Little P asleep with his head on the desk in the chilly back room. He did not wake up when I came in. I stood before him for some minutes, silently, looking around. No lights were on except the small one on the desk, which pooled in a dim, irregular puddle over Little P's head, like water, or blood. A half-empty can of shandy stood among the piles of trash and crushed-out butts. I picked it up and drank some of it, feeling parched. It was lukewarm and flat, but the taste haunted me. I used to buy canned shandy for the motel minibar. Little P and I had spent one fine afternoon with a purloined six-pack when our mother was away, sitting behind the Dumpsters among the dry poppies and sunshine, shouting as the interstate traffic roared along the horizon. That had been a good day; there were not many I could remember on which the horizon had been so bright and dusty and wide. Little P had been only eight, excited by the stealing. Every once in a while he'd held my hand. The thin face under the lamplight seemed to revert back to that little boy, innocent, vulnerable, the veins at his temple palely visible.

Now I had mortgaged his life. A cockroach skittered across the desktop, near Little P's half-open mouth, and he awoke with a small sigh.

"I'm sorry, Little P," I said softly.

He rubbed his eyes. "Sorry for what?" He was still only partly awake and blinked at me without registering any surprise or rancor—only tiredness and a half-dazed quiet.

"I should have come to see you sooner," I said. "Years ago. Mother and I both, we let you run too far, too long."

Little P blew out a breath and reached for his cigarettes, squinting and shifting uncomfortably in his chair.

"If I'd been more responsible, maybe you wouldn't be in this situation right now. I would've dragged you home. I would've found you a job. We'd all be home," I said, "watching *Cosby* or something."

"*Cosby!*" He coughed and spat into an empty take-out container. "If I was back in the States right now, I wouldn't be watching fucking *Cosby*. Tony Soprano, maybe. Bad-ass Jack Bauer. Even if he is some government flunky." His eyes narrowed, sharp, incisive. "Why're you still here?"

"For you," I said.

"'For you,'" he repeated. He spat again and rubbed his mouth. "Meaning?"

"I mean I want you to come back with me."

He made a tsking sound, the show of patience of these last few days wearing thin. "Emerson. Fucking A." His pack of cigarettes was empty; from the desk he took a stale-looking cigarillo. "What, you think you can just bust in here and order me home? Like I'm some kind of juvie? We're not kids anymore."

"All the more reason."

"Don't patronize me, brother."

"Then be straight with me," I said. "What happened to your face?"

"I told you." Becoming agitated. His lighter wouldn't work; he rasped the flint angrily, tossed it aside. "Nothing. A little run-in at a bar."

"Little P . . ." If the threat hanging over his head hadn't been so present, I would have pressed him, but Poison's voice lingered like a specter, draining me of any rights to honesty. If Xiao P go, is too bad, shibushi?

I put my hand on my breast pocket, feeling for Pierre Carcinet's papers. To hand them over would be a truce of sorts, a show of trust; perhaps, in exchange for property, I might get the truth of his life.

But as I started to take the papers out, something caught my eye. Smashed in on a high shelf among some empty boxes and a crate of rice wine: my mother, tilted drunkenly on her side.

"What the *hell*?" I slammed my hand down on the desk.

Little P looked, quickly stabbed out his smoke. "I'm taking care of it."

"I ask you to look after her, and you put her with the garbage?"

"Take it easy."

"Fuck you."

Little P blocked me as I tried to drag a chair over to the shelves and retrieve her. A feint to the right, to the left, but he was too quick, suddenly snarling in my face like a dog, jaw set. Blindly I swung at him. Memories of my mother shuffling up and down the plastic runners in her office at night, face drawn, sleepless over this piece of trash, my brother; the care packages she'd sent; the inheritance.

My fist hit its mark with a blunt crack. I felt a shock of pain like a firecracker in my jaw—but that was his only attempt at defense; otherwise passive, he submitted like a rag doll. A blow to his face, to his face, to his face again.

At last Little P dodged me, grabbed my arm, wrenching it painfully around my back.

"You worthless son of a bitch," I gasped.

He let go. I hobbled away from him, holding my jaw, and lowered myself onto a vinyl banquette.

Little P walked back to his desk and leaned on it, not facing me.

"Bet that felt good," he said presently. "You got some balls after all." He wiped his face with a tissue. His hands were trembling a bit. "Hard to tell under that prissy little front. Tell me, do the ladies really like that ironed polyester suit look? Does that pocket handkerchief make them swoon on the streets?" He paused, wiped his face again. "Who irons those things for you now that Mother's gone, anyway?"

"I suppose you iron your own suits," I said, feeling my jaw.

I guess it hadn't occurred to him until then that we were both wearing suits: mine gray, his black, but both neat, tucked, spotless except for the bits of blood on my cuff, on his shirt lapels. His mouth twitched, tightened.

"It's the *reason* for things that matters," he said fiercely. "Not the appearance. Not the outcome. Maybe we look the same from the outside, big brother, but we are *not* fucking the same."

He smoothed his jacket. "This is invention. This is will. This is self-determination. That"—he flicked a finger at my sleeve—"is fear. Habit. Castration." He brushed his cuffs. He was trembling all over now.

"All right. All right, you made your point. Calm down."

The corner of my mouth bled a little. I dabbed at it with the tip of my finger. Despite everything, I felt suddenly tired and at peace, as if all that was poison had been purged from me. As I sat looking at my brother, pity and guilt twinged lightly in my chest.

"Okay," I said. "Forget it. Let's just forget this. If you won't come home with me, then I'll stay in Taipei. We could, I don't know, start over again. Maybe I can help you."

He turned bleakly. "Help how?"

"I don't know. With the Palace. With Uncle." He twisted his lip. "At the very least we could get to know each other again. Mother's gone, Little P. You are the only one left."

"If you want to help me, you'll get me the will."

Silence. Red and blue lights from a patrol car flashed in through a narrow window, soundlessly.

Little P dragged the chair over to the shelf and brought the box of ashes down. He carried it to the desk and stood indecisively, fingering it for a moment.

"If you stay here, you'll still call the lawyer?" he asked.

"Monday."

"How long, you think?"

"A few weeks. I don't know. It depends on him."

His hands were gripping the ashes firmly, and his eyes met mine, searching. For a long minute, a war of inscrutability was waged, Little P's face as thick and smooth as wax. A tiny filament of resolve took iron root in my heart: he would never undersell the Remada for a quick buck. Not while I had a say in things.

He pushed the box imperceptibly toward me.

"Start over, you say. You say you want to get to know me." He laughed, and for the first time I heard something sort of wild and lonely in him, like a hint of autumn before a long, cold winter. "You don't want to know."

"Why not?"

He sat down in his chair again and swiveled away from me. His disembodied voice came gruffly from behind the chair back.

"You take her."

I picked up the ashes, put them down, picked them up.

"Little P . . ."

"I want the will, Emerson."

"I heard you. It'll just . . . take a little time."

OUT IN the lobby, I collided with Big One, who was trolling the grounds with ponderous aplomb. He poked a finger at the box.

"What means?" he demanded.

"None of your business." I jerked away, drawing my mother protectively to my side. His little, sunken eyes sank further. I should have played it differently—laughed, cringed, flipped the box casually in the air, anything—for he had seen a sign of weakness, of love and need. I could feel Poison watching me from behind the reception desk as I left.

CHAPTER 9

A FEW DAYS LATER, in a dismal little Internet place near Shi Da, I received an e-mail from my boss at Hastie and Associates:

From: James Tillock <jtillock@hastieandassoc.com>

To: Emerson X. Chang <exchang@hastieandassoc.com>

Cc: Emerson Chang <pbear1999802@hotmail.com>

Date: August 20, 2004 6:14 P.M.

Subject: your request and leave

Dear Mr Chang:

We were of course very sorry to hear of your loss Death is the great equalizer and reminds us to cherish each and every moment spent with loved ones.

Regarding your request for extended leave, we are happy to grant it. In fact your situation dovetails nicely with a situation of our own, namely the retrenchment of our biotech teams in the wake of some recent events (litchfield & Johnson, Lunentech, etc. If asked, please refrain from offering any comments on the situation until it has resolved without further rancors. You know what I mean) We have no desire to offend or betray a loyal employee of almost twenty years. Instead, we have put you on official FREE AGENT status until such time as our biotech operations might resume. You are a model team member, Mr. Charng, and we believe you deserve some time for yourself. Consider it a much deserved vacation (though of course indefinite and unpaid).

If therne is anything else we can do for you in your time of grief, please do not hesitate to ask

Warmest regards,
James E. Tillock

I had to read this over several times before I grasped the actual implications behind the cheery-leery tone. A fly buzzed laconically on my arm. All around me, the world continued, oblivious, pimple-faced boys smoking, playing EverQuest, or napping, heads down on their sticky console keyboards while the only remaining anchor of my former life dissolved in a weak platitude about death, some veiled threats, an empty offer of assistance. I looked around for help as I drowned, quietly, in waters of shame and rage. Work had always been a refuge from the failures of my life. Hastie had been dull, perhaps, but I'd taken pride in the neat marshaling of reports; the formulas applied to recalcitrant numbers; even the clean, efficient desktop in my office, wiped down at the end of the day, pens color-coded and arrayed like soldiers in formation—it had all given me a sense of completion, even transcendence. Now, somehow, I had failed, been ejected from that dry, beloved Eden. Without warning, without even the decency to say it straight out. I put a hand to my chest, suffocating in the smoky little room, and went blindly out into the sunshine.

Pride was only the more painful half of it. Without the job, there was no hope of buying Little P out. Some dim aural memory flickered in my ear: Pierre Carcinet and his mention of my inheritance, the property in Taipei. Perhaps the sale of it would offset a down payment on the Remada? But that property—it was my mother's childhood home. Could you sell one ancestral home to pay for the other? Gold for silver, blood for tears. A bank loan was possible—but my mother, in her lifetime, had paid off the Remada in its entirety. The thought of paying interest on it now was a bitter pill. There had to be another way.

I had not told Little P about the mah-jongg game, or about Poison's threat. *Tell him,* warned a small, nagging voice. *He knows them. He's the only one who can help you out of this.* But something in me balked at the prospect of asking him for help; I might almost prefer seeing him whacked to groveling before him. I shook my head violently to clear it of guilt and anxiety: eight thousand; two weeks; you'll still call the lawyer?

As I walked, the alien city seemed to make a show of its difference, its foreignness no longer just a temporary façade but a dawning fact of my new life. Everywhere I went, streets were being dug up with cranes and steam shovels, storefronts being dismantled, sledgehammers and pickaxes being wielded without sentiment or protection, buildings brought down with wrecking balls, no ceremony, broken asphalt dumped in a little area weakly fenced off. Strange faces and ciphers greeted me in block after block of shadowed, featureless high-rises. I ducked down an alley off the main avenue, but the strangeness was worse here: a little open market, tented by a dark awning, full of the smells of sweetness and decay. Chickens murmured in their crates; flies crawled over the sticky, split fruit; while somewhere nearby a hose was rinsing down a butcher's board, the bloody water congealing at my feet. A beggar moved slowly through the crowd, beating his head against the ground.

A two-story Starbucks dawned on the horizon as I came out of the fetid little alley. I almost ran to it, hazarding across the double lanes of Xinsheng Road against traffic. It wasn't the coffee drinks but the promise of quiet cleanliness that drew me, the familiar armchairs and soft, blurry folk with plucked bass over the stereo— a point of stillness and permanence in the wild.

The upstairs tables were nearly empty except for a few students, a group of businessmen making deals over Frappuccinos. I carried my mug to the farthest corner and sat down. After a moment, feeling conspicuous, I took out a little paperback I had brought with me from home and tried to read, but the words squiggled and swam, obscured by the churn of unkillable thoughts: eight thousand; the blade of a knife; Uncle's frozen face like plastic, mouthing its stunted sounds.

"Xiansheng?"

A light hand on my arm dispelled the broken images. A woman peered down at me inquisitively. She had been sitting several tables away when I came in, bent over a book. Even in my distress, I had noticed her: long dark hair, taut limbs, and straight waist, elegant as a dancer. I couldn't understand a word of her lilted Chinese, but the sound of her voice was distinctive, low and sweet.

"Sorry," I said. *"Wo bu dong."*

She paused, examined me with new interest. "You . . . are . . . forn?"

"Excuse me?"

She appeared embarrassed. "You are . . . foreener?"

"Oh. Yes. Foreigner. *Waiguoren.*"

She smiled again, this time at my butchering of the word. She had an unusual face, delicate, doe-eyed, marked with a kind of gentleness that reminded me of both sorrow and wildness.

"You to excuse, please. I see *that*"—she pointed to my paperback—"I think you must to know the English. You know?"

"Well, enough, anyway," I said. Then, because she looked puzzled: "Yes. English, yes. From America."

She clapped her hands in evident delight and clutched my arm again. "Much better! You can to help?"

She fetched the book she had been poring over. It was a computer manual from the eighties, the pages soft and discolored from age, punctuated occasionally with a smudgy black-and-white photograph. She put a finger tentatively on the word *C-prompt* and looked to me, patient.

"C-prompt," I said.

"What, please?"

I rubbed my forehead. "Hard to explain. It's . . . back when you had an MS-DOS operating system . . ." I struggled for the words, then flipped suddenly to the cover of the book: *Introducing PC-DOS and MS-DOS*.

I stole a look at her: that odd beauty, her slim body smooth as ivory but quickened with breath. Surely she didn't spend her days in some cubicle as a programmer.

"Are you an engineer?" I asked. I took out my pocket dictionary and found *engineer*.

She laughed. "No. This book, I find at DV8. You know DV8?"

"No."

"Bar. Pub. Many foreign customer. They leave book, CD."

"Oh. You have an interest in computers, then?"

"No."

She paused, looked down in embarrassment. She seemed pensive, as if she could not decide what to say. Then, impulsively, she reached across the table and took my hand. "You are marry?"

Her touch was warm and searching; I had not felt anything like it in a long time.

"No."

"Too bad." She sighed and shook her head, regretful. "You look like nice man. Can I say that? 'Nice man.' That is the good English?"

"Of course."

She smiled, satisfied. Her pleasure dimmed slightly as she remembered what we had been talking about.

"My boyfriend," she said, hesitant. "He too is the American." She tapped the PC book. "I want to learn for him."

"So he's the engineer," I said, feeling a kind of prick in the chest at the mention of her boyfriend.

"No, no. I want to learn the *English* for him."

"Oh! But . . . you mean with this?"

Crestfallen, she murmured something inaudible; clearly she had put great store in this PC manual, as if it were a book of enchantments.

"It's a good book," I said gently, backing off. "But maybe you should find another one. More useful."

She took the text back, staring down at it in confusion. I was still mindful of her hand on mine, her distinctive, lingering scent of tuberose and something sharper, salt, seaweed.

"You should keep the book," I said. "But you might study some other words too. Better if you had a regular teacher. If you want," I hazarded, "I could help you."

Her glance was so genuinely surprised, so gratified, that I felt extremely guilty, and told myself it was for her, really: she would never get anywhere with that computer manual.

I took her little notebook and pen and wrote:

light
dark
cold
clear
hard

jewel
glass

rock
flame
cave

rain
shine
burn
brush
blow

She looked over the list in silence. "I know already," she said af-ter a moment, pushing the notebook back at me. "Too simple."

"The words are simple," I said, halting. "But you can know the meaning of a word without knowing what it means."

"Shenma yisi?" She furrowed her brow.

"Let's just talk, okay? Using the words sometimes, if you want, or not using them. Or using only the words I've written. For fun." I put my finger on the page. "The cold flame burns dark."

She frowned. "What, please?"

"It doesn't mean anything."

"Then why . . . ?"

"I don't know. Because. Because that's what English is. That's the essence of it." She looked doubtful, and I thought she would probably excuse herself politely, take her book and leave.

But then she put out a tentative finger and moved it slowly, timidly across the page. "The light . . . glass . . . rain . . . is cold clear."

She looked up and laughed.

"Right," I said and laughed too.

"My cold rock . . . burn the glass rain."

"Excellent."

The lesson lasted another hour, or two; I didn't really know. Before she left, she gave me her number, writing it down on a page and adding to it a list of characters, which she pushed at me.

"For you," she said. "For next time. You must to learn." She winked teasingly.

The characters, in their terse complexity, had a look of veiled import, like letters coded in her lovely script.

She gathered her things and leaned over, her dark hair brushing my shoulder.

"Not to drink too much," she said, indicating my coffee. "Too much coffee bad for heart. Car . . . cardio . . . vascular inflammation. My boyfriend," she said proudly, "teach me. Is very healthy. Will to see you next week?"

Her name, she had said, was Grace.

AS I left, the streetlights were beginning to come on, and the air of day-end festivity had taken the foreign edge off the unfamiliar buildings and blocks. Still touched by the lightness of the unexpected English lesson, I had no desire to go back to my room. I was no longer staying with Atticus. His beautiful apartment, with its clean sheets and careful solicitude, made me uncomfortable— something hidden behind the display. Instead, I had installed myself at a budget hotel near the Main Station. It was called the

Tenderness and was as grim a place as the term *budget hotel* could suggest: stained tiles, a stinking drain, gaps between the wall and ceiling so that heat, smoke, and voices circulated in a thick haze.

Atticus had mentioned a rally tonight on behalf of his congressional candidate, at the 2-28 Memorial Park, so I took the train to the NTU Hospital station, thinking I might try to find him. The moment I exited the subway, I heard the dull roar of a crowd like the sound of rushing water, and followed it hesitantly. The park seemed low and unassuming from the outside, but inside the gate, the grounds opened out, the memorial itself rising over the trees like an abstract temple of iron and stone, water running beneath its unfinished framework, an old memory half-destroyed. In its shadow, crowds flowed.

I thought at first that the rally was over, the movement of people was so erratic. Not until I had pushed deeper into the throngs did I understand that something was happening.

"Duibuqi," I said, bumping a woman with a camera. She stood a little apart, training her lens on the murmuring crowd. *"Fa . . . faxian shenma?"*

The woman raised her head, her doubtful look quickly turning to disbelief. It was the girl from the noodle shop, the one named Angel.

"How do you—" she began, and then came a scream. Without warning, the crowd shifted violently, and the shouts swelled into a roaring tide. Someone pushed me; I was thrown off balance, staggering forward, and grabbed helplessly for support, bringing Angel down too.

"Are you all right?" I shouted, then had to roll away as the panicked rally stumbled over us, heedless. A blow to the head blinded me briefly.

Angel, knocked to her knees, struggled up and grasped my arm, half-leading, half-dragging me to a sheltered spot below the memorial, where the water trickled on, placid, through its trough beneath the hanging eaves.

"What's happening?" My voice echoed. Beyond the eaves, the police had moved in swiftly with their riot gear, trying to disperse the crowd. One angry old man lit a match and touched it to his own arm, shouting at a helmeted officer, who blew the flame out and moved him along, his impassiveness like an insult. "I thought this was a rally."

"It was. They whisked Li away," she said, gloomy. "Off in his little escape van. A bunch of Zhang supporters showed up." Her nostrils flared. "They should have expected this. What kind of fool picked the memorial for a political rally?"

"You know what fool."

Another familiar face swam up in the gloom: Atticus, looking flushed and oddly vibrant. He did a double take when he saw me, then smiled. "Emerson! So you did come, after all."

"You *know* him?" asked Angel.

"Family connection."

"That is a good way to say it," said Atticus, then muttered something low to Angel in Chinese.

"I don't care," she said, in loud, pointed English. "It was stupid to have the rally here. Stupid and stubborn. You know what kind of association this place has. Why would you go and open that all up again?"

Atticus frowned, a momentary break in his show of peace. "*Je me souviens.* One needs to be reminded of the past. One needs to remember who one is."

"One needs to cut the bullshit," declared Angel. "One needs to let history die. One needs a good kick in the ass."

"Young people," he murmured. "So much potential, but *vulgaire, toujours vulgaire.*"

"*Je ne regrette rien,*" she said, determined. "Would you rather have that?" She gestured out beneath the overhang, where the police were cordoning off sections of the park with barbed wire, preparing the fire hoses against a small faction of defiant old men and women.

"That is nothing," said Atticus. "Already people are going home. There will be no serious fight. You need not worry about true violence here; only the old ones care. There is not enough passion to light a single fuse in this city."

"No one should be lighting fuses," snapped Angel.

"Emerson, you are contused," said Atticus, changing the subject. He indicated the angry swelling on my forehead.

"I'm all right."

"I wish you had not moved out," he said. "It makes me uneasy to think of you in the city alone, without the language. Consider also the expense of the hotel. I know your situation is not ideal."

"Thank you, Atticus, but I'm fine. Really."

He put on his newsboy cap and said to Angel, "Next week, Guo Xiaojie?"

"Don't think I'll forget this," she said with some disgust. "Passion isn't progress. Inciting violence is not progress," she shouted as he disappeared.

"How do you know him?" I asked.

"I cover the DPP campaigns," she said, staring after him. "Free-lance. The Democratic Progressive Party. Atticus is a Party contact. Well, more like a friend. I guess."

We waited in silence. As Atticus had predicted, it didn't take long for the park to clear. The aged faction dispersed without the aid of fire hoses; campaign signs lay abandoned on the grass. There was barely more than the sound of the water running through its channel when Angel and I emerged from the memorial.

"You hard up or something?" asked Angel.

"What?"

"Something Atticus said. You strapped?"

"Maybe." I bit my lip as the bitterness about the letter from Hastie and Associates, almost forgotten, refreshed itself.

"You need a job, I got a job for you." Angel slung her camera strap over her shoulder. "A share. You help me write the Pennywise Pilgrim series, we split the stipend and proceeds seventy-thirty. What do you think?"

"But I'm not a food critic."

She sighed. "You're not writing for Miche*lin*. You eat; you leave."

"Seventy-thirty?"

"Listen, boy, you want the job or not?"

Annoyed at my indecision, she began walking away. I thought of the Remada, the chipped paint and starched, hard-won history to be put on the block if Little P took it over.

"All right! All right!"

She turned back calmly, looking smug. "Next Friday." She wrote down the address and stuffed it in my breast pocket. "Now what do you say to the nice lady who gives you a job?"

"Thank you," I said, thoroughly beaten. "Wait!"—as she started walking off again. "About Atticus."

"Yeah?" She glanced back at me.

"Have you known him long?"

She shrugged. "Couple years."

"Is he . . ." The right question was hard to compose. My friend, his depth of peace and calm marred by flashes of darkness, his warnings about Little P. "Is he someone you would trust?"

She laughed sharply.

"What?"

"Nothing." She laughed again, clearly amused.

"What's so funny?"

She shook her head. "Let's just say this: I wouldn't trust him farther than I could throw him." She grinned. "But I'm also pretty strong. Next Friday!"—pointing both forefingers at me. Then she resumed walking toward the park exit, still laughing and shaking her head.

CHAPTER 10

I HADN'T EXPECTED ANY OVERTURES OF FRIENDSHIP from Little P, so I was surprised when he called, the next day, and asked if I wanted to join him and Uncle for a spa.

"A what?"

"*Spa*. You know, a public bath."

I pictured mud, oils, big-hammed German women cracking my spine. Nothing could have seemed less manly, or less appealing. But I had to take what opportunities I had with him; he sounded, if not happy, then at least less remote, and I hurried to the sundries store on the corner to buy a pair of trunks.

The spa was on the ninth floor of an old building east of the train station. Little P met me in the dim green corridor just outside the entrance. He cracked his knuckles mechanically. He did not smile, but he held the door for me, and the attendants—mostly bent old men in gray jackets—nodded deferentially, as if they had been told who I was. Certainly they seemed to know Little P and

Uncle. In the locker room, they were helping Uncle out of his tracksuit, his sad, fat breasts quivering as he stepped hesitantly out of his pants.

I followed Little P into the bathing area, a huge gray-tiled gymnasium with windows cut high up in the walls. Shapes milled about in the close steam—heavy, surly souls tattooed along fat backs and arms, a purgatorium of men soaking in the sulfurous waters. Stone benches lined the perimeter of the spa, figures lying prone and sprawling across them, at rest between takings of the cure. High above the pool, a dragon head of mottled jade jutted out from the back wall, its expression glum as it spat water in a weak arc over the heads of bathers. Little P halted suddenly.

"*Oof.* What?" I asked, stumbling into him. His skinny body was rigid, tense as wire, and tuned, seemingly, to the lounge area to our right, where more naked bathers rested, smoked. A tall, pensive man sat on a stone bench facing the water, notable at first glance only for his height and stillness as he surveyed the water. There was something odd about his eyes. A cigarillo dangled from his lip.

"Know him?"

Little P stared. The man had closed his eyes, apparently dozing. You felt that he was mindful of everything about him, whether he saw it or not, like a spider on its web. As we watched, his eyes opened again. His gaze flickered over me, held briefly, and I saw what was so strange: he had a walleye, one pupil focused, the other cocked dreamily toward the other end of the spa.

"Nah." Little P moved toward the edge of the pool, though with some circumspection. "He just looks like someone."

"Did we have to meet here?" I asked as Little P settled himself into a far corner of the pool. I dipped a toe in the scalding water. An attendant had tugged at my trunks as I left the locker room, indicating that I could not wear them into the pool. Poolside, another attendant presented me with a tray of individual cigarettes like hors d'oeuvres at a wedding. I waved him away.

"Emerson." Little P had taken a cigarette; he blew the smoke up toward the ceiling. "You keep standing there looking around, people are going to think you're a fairy. Get in."

I slid into the water, mainly to cover myself. I could make out Uncle a little way down the edge of the pool. The cigarette smoke drifted up, mixing with the steam in a mute, wispy exchange. Bathers crossed the water like shadows of huge fish, or birds; Little P watched them cagily, sunk low.

"You call the lawyer yet?" he asked, after a silent interval.

". . . No."

He eyed me. "What's the problem?"

It was my turn not to say anything. I'd been obligated to leave my glasses behind, and in my wavering vision, Little P gradually receded, became a voice. The sulfurous tinge in the air stung my throat.

"I see," he said slowly. "I see how it is. How much of a cut you want? We can work something out."

"I don't want any cash from the sale of the motel," I said, coughing.

"Well, what then?" He spread his hands. "Shares? Favors? Name it."

"I'm not trying to *profit* off her death. I don't know why you can't understand that."

He sighed. "Listen, you don't have to keep up the front, okay? She's *dead*." He knocked his knuckles loudly against the tiles of the pool. "She can't hear you posing as Jesus anymore."

I splashed water over my shoulders to keep them warm, for a chill had settled in my chest. Little P shifted in the water, seeming to lean closer in, and spoke softly; with the steam, it felt as if we were in a private chamber, a room of the mind.

"I don't blame you," he said. "Sanctimony is the best defense for people like you. It stings, doesn't it? Mama's boy does his thing, day in and day out, and all the immortality he gets is a good night's sleep. You always did buy that crap from Mother. The Chinko-American dream. Family, respect, diligence, prestige. Shit." He brooded, letting his arms and legs drift.

"It's not shit," I said. "I've made something of my life."

The assertion sounded hollow, even before Little P laughed, harsh, disbelieving. Again shadows crossed the pool, dark wings cutting the surface of the water.

"Don't fool yourself," he said. "You and me, we're nothing. Both of us. Don't think I don't know that. I'm not going to leave any monuments behind, and neither are you. But at least I've gotten to the bottom of something in my life. At least I've seen the thing."

Someone had really cranked up the steam. I couldn't see him at all anymore. Blindly, I swiped a hand in his direction and came up with nothing. "Bottom of what thing? Seen what?"

Silence.

"Knowledge," he muttered cryptically. "Forget it. You wouldn't understand."

"Little P, you haven't even tried to explain."

"You're not a human being, you're a fucking saint, you know that? So patient, so innocent. Can't get a smudge on you, ever. You just sit back in judgment, you and Mother, fucking Siamese twins. Does it make you feel *good,* Emerson, to look down on the world? Does it make you feel powerful?

"You know what your problem is?" He splashed water over his head and blew his nose in his fingers. "You never learned to fuck."

"Who told you that?" I whispered, paralyzed. His tirade had grated but not scored too closely to this point, but now, here was my deepest shame, my deepest secret exposed. Not even my mother knew, and Little P was laying it bare in public, like an accusation. The steam had cleared, and I could see him distinctly, tensed with a ferocity that must have been bottled up for years. "What are you talking about? How do you *know?*"

He glanced at me, thrown off.

"What are *you* talking about?" He splashed his head again, stopped. "Don't tell me . . . you've never . . . ?"

I stared him down, face blazing.

His fire was doused by the intimacy of confession. "Well, why the hell not? You had the whole motel to do it in. You lived alone in Boston for a year."

"I don't know." I splashed my chest halfheartedly. "I never found the . . . *appropriate* woman, I guess." True enough, with all the implications of the word *appropriate*: propriety, usury. And how J had used me; how shameful the attempt to play at love had been. I shook it off.

Little P was saying, ". . . right downstairs. Let me do this for you, brother. Cheap cunt, bad boobs, but you get what you pay for.

Sometimes you get lucky, you get a real prize, a young one with tits like milk and lips like sugar, if you know what I mean." He considered. "I guess you wouldn't."

"A prostitute, you mean."

"Yeah."

"I said I was—"

"Yeah, yeah." He waved this away. "It's not the Holy Grail, just tits and ass. Really, that's all it is." He shook his head. "No wonder you're still a virgin. So, are you game?"

"No."

"Come on."

"No. I don't have anything to prove to you."

I turned away, stung, shaken, and splashed water mechanically on my chest. Why was it wrong to hope for love? Why was it wrong to honor my mother—respect the idea of her, even if the reality was flawed?

"Who is that girl?" I asked slowly.

Little P didn't say anything.

"Who's the girl?" I said. "Stop hiding from me. Stop lying. If you want me to call the lawyer, I have to know what's going on. Why exactly do you need the money, anyway? What's the debt?"

The trickling from the dragon's mouth seemed suddenly very loud. I turned back. Little P was gone—vanished, the spot where he had been sitting empty.

I looked about. The same slow, dyspeptic movement of men ranged through the fog, as if nothing had happened. "Little P?"

Uncle had edged closer, looking at me. I got out of the pool and circled the perimeter. Shadows turned to me in the gloom, faceless, indistinct. I pushed past a couple of stocky bathers, thinking I saw my brother at the other end of the gymnasium, but it was an old man rubbing his hollow chest with a towel, sightless, decrepit.

No sign of Little P in the bathrooms, in the corridors. The walleyed man on the bench was gone.

As I came back out into the pool area, I bumped into another man who seemed faintly, unpleasantly familiar. I wouldn't have recognized him without his clothes on, but a pall of cherry flavoring hung around him, thick as honey.

"I'll kill you," I said. "I swear to God, if you have anything to do with this . . ."

Poison surveyed me lazily, fanning himself with a newspaper. "Ah, Mr. Eight-oh-oh-oh." He looked me up and down and sniggered.

"You little . . . turd. Not a cent, I told you. And I will . . . screw you up if something's happened to Little P."

"Not understand." He grinned and sucked his Life Saver insolently. "The English not so good."

"Motherfucker."

"What you say?" His eyes narrowed sharply; all at once he wasn't playing anymore. Big One appeared. Uncle had come up from the pool. He was muttering, agitated but incomprehensible, and as I looked at him, I finally grasped what it was that had been gnawing at me: a flash of knowingness and intelligence beneath the paralyzed exterior—the stroke and paralysis nothing but an act.

In my worry and nakedness, my nerves seemed to be shutting down. As I looked from one face to another, they seemed to blend together; even the faces of the attendants seemed dark and conspir-

atorial, with their sloe eyes and half lids and their solicitous defer-
ence, the way they conferred with each other in slurry Hokkien
and then turned to present a united front against me. The spa now
seemed full of eyes, foreign, evasive, all inscrutable in their hidden aims. I pushed past Poison and hurried to gather up my
clothes.

ATTICUS ANSWERED the door slowly, the latches clicking without
his customary decisiveness. He blinked at me in the corridor, pale
and worn against his blue silk pajamas and robe, thinned hair
frowsy and on end. It was very late, past midnight. I apologized as
he stood back to let me in.

"I've checked the Palace, his apartment, all the shops up and
down Tongan," I said. "Even the river park and the night market."
That last had been an ordeal, combing through the crowds of students pushing violently among the boiling vats and steamers, the
cast-iron griddles spitting oil under the strings of lights illuminat-
ing the alley. "I don't know what else to do."

Atticus rubbed his neck as if it ached and considered, his eyes
cast pensively downward. "And you have not call the police yet?"

"No."

"Good."

He rubbed the back of his neck again, an uncharacteristic motion. He seemed confused, disoriented.

"I am sorry, Emerson. It is very unexpected for you to show up
this way, at this time. I mean only that it is good you have come to
me. The police are not so reliable as you might want; you do not

know who to trust. It is getting better, but it is not impossible to find yourself in the hands of the *hei shehui,* even now."

"So that's it? No police report? No search?"

"He has not been gone more than twelve hours, Xiao Chang. Give things a little time."

"There isn't any time. I keep thinking . . ."

I closed my eyes briefly, but I could not shut out the creeping sense of doubt. *Wouldn't trust him farther than I could throw him.*

Atticus was leaning on the side table.

"You seem very sure about my brother," I said.

"I have know him much better, for a long time," said Atticus, but he was taken aback, blinking owlishly, clutching at the gap in his pajama front. The slip in his grammar too seemed a telltale sign.

"Well enough to know where he goes each day?" I asked. "Where to find him, if someone wanted to find him? Just what has he gotten himself into?"

Atticus looked down. He had picked up one of the shapeless black rocks that lay next to the helmets on the sideboard and turned it over silently in his hands.

"You should not make accusations you cannot prove, Xiao Chang."

"We're not in court, are we."

He muttered something in Chinese and put a hand to his chest, wearily.

"What?"

"I say I am getting too *old* for this." He looked at me, and he did seem old for once, shriveled inside his splendid robe. "I was a Catholic once, did you know?"

"Atticus."

"My father, he was very angry. He hated the Pope. He hated the liturgy. He hated the ceremony and pageant, especially then, when people were so poor. He took my cross necklace away. 'Can you eat this?' he asked, and then he made me throw it in the trash burner. But I loved all the pageant when I was a young man. The idea of heaven. The idea of hell. I eat and shit and sleep, like the animals, but it is only for man that the eating and shitting have the grace of God. It is only for man that the life is connected to the death. What do you think, Xiao Chang?"

I shook my head. "Atticus—"

"Myself, I think it is a lovely dream. Someone, somewhere, in a very cold winter, made up the story to comfort himself and his children, the way you make a fire. Warm and pretty—before it goes out. The faith, it gave me order, and beauty. I wish I could believe still. You do not know how much I wish I could believe. But I cannot. Age has made me incapable. Order and beauty—you do not find them outside life. Only this world, only this once. You must take hold of them wherever, however you can."

"Atticus." I pounded my fist softly on the console. "Why are you telling me this?"

He put the rock down and walked nervously to the window. "I am only trying to explain myself. It is not an excuse. I am getting too old for such complications." He turned to me. "I am your friend, Emerson. I have not lied to you. I swear I have nothing to do with his disappearing, though of course you are right. I do know where Xiao P is. But if I tell you, you must give me something in exchange."

I thought of the Remada, and the mah-jongg debt, and sighed. Atticus, interpreting this correctly, said, "No, no. An exchange of *confidence*." He held up a finger. "No questions asked of me—now, or later. I cannot explain more than I have about your brother. You must not ask me to."

"But why?"

"No questions about no questions. I have already involve myself too much. Agree?"

Hopelessly, I shook his proffered hand. It would be enough to find Little P. All day the prospect of returning to the Tenderness to face my mother had dogged me. *I ask you to look after him, and what happens? He is your own brother.* The dark, familiar weight closed down on me. The effort to earn love, to deserve it—you thought it would end with the grave, but somehow it only intensified, like the pain of a phantom limb, unassailable.

"*Zhende, zhende,* I am getting too old," murmured Atticus as he gestured at me to follow. "I hope you will not judge me too harshly in the end. The final impression, the memory, that is the only kind of afterlife I can believe."

He opened the door to the small room I had slept in before and bowed me in.

Light from the living room spilled over the floor, revealing nothing. The room was empty, the coverlet on the cot pulled straight. I looked around.

"Was there something in here you wanted to show me?" I asked.

Atticus looked startled, followed me into the room.

"*Ai—ya.*" Clutching his silk robe together, he shuffled over to the tiny window and peered out. The window was open. A light, sudden gust riffled through the room like an intake of breath. Atticus reached out to fish something off the metal grille, then closed the window softly and turned on the bedside lamp.

In the small light, Little P's knife gleamed in his hand. He laid it on the coverlet.

"He was here."

"Yes," said Atticus simply.

"But . . . why? What happened?" I crossed to the window, trying to see out into the darkness. "And why would he come here?"

"You must believe me, I wish he did not," said Atticus sharply. He regarded the cot with narrowed eyes for a moment, then—though it looked perfectly clean—began stripping it of its bedding, savage. Little P's knife flew under the dresser.

"What do you think?" he hissed. "Do you think I wish to harbor the damned? To be party to the degradity of the human soul?" The seam of the undersheet ripped as he yanked it from the corner.

Abruptly he sat down, hard, his arms full of bunched linens. He seemed to be no longer speaking to me, or he was speaking to something, or someone, through me. "And yet I cannot do. *Nuoruo!*"—bitterly. "Coward! Coward and weak." Tears glittered in his eyes but did not fall. He half-turned to me.

"But why should it be coward of me to want beauty? Or comfort? Or love. When we die, it is forever. Should we not take as much as we can get, now, before death wipes it all away?"

"Atticus . . . ?"

He roused himself slightly, as if from sleep. "Ah, *bon,* Emerson."

He looked at me—really looked this time, without the glazy half look of terror, misery. He seemed tired and small. "We are what we are; it is what it is. That's all. Most of the time I can accept."

He put aside the linens and got down on his knees, searched until he found Little P's knife.

"Make sure to tell Xiao P it was you at the door tonight," he said, handing the knife to me, blade turned toward himself. "Give him the knife to prove. Otherwise he may think I am lying. That I have betrayed his confidence to others. Of course he still may think I am lying." His mouth flickered wryly. "Perhaps that would be for the best."

"What you said about Little P—about harboring the damned. What—"

"We have an agreement, Emerson, yes? No questions." He reached out and took my hand firmly. Despite myself, I was grateful for him—for his odd desire to befriend me, for his tortured help. "I am still your friend, but no questions. It is very late, or very early. You must go."

Silently protesting, I went to the door, and Atticus bowed me out into the hall. The locks clicked behind me. I thought I was alone, waiting for the elevator, when suddenly I heard him call softly, "Emerson!"

I turned around. He stood in his doorway, battered. His robe had fallen open, mouth parted, and for a moment he seemed to be on the verge of revelation, all secrets to be shed from his brittle frame. Then he cinched his belt tightly.

"I neglect to say good night."

"Good night, Atticus."

"Emerson. *Bonsoir.*" The door closed.

CHAPTER 11

THE PHONE RANG AS I LAY TANGLED IN A DAMP SHEET,
sun slitting around the edges of the broken blind. I'd come
back to the Tenderness in the small hours and fallen onto the bed,
still clutching Little P's knife. Fretful dreams involved my mother,
something hazy and wispy, coded, like a message being tapped out
from the inside of a box, so that, fumbling for my cell, I felt I was
lifting the receiver of a great cosmic line.

"*Wei?*"

No reply. The message being tapped out faded slowly, the wires
cut. The silence on the other end had a personal quality to it, a
lean, hungry shape and form.

"Little P?"

Still no reply. "Little P, where are you?"

He coughed. "How'd you know?"

"I know," I said. "Of course I know." I found myself suddenly
weak with relief, trembling. The body's knowledge was greater

than any rational mind; it knew the depth of devotions and connections that reason could not grasp.

"I guess you want me to explain." His voice was hoarse and low, and there was some kind of ambient noise, as if he were calling under cover of the street.

"No," I said. "I don't. Not unless you want to."

He didn't say anything. I could tell he was puzzled, guarded, as if this might be yet another trick in the minefield. I pushed myself up to sitting position and hung my legs over the edge of the bed.

"I have your knife. It was me at the door last night."

He waited.

"When you disappeared, I thought I'd never see you again. I thought you were dead."

He coughed again. "Better that way."

"Don't say that."

"Why not? Anyway, death isn't the worst of it." His voice was thick and slow, as if he were drunk, or sick. "The worst is when you die and keep on living. Your whole fucking life to live and no relief from it."

"Where are you?" There was some kind of sound in the background; I strained to identify it.

Little P was quiet for a moment. Then: "Would you believe me if I said I wanted to come home?"

"Now?"

"Not now. A long time ago."

"Then why didn't you?"

Silence. The background noise was clearer now: water rushing, the sound of waves washing across the shore, or perhaps it was only static. I had a sudden image of a lovely, peaceful beach bathed in sunset, the kind we used to go to when we were children, up and down the Pacific shore.

"I had my reasons," he said. "I never meant to abandon her. I never wanted to stay here. But I couldn't come home."

"Why not? You were the apple of her eye. There's nothing you could have done that she wouldn't forgive you."

"You can't understand." He coughed again, sounding wretched. "It doesn't matter anymore."

"Where are you?" I repeated.

"It's not important. I called to ask you a favor. You said you wanted to help."

"I do. I meant it."

"Well then." Did I detect, in the slight pause, a kind of embarrassment—a kind of pride? "I need money."

"I just gave you five hundred a couple of weeks ago."

He cleared his throat. "Not enough. Not this time. I'm not asking for a handout, I'd pay you back. All I want is a little loan."

"How much?"

A pause. "Two grand. U.S.D."

"Two *thousand*?"

"You stayed behind to help me."

"I know, but—"

"Then *help me*."

The line seemed to go dead but for the sound of the sea in my ear.

"Hello?" I got up, agitated. *"Hello?"*

Little P's voice came back. "I wish I could just stop running."

"Who is it, Little P? It's— Is it Uncle? Or—the cousins? Who are you afraid of?"

"*Who* is incidental. The question is *what*."

"What do you mean, 'what'?" I thought immediately of restive ghosts, the incubus and the succubus eating the history of the flesh, turning old regrets into night sweats, terrors. I pictured a spirit sucking out my brother's breath.

"Help me."

"All right. All right. Where are you?"

"I can't say. It's okay, I'm safe for a while. But next Wednesday, midnight. Bring the money in cash. I'll tell you where."

"All right. Listen, Little P—"

But the line was really dead this time. I threw the phone down on the bed in frustration.

The box of ashes stood upright on the nightstand and held my eye. *Death isn't the worst of it,* Little P had said. *The worst is when you die and keep on living.* He had been right when he said I couldn't understand. My life had been a long gray stretch dogged by fear and loneliness, a little sorrow, a little boredom. And yet if someone had held a gun to my head, I would have begged for more. I wasn't a nihilist, not like Atticus; I thought perhaps there was another world beyond death. But it didn't matter, for another world was not this one.

I had a sudden urge to open the box, to see once and for all what change death had wrought. Did she smell of antiseptic still? Did the bitter, herby scent of her medicines inhere in her ashes somehow? And her dreams of Princess Diana, her propriety and gossip, her impenetrable core of love, her abiding ideal—where did all of those go, in the final incineration? What was there left to remind me, not just that she had existed once but *how* she had existed?

I did not open the box. Instead, I took out my little travel iron and filled the reservoir with gray tap water, plugged it in. The dinginess of my little SRO had gotten me down temporarily but no more, not anymore. Was it not too late to turn things around? Little P had said as much with his haunted plea: *Help me*. There was something I could do. The little timer pinged, the water bubbled like a deep breath in the silent room. I hung my suit over the door and pulled the creases straight while I blasted them with steam, like cleaning armor before a battle, or repeating the rosary. From now on, I'd keep my suits clean and shirts pressed, my temper even, my thoughts calm. I would save my brother; I'd get him out of here.

"WHERE DO you think they *come* from?" she asked.

It was late Friday night, and we had found ourselves in a kind of underground bar, a steel-and-chrome affair that hummed and thumped with strobe lights and R & B, and a mindless bass line throbbing like a swollen vein. I had met up with Angel earlier for a restaurant review, a meal of simmered goose and blanched lettuce and beer, which she had drunk with a hard-bitten vigor that seemed premature, given her age. The geese, stripped without ceremony, had been boiling away in a drum on the sidewalk, feet sticking up above the rim of the broth. " 'A true local experience,' " Angel pronounced, writing furiously in her little notepad. Then she crossed this out. " No. 'The food of the proletariat. The food of the people.' "

"Hardly," I said. The bill had run up astonishingly, three times what a meal of beef noodles would have been. I watched her write. "Aren't you patronizing your public a bit?"

"Oh, neohippie tourists eat this crap up."

She rested her chin on her pen and looked at me pityingly. "It's called the Pennywise Pilgrim series. Neohippies always have trust funds to burn." She shook her head with some irritation. "Just eat your goose, boyo. I know what I'm about."

Afterward, I had wanted to say good night and go back to the Tenderness, but Angel had insisted on a drink. The Roxy catered to foreigners, but there were a good number of locals here on a weekend. I could see one pimpled young man trying to gaze down a Taiwanese girl's dress. Some shoving and shifting in the crowd; the Budweiser girls approached, making their nightly rounds; a triumvirate of vice—cigarettes, beer, I forgot the third—employed girls in skimpy clothing to hawk their products independently in the bars. The Marlboro girls wore big white ten-gallons and matching high-heeled boots with tight shorts, and would let you wear their hats as part of their promotion. Angel had gone off to get a whiskey. A Bud girl insinuated herself into my little corner of the crowd and began her spiel in a high, squeaky voice.

"Lai yi ping," I told her. Her jeans rode low, revealing delicate hip bones. I observed them with mingled lust and melancholy. At the same time, I felt unreasonably protective of her, in a way that I would never have felt toward a boozy white stripper in Las Vegas. "Our people," my mother used to intone, magnificently, like an Indian in an old TV movie, "our people." I didn't even like Bud.

"Pig." Angel had sidled back with a neat whiskey.

"Sorry."

"Not *you*." She indicated a sorry-looking specimen who was cozying up to the Bud girl; he stroked her neck and whispered words festooned with spittle into her ear.

I sighed, ready for the coming screed. Angel, I had discovered, had recently graduated from college with a communications degree, and her father, at a loss, had shipped her off to relatives in Taiwan. Before the Pennywise Pilgrim series had fallen to her, she had been fired by both the Nationalist-run *China Post* and its DPP rival English daily, the *Taipei Times*. The disputes were not political, as far as I could tell; Angel only objected to the practice of running advertising specials as news without identifying them as ads, and also the fake bylines. Fair enough, but she had called the editors turtle eggs and sons of turtles and stormed out in a huff. Her Chinese was fluent, but she had a short temper, and seemingly not many friends. An only child, I guessed. She pushed her chin out aggressively and settled her glasses on her nose.

"Why don't you *do* something?" she hissed. She had an underbite, which allowed her to say things quietly without appearing to move her jaw.

"About?"

"The rape! The pillaging of our women!"

I looked over at the boy, the weak chin and lank hair, the way he ingratiated himself with a sweaty hand as she laughed and continued her little beer advertisement. A toad at home; here, a pale, exotic prince. I felt a throb of envy.

"Well, it's not as if he's holding her against her will."

She sighed. "It's the *prin*ciple, not the *thing*. You really think this is just about sex?"

"I don't know." My martini had been made too dry. "It doesn't look like much else."

"Well, it's not just *sex*. If it were, these . . . *folks* . . . could just go buy a big fat hooker in L.A. But they come here. Why?" She drained her whiskey and raised a finger like a wise old professor. "Because they want a pretty, meek Oriental girl kowtowing to their will. Your blood sisters are being groped by the social dregs of the Western world, exploited by capitalist pigs! And for what? To boost the self-esteem of losers who couldn't catch a cab with their looks in America. Tell me that doesn't piss you off."

"It doesn't piss me off," I said. "It makes me jealous," though in fact I did feel the stirrings of some resentment, too irrational for action. If a woman didn't like you, she didn't like you. The Bud girl was laughing, letting the boy wear her baseball cap. "Anyway, who's cashing in on her profits?" I nodded toward the silent presence near the door. "Her boss looks rather local to me."

She frowned. "This is all about demand," she said. "He wouldn't be doing this without demand." Suddenly she punched me. "I can't believe you bought a beer from her."

"It's her job."

"It's a form of prostitution!"

I was starting to get angry. "Let's just be clear here. Are you mad because men are exploiting women, or because the West is exploiting the East?"

"Either. Both." She looked taken aback.

My beer arrived, and the Bud girl stripped me of one hundred *kuai* over the quoted price plus tip, disappearing expertly with my change.

Angel went off in a huff to write up her restaurant notes in the corner, leaving me alone with my beer. I ordered another martini. I had had rather too much to drink; the bar now seemed smaller, hotter, and more cramped, the soft light from the recessed alcoves in the brick obscuring rather than intimate. More people had come in, the crowd spilling out onto the dance floor, where a mirrored ball revolved, flecks of light drifting dreamily through the air. As I looked around the room, I seemed to see it, unwillingly, as Angel did—cold transaction, trading and sales where formerly I would have thought friendship or, possibly, an awkward kind of love: a possessive hand on the elbow, a finger on the lips. A thumping, throbbing set had started up again, and the couple next to me tongued each other, pressed up passionately against the wall. I felt myself palpably aging as I stood in my suit and sipped my Bud; I thought I might prefer to be back in my room with my mother and a Hershey's bar.

"Emer-son?"

A figure moved toward me through the thick sea of sweat and smoke: Grace, pale, luminescent—a cool spot in the hot, damp underground. For a moment I thought she had searched me out.

"How did you find me?"

"The cold light blue on glass," she said.

"What?"

"I have practice," she said, slipping her arm through mine in a best-girlfriends kind of way. "My boyfriend, he have not hear me yet. For the surprise."

Of course; she had come with her boyfriend. My heart fell as she scanned the crowd anxiously, squeezing my arm.

"I want for you meet him."

"I really don't think that would be . . ."

Against my weak protests, she led me firmly toward the end of the bar and presented me. "Emerson, I like for you meet A. A, *ta shi* Emerson."

Late forties, maybe fifty, with short bleached hair and a dark tan. You wouldn't call him fat, but he looked oddly overstuffed in his T-shirt and khakis, and seemed melancholy and uncomfortable, shifting on his stool. He did not smile as he shook my hand.

"Drink with us, please?" Grace, delighted, nudged me toward a seat. A moved over with ponderous effort, not speaking. His unfriendliness made me nervous.

"What are you having?" I asked, signaling the bartender.

A shrugged and made his own cryptic signal to the bartender. He had been nursing what looked like a glass of chocolate milk.

"Whey protein," he said, fishing out a couple of almonds that had drowned at the bottom of his glass before handing it back to the bartender for a refill. "I keep a jar of it here, special, for days like these."

"Oh," I said. I tried to think of something to say. "You must work out."

He perked up momentarily. "I had a killer session today. Four sets of reverse hamstring curl, four sets drag curl, four sets lat, and *five* sets cable crossover."

"Oh."

"Intense, I know." He popped the almonds in his mouth. "See these tie-ins? Between the delts and triceps?" He fingered his upper arms critically, as if judging a piece of fruit. "Gotta get 'em crisper. More defined." Then he lapsed back into silence, brooding. I had the sense that he hadn't registered our presence particularly; he talked like a man speaking to himself.

He eyed my martini and beer with sudden focus. "You gonna drink both of those?"

"I was, yes."

"Mhmm." He crushed an almond in a clean ashtray and sprinkled it in his glass.

"It's just gin. Gin and a beer."

" 'Just' gin. You know you excrete calcium at a rate of two to one when you drink?" Reckless, he crushed another almond.

I glanced at Grace, who was resting contentedly against A's arm.

"That's not even the main thing, though," he continued. "The main thing is, alcohol weakens you psychologically. You lose vitamins and minerals, but even more, you lose focus, will, and the desire to succeed."

"Not much for me to lose on that count."

"Is that a joke?" he asked, not belligerent but plaintive, confused, as if he really wanted to know. I swallowed the rest of my cocktail.

"Only kidding."

"I thought so." He sipped his shake. A sudden bitterness made his voice break. "Ha ha ha. Right. You think it's funny? It's not funny."

"I didn't mean anything," I said, taken aback, but he overrode this, gathering his fury.

"No one cares in this pathetic little backwater. Look at this place. The ancient wisdom of the Orient—ha! Can't even build a proper gym. All anyone cares about here is money and clubbing and what kind of car you drive. But hey, I don't blame you," he said, laying a heavy manicured hand on my shoulder. "I feel for you, man. Like a phoenix for the ashes. Have another one. On me."

He threw a few bills down on the counter. "Come on, Grace."

He stalked out, stiff and ponderous with muscle. Grace made an apologetic face before running after him, leaving me alone with my drinks.

"Who's that?" asked Angel, sidling up.

"Nobody," I said, draining my martini. "I met her at Starbucks."

I SLEPT a little on the short cab ride from the Roxy to the Tenderness, and when the cab pulled up, I lay blinking up at the seams in the ceiling. I had had my dream again: the coffee, the trolley, the pink, hazy sky as I rode toward my office in the financial district. There had been something qualitatively different about it this time, though—a feeling of strangeness, as if the dream, which had also been my waking life, had separated from me and now floated authorless in the fund of half memory and invention. Distantly I recognized the office desk and the plants and the dusty computer monitor as mine but distantly, like an archaeologist coming upon artifacts of his ancestors. The dream left me desolate. I paid the fare and got out.

The hotel was chilly, a perpetual draft blowing from the vents overhead. Angel had clapped her hands in disbelief when she first discovered where I was staying, and laughed. "But that's a *love* hotel!" Tired, I tried to think of Grace again, but Angel's round face kept interfering. I had not said good-bye; she would be angry. The elevator walls were covered with small, grimy mirrors printed around the edges with advertisements.

I rolled back my sleeve and flexed my biceps tentatively. Tiny Emersons peered back.

In my room, shedding my clothes, I was too tired to turn on the light. In the darkness, I bumped hard against the chair and paused, feeling about with my toe. Something was not quite right.

I ventured farther into the room, tripping over something in the middle of the floor. My window caught the light from the street; I pulled back the blind and looked around.

The door to the closet swung loosely on its hinges. In the false white light, I saw that the mattress had been overturned and the desk drawers upended on the floor. Clothes, underwear, a notebook or two—everything was scattered where someone had pawed through my carryall. The old, derelict radio lay drunkenly on its side. The pages of my mother's will fluttering like leaves.

I don't know how long I stood there before the instinct for order seized me and I knelt down to pick up a few sheets of paper. They were covered with grit and a fine, stubborn dust that clung to my fingers and clothes. I brushed at it, but it only ground more deeply into the fabric and skin. My mother's box lay on its side in a far corner, and I understood that the dust was not talc or some kind of litter. It was ash, ash, ash, all over my hands.

CHAPTER 12

MY FIRST INSTINCT WAS TO CALL THE POLICE, but when the dispatcher answered, I had to hang up. Several minutes spent thumbing through my English-Chinese dictionary for the word *thief* yielded nothing. *I've been robbed.* The thought came very slowly, hardening like wax into the form of fact. Then: *I am reading the dictionary.* I tossed the book aside. Little P's phone was off again; Atticus was not home.

"*Wei?*" Angel always sounded brusque on the phone. At least she wasn't asleep.

"Angel? It's Emerson."

"*Oh.*" She was still angry about the Roxy, then.

"Are you . . . Can I trouble you to come down to the Tenderness for a minute?"

"Can I trouble you to give yourself a good cock punching for me? No. No, I'm busy right now. Tata."

"Don't hang up! Please, please, Angel. It's a small emergency."

"What up, boyee?"

"Just come, if you can."

She arrived shortly, her little bulldog face pushing anxiously in front of her. I had swept the ashes into a heap with a piece of paper, but otherwise things were as I had found them.

"Shit," she breathed as she came in. Then she blushed and looked away. I was still half-undressed; hurriedly I zipped up my trousers.

She called the police, and an officer arrived to take a report. Angel kept indicating me with a careless thumb, saying, *"Ta,"* and it was strange to think of myself in the third person.

"Did you see anyone when you came in?" asked Angel.

I shook my head. The officer made notes as he walked about, lifting the derelict drawers with a toe and examining the lock.

"What's he saying?" I asked.

"He'll file a report." She shrugged. "But they're not going to spend their time chasing down some teenager for stealing a few things from a foreigner in a love hotel. Besides," she said carefully. "He thinks we're together."

"So?"

"So? So he thinks you had it coming. It looks like the other guy's revenge."

The officer interrupted her, indicating the ash along the floor. Angel glanced at me quickly and answered in a low voice. He was a tall, stringy man with a bored expression, but at this his eyes widened. He adjusted his cap heavily and made a few more notes, then spoke to Angel.

"Are you missing anything else?"

"No. Fifty U.S. dollars, a watch, a pair of shoes. I think that's all." Then something crossed my mind. "Wait."

I went over to the makeshift desk and sifted through the papers on the ground. "My passport. My passport is gone."

"Oh, Emerson." Angel relayed this to the officer.

When he was gone, Angel went down the hall to use the bathroom, closing the door behind her. I walked over to the pile of ashes and knelt.

Grayness and a fine particulate; a pale white powder that suggested parchment, or the color of my mother's skin. So at last I saw her transmuted into her new form, silent, in some disarray, no less forbidding now than in her actual person. Proving, I supposed, that some kind of spirit did inhere in the basic matter of things. The thought should have been a comfort, but it filled me instead with a slow, suffocated dawning and dismay. If she had been nothing but dirt, nothing but dust and ash, how much easier it would be. I put my hand out, ran my fingers softly through the powdered grit. Not so much like ash as hard little seeds, inert but waiting.

"Can I have your purse?" I asked Angel when she returned.

"My . . . this?" She had a red beaded silk purse with a zippered top and a braided cord slung over her shoulder. Against her dun-colored fatigues, the pouch looked odd and migratory, like an exotic bird blown off course. She was unwilling, but these were extreme circumstances. Reluctantly, she emptied the contents and put them in her pockets.

Together, we managed to get almost the whole of my mother into the silk lining. I zipped the top and hung the bag across my chest, testing. The weight rested lightly but with heft against my side.

"It's just temporary," I told Angel, who was smoothing her blunt-cut hair behind her ears in a studied way. "Until I find her a permanent home."

Unexpectedly, Angel's face grew cloudy with emotion, and she seized my elbow, giving it a hard, painful squeeze.

"You can't *stay* here," she said. "I never thought you should stay here. It's not *safe*. What if they come *back*?"

"Don't be silly. There isn't anything to come back for," I said but without conviction, for her words raised the specter of Poison, his gray little teeth grinning at me and the smell of cherry candies as he said, "You *have*." He didn't know where I lived, of course, but there were any number of ways to find out. He might have followed me; Atticus might have told him, or Little P, unaware of the debt. I would have to be careful now; perhaps I was being followed; something would have to be worked out. The late hour and the alcohol made my thoughts thick, gauzy. I pawed through them heavily to hear Angel saying, "Come back with me. At least for tonight."

I had no choice, really. Angel had ridden her bike; I clambered up precariously behind her, clutching my carryall, and off we went, she pedaling laboriously as I wobbled along.

It was the hour of the night when cities show themselves. Traffic lights blinked, off-line; street dogs wandered in the alleys, carrying away trash and scraps, shitting in the gutters. The pavements gave off steam like a long, collective breath, and the smell of open drains hung in the air. In my mother's stories about the old country, Taipei had been a land with a single train going to and from school, a church and a priest, fresh sugarcane, candy stores, earthquakes, curfew. One more death, I thought vaguely, sleepy—death of a memory, of an image.

"Quit *listing*," said Angel, swerving. My head jerked up; I had fallen asleep. "Or else we're going straight into the gutter."

When we reached Gongguan, the night market had all but died out, stalls shuttered, the second-run theater closed, only a few noodle shops doing small business, like candles in the dark. Angel propped the bike in the entryway, and we went up. She waved me into the apartment furtively, like a convict, without turning on the lights. She lived with her grandparents. We seemed to be treading down a hallway of books, scrolls, another little shrine with incense burning in the corner.

She slid a pair of paper doors open and paused. "There's only the one bed," she whispered.

"Fine," I said, too tired to register this completely. The mattress lay directly on the tatami floor and smelled of camphor, the way my mother's closet had, long ago. Time seemed to fold in on itself as I shed my suit and lay down gratefully: five years old again, drowsy with fever, burrowed in the warmth of my mother's bed. Footsteps in the hall; voices (for my father had still been alive then) low and soothing outside the door, bodiless but palpable, as if to say that I would never be alone. Soon my mother would come and place her hand on my forehead, a gesture of tenderness that haunted me still, for I had never found its equivalent since. I would reach out and touch her face in the dark. My fingertips found a patch of warmth, and I traced it achingly.

Until the dream faded, and I became aware that it was Angel's skin I was touching, soft, indeterminately white and silky. Unclear, even, what part of her I had put my finger to: an arm, a breast? She did not say anything, or move, though from her breathing she was clearly awake. A question hung in the camphored air. Rigid, awake, I could not answer it. She was my friend, but even loneliness could not conjure love where it did not exist. Quietly I withdrew my hand and rolled over, away from her, clinging to the edge of the mattress as if to a floating spar. She shifted tentatively in the bed, her leg barely grazing mine; the touch was gently baited, like a hook in my skin. Still, I couldn't respond. It took a very long time to fall asleep again.

IN THE morning, the piece of sky out the window was a thin whitish blue. I rolled over, a dull memory of distress circling the bed, weighing upon me more heavily as I dragged up toward the surface of wakefulness, until I finally remembered: my passport.

Angel was gone. I swung my legs over the end of the mattress and sat up painfully. It was not just my passport; all my official documents—driver's license, social security card—had been in the little desk at the Tenderness, and were now gone. How odd that something as dry as a government document could have such a hold over you; I felt suddenly exposed—as if all these years I had been a U.S. citizen only nominally, and now that right had been rescinded, through fate, or through the invisible hand of some central intelligence.

Voices rumbled beyond the sliding doors: Angel's thin, strident one; and a lower one—an argument of some kind. Suddenly Angel yelped and footsteps approached, sharp and canny. I leaped up and drew Little P's knife from my carryall, clutching the bedspread around me.

"Emerson!" Angel's face appeared as the doors cracked apart. "I'm sorry, but he kept saying . . . and he wouldn't take off the—"

The doors banged as someone behind her forced them fully open. A man in a black motorcycle helmet stood in the doorway, tense. He didn't move, only raised his head toward me in silent, chilling recognition. I knew immediately it was Atticus. His dark, mirrored visor was still down. The effect was malevolent, anonymous, and instinctively I tightened my grip on the knife, even as I said, "It's all right, Angel. Leave us for a minute."

She wavered, uncertain, then left with a dubious, angry look at Atticus.

I motioned him into the room, then went over and shut the doors behind him.

"What is it?" I asked. "How did you find me?"

The helmet was not just faceless but voiceless; he seemed mute. His frail frame, usually so straight and proper, sagged heavily against the back of Angel's rattan chair. I reached out and lifted the visor.

"Atticus . . ."

His bruised, bloodied face looked back at me, eyes bright with tears, or fever. I pulled the helmet off quickly. He had a lump on his forehead, and his scalp bled. I found a Kleenex and a bottle of water in my carryall and dabbed at the blood trickling down his temple.

"I did not wish to implicate Guo Xiaojie," he said. "So I keep my helmet on. It is bad enough without suspicions. I went to the hotel, but you are gone. I suspect you may be here."

"What happened?"

He took the tissue from me and held it to his head. His gray fingers trembled.

"I was at home," he said wearily. "Drinking coffee and eating my toast. Planning for the day. Two men come to my door, they say they are from Zhang's campaign, they want to talk." Zhang was the Nationalist candidate in the upcoming election, a short, bad-tempered man with a strident voice who had twice evaded charges of bribery. Earlier in the month a radio host supporting his rival had been attacked outside the station, but there was no proof that Zhang had ordered the hit. "Of course I don't want to talk. I think I know what they want. I have evidence, you know, Xiao Chang."

"Evidence of what?"

For a minute a smile seemed to flicker on his face, far away. "Scandal," he breathed, conspiratorial. "Sexual scandal implicating Zhang. This time with proof. Pictures. Witness."

"I'd rather not know, Atticus." For some reason he was making me nervous.

"Oh, it doesn't matter," he said. "In a week, two weeks, everyone will know."

"They didn't come about the proof, then?"

He shook his head. "Let me finish. I let them in. I thought, if they are actually from Li's campaign, and intend to harm me, they are acting very funny. Why would they announce themselves? Not very politic, *non?* Even Zhang is not so graceless. So I open the door." He looked at me. "Stupid, I admit."

"And then?"

He dabbed his head more vehemently, not speaking. I imagined that he was replaying the event in his mind.

"Xiao P has asked you for money, has he not?" said Atticus slowly. There was an odd, mechanical note in his voice, as if the words were being drawn from him unwillingly.

"Yes," I said. It was not a question I had expected.

His fingers moved over his bruise and pressed, hard, as if he wished to intensify the pain. Beads of sweat stood out on his face.

"There are people," he said, "who have an interest in these monies. Who are not willing to let it rest simply with Xiao P."

"But Little P said I didn't need to bring it till Wednesday."

"You have the money, Xiao Chang?"

"Yes. Some, anyway. Enough for this."

He straightened up. A shadow slid over his eyes, and he pursed his lips. "But this is, as they say, only the tip of the ice glacier. Xiao P is very much in debt. If he should need more, will he come to you, do you think?"

My cell phone beeped suddenly.

"Probably. I guess." I sat down on the bed, all at once nauseated by the conversation. "I don't know that it'll do much good. *He's* the wealthy one, now—almost. The motel is his, or will be." A twinge of guilt as I thought of the papers in my carryall. "My mother left me a parcel of property here in town. Somewhere in Songshan. I was planning to go see it next week. But she grew up there. It has sentimental value. I don't want to sell it if I don't have to."

Atticus walked agitatedly over the tatami, a strand of bloodied hair like a gash across his forehead.

"Property," he echoed, incredulous. "In the city? Here?"

"Yes."

His frail chest heaved up and down lightly now, like a bird's.

"Why?"

"I wish you had not told me this," he said, his voice rising, no longer the bleak, robotic monotone. He crossed quickly to the sliding doors, as if to check that they were secure, and then he came over to me.

"Xiao Chang, you must listen," he whispered. "I will keep my mouth shut, but do not tell anyone else that you have a property to liquidate."

I drew back, startled. "But . . . why? It's too late, anyway. Angel already knows. She had to help me locate the real estate agent."

He sighed. "How can you be from the San Francisco city and not understand property worth? Do you not see how valuable this would be in a city like Taipei? They have to build to the sky as it is. Guo Xiaojie is no problem, I think; you may trust her. But nobody else, do you understand?"

We both blinked. I pulled away from him.

"No, I don't understand." I stood up and pointed Little P's knife at Atticus. "I'm tired of being scared without any explanation from you! Any proof! You hint at things, you deliver these pronouncements, but it's like you're . . . daring me or something! Like a game. Play detective. Connect the dots."

Atticus blanched. "Believe me," he said, "I am never more serious in my life, Xiao Chang. It is no game. And I would not risk it if you were not a friend."

He was sincere; I believed what he said; and yet, there was something not quite honest in him when he called me his friend, said he risked everything for friendship. He picked up his helmet and put it on.

"Get out of here while the time is still good," he said softly at the door. He flipped the visor down. "Going," he said and was gone.

My cell phone beeped again. Distracted, I looked down at the little glowing message.

$8000? it said. Then, YOU NEVER TO FORGET.

I FOUND Poison in a little back room of the Palace, watching *The Sopranos* on a busted television. He was alone, for once, and subdued, sprawled on a banquette in his undershirt and flip-flops, eating a bowl of pork and rice. I did not knock; he sensed someone in the doorway. Slowly he stopped chewing. I could see the back of his neck tense. Then, in one swift movement, he whirled around to face me, back to the wall.

"Your brother not home," he said and waved the remote; I suppose he meant to defend himself with it.

"I'm not here for Little P."

"Uncle go with him."

"Not here for Uncle either."

"So?"

In his boxers, he looked like a white spider, cunning, sickly, and thin. Without Big One and his entourage, he seemed diminished, and unexpectedly, I felt a kind of pity. I looked around at the stained ceiling, the broken TV, the shop light that swung dangerously low and precarious from a wire. Even the Remada in its earliest years had been better than this. A cheap Impressionist print hung incongruously beside the television—Monet's *Water Lilies*. Someone had bought the print and put it there; the fact seemed to speak of a dreaminess somewhere in the Palace, an ill-defined longing for water.

"You like this business you're in?" I asked.

He blinked, thrown off. "What mean?"

"This KTV. The karaoke."

"Wo xihuan." But he didn't sound convinced. He darted a narrow glance at me, wary. "Like or not, what matters?"

"Your English is very good," I said. "Surely you didn't learn it just to run a second-rate karaoke den."

I don't think he knew the term *second-rate*; he seemed uncertain whether or not to take umbrage.

"Architect," he muttered. "I like to be the architect. Pei Ieoh Ming."

"So why didn't you?"

"Have not the school." He looked at me directly this time, eyes blazing. "Must to the U.S. for the school. No money to go. The architect is also no money, say my father. Is right. Is no money."

He kicked a take-out carton halfheartedly out of his way and wiped his greasy mouth on his shoulder. A dilapidated fan sputtered in the corner.

I removed an envelope from my breast pocket and placed it on the table.

"What is?"

"One thousand U.S.," I said. "In *tai bi*."

First he looked startled; then he grabbed for the envelope with both hands. I drew it back a little.

"This is conditional." He made another swipe; again, I pulled the envelope away. "Leave Little P out of it. This is between you and me."

He grabbed the envelope without concession and counted out the money. It took a while; I chewed a hangnail. The Taiwan dollar was one of the weaker currencies, with many zeros after its conversion.

When he was satisfied, he gave the bills an approving pat and turned to me. "I say eight thousand, not one."

A bastard, when one really came down to it. All pity shriveled and died by the light of the shit-eating grin he gave me.

I leaned in close. "You touch my brother, you get nothing."

He blinked and dug a nail into one of his little rat ears, flicking his waxy fingers to the floor. Then he laughed expansively and held up his hands in a gesture of good-natured surrender.

"Okays, okays," he said. "I said I am the nice guy. We say, you give me eight-oh-oh-oh by *zhong qiu jie*." His eyes narrowed. "You know what means *zhong qiu jie*?"

"No."

"*Ai-ya!*" In one explosive movement he upended the makeshift bar. "*Gan ni ma! Fuck your mother!*" Vodka and corrosive whiskey leaked out onto the floor. "What *do* you understand? Nothing! Nothing. Son of a turtle's egg! You are not the fucking Chinese. You are not the fucking anything! Talk, speak, but understanding *nothing*! Maybe you understand this?"

He grabbed a bottle of vodka and smashed it, then backed me to the wall, the jagged end of the bottle to my crotch.

"*Zhong qiu jie*," he said, suddenly calm. "Mid-Autumn Holi-day. Very nice. Moon very big, very bright. Look up to the sky, see the

Princess Chang-e waiting for lover. Maybe have barbecue. Very nice." He dug the bottle in slightly, grinding it against my zipper. "This year *zhong qiu jie* is October. One month. Little more than one month, I give you. Very"—he searched his vocabulary list—"big heart, no?"

"Just leave Little P alone," I said through my teeth.

He let me go, pushing me roughly toward the door.

"You not to worry about Xiao P," he said, soothing. "We leave his finger alone. Finger is not good, not *special*. I work in the out-doors market, I know. Finger is bone. No meat, worth nothing. But the *cojones*"—he smiled and cupped his groin tenderly—"the *cojones* worth big buck. Eight-oh-oh-oh, maybe?"

"I don't speak Spanish." I cradled the purse of ashes against my chest and backed away. "Seven thousand," I said. "And you don't touch him. Fingers or balls."

CHAPTER 13

MY INHERITANCE LAY IN THE SHADOW of two flanking apartment buildings, down a narrow lane. It was low and dank, made of a kind of stucco, with a roof of leaking corrugated tin.

"Here," said Angel, pushing at the gate. A rusted padlock scraped and fell into the weedy overgrowth. The yard was sealed off, broken glass embedded along the top of the walls to keep intruders out. Inside lay a private Eden lush with neglect. Grass, sumac, a splash of overgrown ragweed in the corner. Mosquitoes swarmed up from the weeds leaning high against the house and bit at my hands.

The real estate agent trampled a path to the front door and let us in. It was an odd thing, to see the place where you had begun: you imagined mystics and incense, a wizened old sage, and got instead packing boxes, water damage, mold climbing the walls. Maybe it was only neglect, but it seemed to speak of a more basic meanness. The agent chattered as we moved through the small rooms, as if I were a buyer, not a seller, but it barely registered. I was thinking of my mother, who had never been at home among the grizzled, dopefied tenants of the Remada. She had always longed for one of those huge tract homes with its naked aspirations and ugly symmetry, a three-car garage, respectability. Her first and last actions of the business day had always been to check her appearance in the cracked glass over the register, for she would not be seen without her hair combed and her harsh white makeup applied.

"*Aiii-eeeek!*"

Angel shrieked from a back bedroom. I dropped a box of musty linens and ran to her.

"Look out!"

Something soft and winged strafed my head as I charged into the room. Soft-bodied bump; scrabbling, scritching in the eaves. Dirt rained down into my collar.

"Kill it!" shouted Angel.

The agent screamed like she was being stabbed. "Kill it!"

I picked up a ceramic pot that was near to hand and threw it. The bat redoubled its frantic efforts, wings blurred, clattering like a pack of cards. A battery of glasses and cups hurtled through the air—Angel, blindly picking up and throwing whatever she could.

"Quit it!" I shouted. "Just calm down!"

A length of heavy pipe did it at last. The bat peeled suckingly off the wall, impaled on the pipe's joint end.

"God, what a mess," said Angel, looking around at all the smashed pottery and glinting shards as if surprised.

I sighed and tossed the pipe away. It smashed against a shelf with a tinkle of glass. The agent, recovered from her fit, patted her hair and began her bright, chirping spiel again, though her smile had slipped a little.

"She wants to know what your timeline is," said Angel. "She thinks, with a little work, it'd be worth at least five hundred thousand . . . certainly an optimist"—lowly, under her breath. Then, "Hey! Are you listening to me?"

I had approached the dark corner where the pipe had fallen. Something in the configuration of the shelf and the dirt-filmed mirrors made me move closer.

It was, I saw, a shrine—an altar exactly like the little shelf reserved for the garlanded portraits in my mother's apartment at the Remada. The two frames were not mirrors but photographs of my grandparents, the glass overlaid with dirt. The shelf held an arrangement of candles, wicks burnt out; a vase; a little bowl of blackened fruit. The chiming grew stronger, two bells sounding off each other, the tones threatening to resonate together in a single note. I had already seen the shrine at Uncle's house, of course, but this was different; something about it would not let go. Not the portraits, which after all Uncle had had too.

Then it came to me. It wasn't just the objects themselves; it was the arrangement of them that showed so clearly the imprint of my mother's hand. The candles laid in threes, the swag of the garlands, the brittle plastic flowers carefully fanned out and centered between the portraits. In them I could see the little altar in the motel, as if peering through a rent in the curtain of years. A signature, a message read aloud after the source was gone.

The agent prattled on. I turned to Angel. "Tell her to get out of here, will you?"

"Huh?"

"I said I'm not selling."

Her mouth fell open slightly. She looked at the smudge the bat had left. "Then . . . what are you going to do?"

For the first time since arriving, I felt a flint of happiness strike in my heart. "Live here."

THE PLACE Little P had asked me to meet him was around the corner from the Palace, a bilevel *xifan* eatery full of steam from the huge vats of congee, and the tiny jewel-like colors of the little side dishes lined up along the buffet. Though it was midnight, the place was busy: tech men just off work in their bland white oxfords, scanning the newspaper for the Taiwan Index; students; a crowd of old men gumming their food, shouting at one another. I had put on the better of my two suits as a kind of ceremonial costume for this exchange. The great wad of cash lay in my breast pocket, loud as a shout; I crossed and recrossed my arms to hide it.

Half an hour passed without any sign of my brother. Finally I got up and walked down the street to the Palace.

One of the clerks dozed at the reception desk, a cigarette burning in the ashtray, pinned possessively by a greasy, nicotined finger, even in sleep. The lobby was deserted, although I could hear both the nasal strains of an old Shanghainese pop song and the boom-and-bust bass line of some hip-hoppy track coming from the upstairs karaoke rooms. My mother had liked those pop songs from the mainland herself, the old, plaintive ghost of Shanghai glamour singing sadly about the age of blossom, islands in the graveyard. A strange underwater atmosphere prevailed as I moved toward the office, the thin melody distorted, echoing. I opened the office door.

"I hope—" I began, then stopped.

Little P was on his knees, facing the far wall with hands on head, his back to me. A gun, a hand, a black uniform. All these things registered discretely as I stood dumb at the door.

The man in black grabbed Little P by the collar and spun around, catching my brother in a headlock and pressing the gun to his temple in defense as he turned to glare at me. Tall, sallow, he was familiar: the man at the spa, the long-faced man with the slow eye.

He hissed something at me, finger on the trigger.

"Please," I said, quavering. The words fell weakly in the dreadful silence. "Anything. But not him. Take me."

This seemed to enrage him, though he could hardly have understood the English. The cop—for his uniform was that of an officer—tightened his choke hold on Little P and grunted through his teeth.

Little P clawed at the man's arm.

"Ta," he said, his voice rasping, choking. *"Ta you." He has it.*

The officer looked at me with new interest.

Trembling, I withdrew the envelope of cash and held it out to him. He motioned me closer with a jerk of the head. When I was close enough, he snatched for the envelope. I clutched it to my chest.

"Ta," I said, shaky, pointing at Little P, making clear this was a trade.

He released Little P, pushing him roughly back against the wall. Little P coughed and choked. I handed over the envelope, and the cop directed me toward the wall with the nose of his gun.

As he counted, I bent over my brother, whose rasping breaths were getting easier. I put my hand on his back, but he swatted me away violently, as if I'd burned him.

The cop pocketed the money. I expected him to leave, but instead he went to the office door and closed it. A panicky feeling made my heart race, as it used to when the lights went down in theaters. There was to be a second act.

He strolled deliberately over to the desk and picked up a book, thumbing through it at leisure. Every so often he ticked his ring against his nightstick, slow, calculated—*tick tick,* like chips of gathering tinder. He put the book down and made a slow circle around the perimeter of the desk. A toothpick dangled from the corner of his mouth. Someone—the water lilies person, I assumed—had hung a poster of *Nude Descending a Staircase* on the wall, and he studied this for a long moment, shifting his toothpick from one side to the other.

Suddenly he laughed. He had a high-pitched giggle, joyful and pure as a madman's. He swung around abruptly and spoke to Little P, his voice low, pleasant, tinged with an undercurrent of polite, deadly calm. Little P answered without looking at him, or me, staring at the floor. It was an argument of some kind, a negotiation perhaps. I watched the cop warily. His slow eye gave him a blind expression. You couldn't tell where he was looking, what he might do next; it was like circling a two-headed snake.

"You have your money," I said. Anxiety made my throat close up on the words. "What else do you want?"

They ignored me, murmuring low and harsh. The cop made another measured round of the desk, stopping right beside me.

I didn't see it coming at all, so that when he pistol-whipped me across the face, the shock splintered my vision—a bright white flash, the taste and texture of bitten metal. The ceiling lowered, pressed upon me.

"What do you want?" I clung to the edge of the desk, stunned, vision blurred by tears. The cop backhanded me again, and again. Pain shot down my scalp, tingled in my groin. I yelped. "What do you want?" Through the mist of shock, I peered at Little P, who seemed in my dimming sight, strangely isolated, passive—no protest, no surface emotion, just a flat, unreadable expression.

When my vision cleared, the mouth of the gun gaped in my face, issuing a faint breath of graphite, cinnamon.

"What do you want from me?"

No answer. Stillness, silence. Little P was watching us simply, without speaking.

They remained this way, locked in dreadful defiance, until finally the officer lowered his pistol. He stood, looking for a moment blind and uncertain, before recovering himself. Some muttered expletive as he stalked toward the door.

"Qian wan bie wangle," he said, glancing over his shoulder at Little P, who merely stared back. The cop shrugged, picked up his cap from a banquette, checking the inside of it before putting it on.

But when he reached the door, he paused, drew his gun, swift, smooth, and fired.

"HE WAS holding that book upside down," I said to Little P.

"What book?"

"The book he took off your desk. The thesaurus. He was reading it upside down."

The *xifan* eatery was still warm and crowded. Little P had gotten a bottle of Taiwan beer from the refrigerator and drank it wearily, leaving his porridge almost untouched. I had no appetite either; my nose was bleeding, and my temples rang. The cop's shot had narrowly missed my shoulder, and I could still hear the singing of the bullet, feel the raw place in my throat where a shriek of terror had torn out.

"Officer Hu," said Little P. "He likes to think he speaks and reads English. He also likes to touch my things. Intimidating, he thinks."

"For my money, there's nothing like a good old-fashioned gun for intimidation."

Little P took another swig of beer and said nothing.

"You owe me," I said, sopping up blood with a handful of tissues. "You owe me an explanation at least."

"Simple," said Little P. "Hu wants his protection money."

"Protection money for what?"

"For *protection*," said Little P impatiently.

"I mean, from whom?"

"Everybody," he said. "From our competitors, from the local toughs. From the police too."

"What would the police do to you?"

"Shut us down," he said.

"On what grounds? Fire code?"

"There's no fire code." This was true. The building across from the Palace had no windows, only little bread box–size holes for air-conditioning units in the summer.

"Well, then."

He put down his beer. "Emerson, do you have any fucking idea what the Palace does?"

I flushed. "Why . . . KTV," I said, faltering. "Karaoke and snacks and beer."

He snorted. "If we were counting on the karaoke for cash, we'd be screwed ten times over by now."

"Drugs," I said. My heart seemed to push up through a funnel. "A front for the international drug cartel."

"Don't be an asshole," he said, irritated. "Do we look sophisticated enough for that?"

I thought of the clerk sleeping at the reception desk and concurred.

"Well, what then? Gambling? Theft?" I threw out all the vices I could think of.

"Maybe it's just as well." He lit a cigarette; he was in a reflective mood. Knowledge and ignorance; my heart seemed poised evenly between the desire to know and the desire to remain oblivious, just a little longer.

"The cash," I said. "That satisfied Hu, no?"

"For now."

"How about the check I wrote you earlier? Did that help?"

"Would've."

"You already spent it?"

He examined the end of his fag.

"For God's sake, Little P."

He flicked ash at me. "If you want your money back, just take it out of the motel account."

"I'm not asking for my money back." I shook my head, frustrated. "Even if I did pay myself from the motel, so what? So then you would owe the Remada. What's the difference?"

"What's the difference?" His face flushed, the first display of emotion I'd seen all night, and he lunged across the table in a sudden rage.

"The difference is the Remada is *mine*," he hissed. He had my collar, and I could see the line of scarring that the stitches would leave in his forehead. "Mother left it to me! You have no right to keep stalling. Who's the lawyer? Give me his name!"

"No," I said faintly.

I suppose he didn't deal with defiance very often; his expression was cold, stonelike—underlaid by desperation. But for once I didn't care. I was chilled by the faint prickings of knowledge—something I'd seen in the back room there at the Palace.

"You didn't make a move," I said.

He coughed, rubbing a red angry mark on his neck. "Move for what?"

"That whole time he was beating me up, you didn't say a word. The guy would've *killed* me, and you just sat there like it was—TV."

"Oh, fuck me," he said, grinding out another cigarette in disgust. "A guy shoots a gun at you less than half an hour ago and all you can think of is this Army brothers, Knights of the Round Table shit? No wonder you never got it on."

"I want my money back." I got up suddenly and prepared to take away my tray. "The two thousand I gave to Hu and the check I gave you. No more handouts."

He sighed. "Don't go, Emerson."

I picked up my tray and moved toward the trash bins.

"I'm sorry."

I was almost to the stairs when he finally stood up and called across the room.

"That was an act of fucking *preservation*."

I turned to look at him. The other diners stopped talking, looked too.

In the dim, golden light and sudden silence, he seemed the very image of humility, battered, bloodied, with a thin, sharp wariness— a kind of liar's Christ.

He spoke again. "He was testing me."

"Sit down, Little P." I went back to the table, ignored the stares.

"He wanted to see what kind of currency you were. If I begged or screamed or showed any sign, he'd have his eye on you. He wasn't going to kill you, brother."

"Well, he does a very convincing psychopath." I touched my nose. The blood had thickened, slowed. "I don't understand."

We sat without speaking. The other patrons buzzed quietly. The proprietress came by with a damp rag, wiping down the tables, smelling of cheap perfume and disinfectant.

"Does it have to do with the woman?" I asked suddenly.

He stared. "What woman?"

"The woman upstairs in Uncle's apartment."

His eyes flickered. "You're crazy."

"I saw her," I said warningly.

He didn't have any cigarettes left; his fingers found a corner of napkin and shredded it mechanically.

At length, he looked up and said, "That's Poison's girl."

"Don't treat me like an idiot. Poison's as gay as a summer afternoon."

"Bullshit," he said, looking shaken. I hadn't even known I knew until now; it was merely something about the man that fit, suddenly, like a key in a lock.

"She's Poison's girl," repeated Little P.

He got up and walked out. I had to grab my things—jacket, ashes—quickly and trail him out to the street.

"Why won't you tell me anything?" I had to hurry to keep up.

"Emerson."

He wheeled abruptly. For a moment I thought he was going to hit me, and then I thought he was going to hug me. The red glow of the paper lanterns made it difficult to tell; the light was no more than an illuminated shadow in which I could see Little P only darkly.

"Don't stay here," he said. A note of urgency made his voice harsh and low. "If you want to help me, give me the lawyer's number and go home."

"I can't go home," I said doggedly. "Even if I wanted to, I really can't, now." I told him about my passport, about the wallet with my IDs.

He planted his feet and didn't say anything at first; he seemed to be thinking, formulating, calculating.

"I can get you a passport," he said slowly.

"What do you mean?"

"I mean I can get you a passport. From any country that's got an embassy in KL. Be anyone you want to be," he said. He took off his glasses, and the light of commerce shone in his eyes like candles. He leaned closer. "I'll make you a deal, brother. I get you the passport, you give me the lawyer's info. And then you get the hell out of here. *Haobuhao?*"

I searched his face. There was no false enthusiasm there, no particular guile; he really meant it. He didn't understand, then—not at all. He had sized me up, taken the measure of my needs and desires, and then tried to bargain with me: my brother, and the Remada, for some stupid government document, a laminate book with some meager, artificial facts typed in. How could he believe that such a trade was fair, or even close? Perhaps he thought I had some attachment to the bare fact of home itself. California—America—with its great coasts and sun-filled reprieves; its mythologies and corruptions; its short flame of history; its violence, shame, ambition.

But wasn't Little P too a kind of home? Whatever he was involved in, my mother and her boundless ideal lived in him too: in bone structure, in memory, in the common language of the blood that distance, even time, could not quite erase.

Belatedly, I remembered Little P's knife. I drew it out of my pocket, hesitated. Then handed it to him: a kind of penance, a kind of letting go.

"I have to think about it," I said.

He put his sunglasses back on. "Don't think too long."

CHAPTER 14

THE NEXT DAY I OCCUPIED MYSELF with cleaning out the new house and moving in. Angel, who gave me some cast-off furniture belonging to her grandparents, was dubious, but despite the bats and creeping mold, the little, low shack felt safe in its bower of subtropical green and mosquitoes; no one would find me here. Debt loomed: Poison and his broken bottle; the cop with his schizoid walleye, giggling as he pointed his gun; Little P. All this I tried to sweep up into trash bags, to incinerate when the garbage truck came by in the evening, playing its tinny, mournful rendition of "Für Elise." By candlelight (there was no electricity), I scrubbed, dusted, washed my shirts, read through my Chinese phrase books, and, dozing, dreamt the old dream of coffee and office buildings, riding the trolley to work. But now the dream diverged: there was no more office building, only a crater in the earth, and when I peered down into it, there was my mother in her hospital bed, dying, wordless, looking up at me with pain and dark recrimination in her eyes.

"Mother," I said aloud. A scrambled moment as the last vestiges of dream lingered. Then I was awake, and my voice hung awkward in the silent house.

I had held the ashes all night. Warmed, supple, through the silk they felt almost alive—almost. Sun had made its way into a corner of the tangled garden outside: the promise of a clear day for once. Why then did it seem so haunted, so bittersweet?

Then I remembered. Today was the last day of my stewardship. Atticus had found a temple for my mother in Beitou, north of the city proper, and we were scheduled to meet with the director this afternoon. In a basket by the door, I had piled my offerings: a bag of oranges, a pear wrapped in its own soft pillow and cellophane. Atticus had explained that I could bring an offering for her.

"An offering? Like a sacrifice?"

He smiled patiently. "It's not so primitive as you think. It can be fruit or drinks or crackers. Did your mother like something in particular?"

"Snelgrove's ice cream," I said. "And XO chili sauce."

We were sitting in his apartment, his lofty, skyward windows a shifting palette of sun and gray. He had bought a bright orange orchid from the weekend flower market and was trying to decide where to place it permanently in the spartan expanse of the living room. The walls had been newly painted in a sandy color, and the floor had been scrubbed and oiled.

"Maybe just some oranges," he murmured. "That will be easiest."

He sat down opposite me. "You have seen Xiao P lately?"

"Yes."

"Ah," he said carefully. "And how does he seem?"

"He's okay. I guess." I watched him fiddle with the foliage. Abruptly, I asked, "Is the Palace a money-laundering operation?"

He looked startled. "Did Xiao P say that?"

"No. He said your main revenues are not from karaoke customers."

He turned the orchid a little on its tile, so that the showy bloom faced the window. "He is mistaken in that. As the bookkeeper, I should know." He pursed his lips as he said this, however, preoccupied. "What else did he say?"

"He wouldn't tell me anything."

Atticus stroked the luminous petals pensively, checking the underside of a leaf for signs of blight. After a moment, he looked up.

"You will forgive me, Emerson, but I have a friend coming in a half hour."

"Oh." Frustrated, I stood up.

"No, no, no. Stay until he arrives. He is an old friend of mine. We lived in New York together. We are organizing a rally for a legislative candidate put up by the DPP. You know the DPP?"

"Democratic Progressive Party."

"Yes. Nationalists, with a small *n*. Pro-independence." He clenched a fist and his mouth hardened. He took a small pair of clippers from his pants pocket and began clipping the strings that held the orchid's stem to a stake.

"Was your mother pro-independence?" he asked.

"I don't know." My father had been blacklisted after graduate school for holding dinner parties at which they sang Taiwanese songs. "She was against the Nationalists, I suppose, but I never heard her say anything directly about current politics, Taiwanese or American. She liked Reagan because he was in the movies."

I watched him clip a few more strings.

"Why . . ." I hesitated, curious. "Why do you want independence?"

Atticus looked sharply at me.

"I mean," I stammered. "I just want to understand. I've never heard anyone—here—say anything against reunification. They already do a lot of their business on the mainland anyway. They have family there. The push for independence, it just seems like it runs on—I don't know. Dreams, theories. Ideas, maybe. But only that."

Atticus's face had darkened. *"Only,"* he repeated. *"Only?"* He tilted his head. "Why so little respect for ideas, Xiao Chang?"

He looked down and adjusted the pot on its tile, turning it infinitesimally to catch some elusive angle of light.

"Do you know what happened when the Nationalists landed here after the war?" he asked softly.

"An incident." I tried to remember what Angel had told me. "A shooting over taxes in a public square. Chiang Kai-shek's soldiers killing local merchants."

"The shooting was just the end result. I mean before that."

"No, I don't know."

"There was a betrayal. Taiwan, it has never been autonomous. It is too strategic, speaking of geography, for people to let it alone. Holland, Spain, and Portugal, all of them had settlements here. The Manchu took it over a few centuries ago, and immigrants from the mainland have settled the island for over two hundred years. It was . . . an outlier, a prefecture of the Chinese kingdom—they neglect it sometimes, but still, Taiwan was part of the empire.

"Now Taiwan was given to Japan at the end of the Sino-Japanese War. A big dishonor for China; you cannot imagine the shame. You must understand: China considers—still considers—Japan the inferior force. A barbaric country. To be defeated by Japan would be a terrible humiliation, as deep as the humiliation America would feel if it was defeated by China, maybe."

He smiled mischievously. I waited for him to go on.

"And the Japanese occupation was not kind. The island resources, they diverted them to benefit Japan only. Only Japanese could be spoken. Naturalization of all Taiwanese was enforced. Meaning, partly, that your Chinese name was wiped from public record and they gave you a Japanese name instead. To me, that is a special kind of insult, the worst kind. To take somebody's name away! You know that story, what is it called? About the dwarf and the hay?"

" 'Rumpelstiltskin'?"

"Yes, that one. The woman, the queen—she guesses his name at the end. And the dwarf, he loses his power and disappears.

"So you see how much it meant to us when the island was returned to the Chinese at the end of World War Two. A return to the motherland: that is how we thought of it. My mother cried, she was so happy.

"But you must understand, the return was just part of the war strategy. The Kuomintang, they did not come here to embrace us. They were preoccupied with defeating the Communists on the mainland, and when they came here, they stripped us of every-thing just to keep the campaign going. Rice went to the army; public funds were drained. There was garbage," he said moodily. "Garbage rotting in the street because there is no money for pub-lic works."

He flashed a shamefaced smile. "That is a small thing to be an-gry about, I know. After all, people disappeared later, under mar-tial law. Some of them turned up dead. Some are still missing. But the garbage is the thing I dream about. It is the little things that make a civilization. You know Eliot? 'The Hollow Men'?

" 'This is the way the world ends,' " he sang:

> This is the way the world ends
> Not with a bang but a whimper.

He stirred the potting soil with a finger. "You can tell by the ar-chitecture that Chiang and his army never wanted to stay." He ges-tured widely out the huge windows. "It is so temporary, everything is so cheap and falling down. No beauty anywhere, no investment in anything. The place looks like a big shantytown. At least the Japanese, they built the roads and the train station and the school during their occupation. And yet the Kuomintang, they expect loyalty. They expect loyalty to the idea of being Chinese. One China! One China!" he said mockingly.

He lapsed into silence, turning the plant on its tile again.

The intercom to the entry door buzzed, and I jumped. I had for-gotten about Atticus's friend. Atticus buzzed him in. I gathered up my things.

"Did you know," Atticus said, walking me to the door, "that in Xinjiang they force people to use official Beijing time? Xinjiang is hours ahead of the capital! But business is done according to the official watch. Beijing says this is a unifying practice."

He laughed, a note of scorn uppermost in his voice. Then he grasped my arm tightly. "So you will forgive me if I seem a little ideological in my beliefs, Xiao Chang? One has to fight an idea with an idea. I cannot *stand* an authority that expects blind following, blind loyalty. I cannot *stand* it. I have rejected everything in my life that requires such blindness from me. Even God. Even the Confucian teachings—even those. I have not swept my father's grave in ten years," he said.

He let go of my arm and stepped back, reverting to the calm, solicitous man I knew. "He beat my sister when we were young. A good Confucian son would forgive him and take care of his grave anyway. But how can I? She walks with a limp now. She is blind as well."

"I'm sorry, Atticus."

He waved this away. "She, of all people, forgave him. She lives in a disability home in the U.S. now. That row of statues on the shelf there, she is the one who made them. Strange, no? They look almost like people."

He picked up one of the figurines and held it out. It resembled a faceless Madonna, black and kneeling.

"She also painted them herself. She says the colors have a feel. She says black is peaceful."

He sighed and held the door for me. "I am sorry, Emerson. I did

not mean to lecture. Bring some oranges for Friday, yes? Good. See
you then."

THE TEMPLE ossuary was a white pagoda with many rows of long
tables set up in the front courtyard under a pavilion, facing a
blackish statue of Matzu, a local deity. A weathered-looking stall
across the street sold offerings: oranges and guavas, ghost money
for burning—silver and gold spots painted on heavy brown paper
and bundled together with twine; squares of the same heavy brown
paper printed with drawings of shirts, pants, telephones, and
VCRs. As I looked over their stockpiles for the dead, the proprietress and her daughter tried to interest me in a cloth representa-
tion of a house, but I shook my head. My mother hated maintaining
property, and I had the oranges already. Still, I felt that I should
buy her something else.

"I guess I should just give her money," I told Angel, distressed
by the number of choices.

"Sure. Practical."

"It does seem depressing." I paid the proprietress gloomily.
"You'd think death would be a respite."

"Want a Coke? I have a Coke in my backpack," she said.

"My mother drank Pepsi."

As we crossed the lot, the wind came up, whipping the pavilion
and pulling the canvas taut with a crack of thunder. Despite the
cold, several people were making offerings at the long tables, sticks
of incense in hand and heads bowed in obeisance before an assortment of gifts: a liter of 7UP, a bag of tangerines. Smoke drifted

over the grounds, dissolving into the white sky as if the sky itself were no more than a continuance of ash and cinders.

The administration was housed in a low pillbox to the side of the pagoda. Atticus was already in the main office. The director greeted us quietly and sat down to check something on her computer. The room was heated by a single kerosene element, and its walls were whitewashed, so that I had the disjointed sense of being near the sea. I sat down uncomfortably on a rattan chair as Atticus read over the contract for me.

I had expected to feel a surge of solemnity and weight, but the reservoir of tears that I thought was dammed inside had dried up, and instead I felt flat and detached. So this was what death eventually came down to: contracts, filing cabinets, outdated computers, a stack of dot-matrix printouts, and an enormous analog clock on the back wall with the hands stuck at nine and seven. Faint, tinny AM voices issued from the director's little ghetto blaster.

"Do you want monks?" asked Atticus. "You can get Taoist monks to pray for her, I think. An extra fee."

"She wasn't that devout." The numbness in my breast was starting to thaw. "She gave a little money to a Buddhist organization in California. Is this a monastery?"

"It is not. You can contract with a monk separately."

When we were done with the paperwork, the director took a set of keys from a drawer and motioned me to follow her. Both Atticus and Angel declined to come along.

I followed the woman out to the graveled lot and then up the stairs into the crematorium.

I suppose I had been expecting the funerary pomp that had

adorned my father's columbarium—the fountain, the fake flowers, the meticulously groomed carpets—but the interior looked rather like library stacks, the aisles narrow and claustrophobic, the metal lockers bare and numbered in black stencil. We toiled through wing after wing of anonymous grids, and I had no sense of haunting, as I sometimes did in cemeteries and crypts and even museums. A janitor was mopping a long, featureless canyon of ceramic tiles as we mounted the central stairs.

The burial space was on the third floor, in an awkward position in a stuffy corner. The director stopped abruptly and shook out her keys, which made a meek chime against the wind whistling around the flanges of the pagoda. The director opened the locker and left me with my mother.

I took the purse off and laid it on the ground. The cord was dirty and frayed from wearing it against my neck, and I was suddenly grateful for the heavy lockers and the solid, institutional floor. I had bought an urn with a sprig of willow carved into the brownish glaze, and now I unwrapped it, placing it carefully beside the lockers, and unzipped the purse.

A cloud of fine dust rose as I stirred the ash gently with a finger. I would have liked some kind of acknowledgment to attend the transfer, a few final words of religion or peace spoken by someone who knew them, but it was just me. I crouched down on the floor and addressed the purse softly.

"Here you are, Mother." This came out plaintive rather than upbeat. "Here you are."

I waited for what seemed a decent interval. Then I dumped the ash into the urn.

"Don't worry about Little P," I told her.

It felt silly to be talking to a heap of cinders. Before, I had mourned the loss of her as a discrete body. A corpse I could follow in my mind's eye, even into the ground, but the consciousness of dust was a place I could never enter, never batter my way into through grief, dream, or imagining.

Now I was mourning the imminent loss of her as a body at all. I didn't, I thought, staring down into the little black cavern of the urn, really believe in the existence of anything apart from bodies. The janitor made his way up the stairs and began pushing his mop around down the hall, humming closely. No souls, no transmigration. I was therefore locking away the last I would ever have of my mother.

WHEN WE got back to the center of the city, it was already quite dark, and contrary to the morning's predictions, an unseasonable rain slicked the roads. The trains expelled commuters in long, stale breaths; the evening vendors selling sausage and candied tomatoes were out on their isolated corners, heat lamps shining like jewelry inside their warming cases. Angel had pulled out her cell phone and was consulting her voice messages briskly as I waited. Despite her signature fatigues and shapeless silk jacket, she looked different somehow, some kind of orangish glaze on her mouth, and her head seemed bigger.

"Well." Angel snapped her phone shut and looked at me dubiously. "I guess I'll see you at home."

"Wait." I stammered a little; the thought of going back to my silent bower was at the moment so monumentally sad. ". . . a drink?"

She brightened a little and stuck her hands in her pants pockets, a sign that she was pleased.

We went to a foreigner pub near Yongkang, the interior of which was hung with Bavarian crests and tattered German flags. Only a few customers idled around the heavy wooden bar: an Australian and his girlfriend, and a tall, burnished American in a white lawn shirt perched on his stool, playing with an olive. He ignored us as we sat down next to him, giving a barely perceptible nod to Angel's hello before curling his body slightly away, as if to protect the olive.

"Love Buddha," muttered Angel.

"What's that?"

She indicated the American imperceptibly with her head. "Love Buddha. Him. You only find foreigners like him in Asia, I guarantee. A Love Buddha. Yellow fever."

I looked at him dully. "He looks perfectly normal."

"Ha. Blond, blue-eyed, not quite good-looking? Check. Drawstring pants? Check. Leave it to a professional, boyo, I can tell you exactly what he's like. Martial artist. Drinks healing green tea and believes in peace. Sanctimonious bullshit. Speaks only to locals. Won't talk to other Americans—will actually *ignore* you if you speak English to him on the street. Afraid of tainting his beautiful Oriental dream. He probably does *tai chi* with the ladies' groups in the park. Eventually he'll go home and write a memoir about his time in the mysterious Far East, how the natives all accepted him as one of their own."

She scowled at him. He frowned censoriously and edged farther down the bar. The bartender, a pretty young woman with blackened teeth, came over and spoke to him. With her he haw-hawed in muscular, flexing Chinese as if they were tremendous old friends.

Angel ordered a neat whiskey, and I had a sidecar. When the glass arrived, she lifted it toward me in a kind of salute. Then she said quietly, almost conversationally: "I know you didn't do it, Emerson. I know you've still got her in the purse."

The casualness with which she said it made her seem momentarily cruel. The regular knock-knocking of my heart desisted, suspended like a breath before dying. I reached for my glass. "I don't know what you're talking about."

"C'mon, boy. I'm not outing you. I just want you to know that I know. So you don't have to pretend with me, you know?"

There was a cracked mirror behind the counter. In the dim bar I looked and saw for the first time how much of my mother there was in my face. The nose and ears, and especially the narrow eyes, which observed me with mute sorrow and confusion at the uncertain resurrection of a woman who should, by all rights, have been laid to rest by now. I felt for the purse, which was tied up under my jacket; I hadn't wanted the temple director to see. I took the purse off and laid it on the bar, where it sagged, bending toward us in a bow of humility.

"I couldn't." There didn't seem to be any better or more descriptive words for the fact.

"I have to protect her," I said, so fiercely that my voice cracked. "Had to, I mean. My father died when I was eleven. My brother was still a baby, and we didn't have any relatives around, or friends. You try to be good, at that age. You haven't learned that model behavior isn't a form of currency. I tried to be a good student. In fourth grade, Dickie Deaver stole my lunch money every day and I never complained. One day I was playing with my viewfinder and he threatened to smash my face in if I didn't give it to him, so I let him have it. When I got home, I told my mother I'd lost it, and she thrashed me. We weren't very rich then," I added lamely, to excuse her. I took a peanut from the bowl. The nut meats were small, dark, and wizened, like little mummies in paper shrouds.

"I'm not busting you," Angel repeated, surprisingly gentle. "I just wanted you to know I knew."

"Let's not talk about it anymore," I said. "Let's talk about you for a change."

"I am one hundred percent single," she said confidently.

"Oh." I blushed a little at the revelation. "No boyfriend back home?"

"I had one once," she said and frowned. "A Catholic. I never understood about the Protestants before, but I do now, believe me, boyee! He's the reason I'm an atheist."

"What was wrong with him?"

" 'Love the sinner, hate the sin,' he used to say about gay people. And fornicators. And Democrats. That schmucky pious saying let him go all around campus feeling like Jesus while he slept his way through the Young Republican Club. 'I forgive you, even though you live in sin,' he'd say after—well, you know, after. It was okay for him, because he felt bad after and would cry a lot. '*I forgive you*'? Maybe that was what Father Williams said to him when he was little, after their weekly confab in the confessional, and I'm not talking about confession. Also, he had a painting of Reagan over his desk. I mean, one he painted himself."

I shook my head. "Then why did he go out with you if he wanted to bed a socially conservative Republican?"

"I think I was his Magdalene," she said without irony. "His exquisite taste of secret depravity. That's the only thing I'm proud of in the whole thing. I hope he rots in hell because of me."

"How romantic," I said. "And there's been no one since?"

"Not a one." She looked at me with a kind of weird intensity; I chalked it up to the whiskey.

"But you're only twenty. When I was your age—"

I stopped; I had not thought of J in some time.

"When you were twenty?" Angel prompted.

"Nothing. I had a . . . relationship." The word sounded dismal and dry compared with what the thing itself had been. "I thought she loved me, but it seems she loved someone else."

"What happened?"

What had happened? Nothing. Something.

"Look, I'd rather not talk about it."

"But why? If it was twenty years ago—"

"Angel," I snapped. "Have another drink."

But after we had finished our drinks and gone home, and I was alone in my leaky house with the ashes tucked back under my pillow, I stared up in the dark and the sound of water came trickling back. The day had been hot and damp, and the tepid pond had lapped the shore. Our legs had touched; J had seemed expectant, languid. It was the most natural thing in the world to lean over, touch her waist, and kiss her. A brief, sweet, pendulous moment when she seemed to submit—and then the kiss went too far. I broke away, gasping.

"How long is this going to go on?" she called, following me up onto the bank as I retreated along the path through the woods.

She brushed aside a branch and stood at the edge of the copse regarding me. The water had dried on her skin. A kind of loneliness tore at me.

"I'm tired of it," she said. "You want me; you don't want me. I've been patient, but I'm getting too old for this. You have to say the word yourself. What do you want?"

"You," I said, afraid. "But not just any old way. Not just some kind of, I don't know, animal rooting around in the mud. The moment has never been right. Just give me some time."

"Emerson." In the muddy light, she sighed, looked at me with pity and exasperation. "Don't you know?" She touched my cheek.

Later, I would think of her touch as a killing one—the gentle, hypnotic stroke that lulls the unsuspecting to sleep. In the end, the ashes beneath my pillow had proved more constant than J had, less duplicitous, less bound to make a point about the harshness of the world.

CHAPTER 15

ZHONG QIU JIE APPROACHED, relentless: three weeks, then two. Angel, who knew nothing of my money and family troubles, took me on a review circuit of teahouses all over the city: civilized, little, dark places with smoky teas and carved pots; bubble-tea stands; a minimalist tea café with industrial seating and some kind of bizarre theater troupe rehearsing behind a blank white sheet. In the garden courtyard of a rich, pensively designed teahouse, notes of the *erhu* fell like droplets in the lambent light of late afternoon.

"Do you taste the oils?" asked Angel.

"Hm?"

"Oils." She pointed at something, an imperceptible film on the surface of the tea.

"Oh." I tipped my cup and squinted, checked my cell phone.

Angel punched me in the arm. "You've been looking at that thing all day," she complained.

I merely shook my head.

"It's that girl, right?"

"What girl?"

"Starbucks girl. Million bucks girl. Still waiting on her, right? That's so quaint."

"I'm not waiting on anyone," I said, in no mood for Angel's pokings and proddings. I had left messages for Little P all week, none of which he had returned. Though Poison had said Mid-Autumn Festival, there was no reason to trust my rat-faced cousin. The *erhu* plucked, the fountain in the courtyard plashed. The artificial quiet grated. Restless, I spilled my tea.

"Sorry."

"Go home," said Angel irritably. "Call me when the chickie dumps your ass. I'll be laughing too hard to say I told you so."

Outside, I dialed Little P again and got no answer. I started for home, wishing too late that I could go back to the teahouse with Angel; the peace there was better than this aimlessness and worry.

The market arcade near my house was eerily deserted, awnings flapping, plastic stools stacked—too early for dinner, too late for lunch. At the mouth of my street, I paused, uneasy. Was it paranoia or fact, the feeling of being shadowed? I looked around. Of course there was nothing. I'd make myself some tea. I unlocked my gate, trod the path through the weeds.

As I shut the gate, something winked in the grass. A piece of embedded glass had been knocked from the top of the wall. I picked it up carefully, intending to throw it away, when I looked at it again.

Blood, the thinnest film of it glazing the glass edge. I touched it, pulled my finger away. A cat, I told myself. But as I stood in my darkening yard looking at the glass, I knew that was an evasion, like the artificial peace of the teahouse. The truth, I felt, was very near to hand.

A plastic bag full of newspapers had been left at the front door. Fearful, I approached as if it were a bomb. But the weight of the bag was organic, soft and meaty, not mechanical. A curious smell, sweetish but rotten, rose into the air as I opened it. I pulled out the newspapers, unrolled them.

A fist-size mass glistened red in the nest of wet, blood-dark papers, tentacles of gray snaking it through like veins. I dropped the bag, backed away. Not human, I thought—prayed. At least not human. Dog, bull, pig—anything else.

A stained card had fluttered to the ground and stuck in the grass. I leaned over and read the neat, childish hand. A sentence, scrawled in pencil, almost obscured by blood:

"This means cojones," it said. "maybe you speak the spanish now?"

THE NEXT day a crowd had gathered in the street outside the double doors when I arrived at the Palace. The mood was festive; they were watching with evident enjoyment as a covered flatbed truck tried to maneuver out of the narrow alley off the street.

Little P was at the wheel, apparently whole. My chest loosened, blood moving painfully again. I knocked on the window.

"Get these fuckers *out* of here," he shouted. The truck's fender shrieked against the side of the building, and the crowd muttered appreciatively. "They're blocking the whole street."

"How'd you get this thing in here anyway?"

He wiped his forehead. "Are you going to help me or what?"

"*Jieguo . . . jieguo yixia . . .* " I said feebly, sweeping my arms in circles. There was a shuffling, like a mild ripple on a placid lake, but otherwise no response. I went back to the window.

"Nothing doing."

"Shit."

"Little P, I need to talk to you—"

"Son of a cunt, Emerson, not now!"

"But I—"

"Get in!" he barked. "Just get in!"

I ran around to the passenger side.

"Hold on." Grimly, he set the truck in gear. We bucked backward, angled, snapping off the right mirror cleanly. The crowd cheered; a woman picked up the mirror from the ground and waved it at us like a flag.

"Where are we going?" I asked, once we were settled into the flow of traffic. Little P kept glancing in the rearview mirror.

"I got some business in Jilong."

North of the city, on the coast—a port town. I couldn't ask why: he was wound up. The truck was government-issued, the kind they used for construction, and battered, misaligned. Little P drove fast and reckless along the highway, cutting off semis, veering onto the rutted shoulder several times. Two trucks converged ahead of us, the space between them narrowing to a slit. As we shot through it, I gripped his arm involuntarily.

"Look out, Little P! *Little P!*"

He pressed into the next lane and shot out safely onto the interchange.

"Take the wheel," he said.

"What?"

"Take it." Abruptly he stood up and shifted out of his seat. The truck veered to the edge of the road, clocking 130 kilometers; cars blared behind us. I lunged across him for the wheel and pulled us back onto the asphalt.

"Are you crazy?" I shouted.

"It's just a regular clutch transmission. You'll get the hang of it," he said, flicking ash from his sleeve. He had a cigar this time, which he lit with eerie calm as I struggled to hold the truck steady. "I'm doing you a favor."

"Go to hell." The truck wavered and barreled left.

"It's an object lesson. You know what your problem is?" he asked.

"*My* problem?"

"You're afraid to die."

Despite the lanes of traffic, I glanced over at him. He was without irony, without humor. "And you're not, I suppose."

"No," he said simply, jaw bunched. "I'm not. Or I'm learning not to be. It's the key to enlightenment, brother."

"Key to the insane asylum."

"Key to immortality," he shot back. "Those guys who walk through fire? They know. Nothing can touch you if you're not afraid of death. No consequences, if you're not afraid to lose."

He was in a weird mood; a sheen on his eyeballs made me think uppers, but I couldn't be sure it was drugs. It was not the time to bring up Poison, or the package left on my doorstep.

For the rest of the ride he was quiet, except to give me directions. Every now and then I stole a glance at him. I hoped the talk about death was figurative, but the way he had abandoned the wheel of the truck suggested not. *I don't want to know.* It would be so easy to simply get my passport and go home, forget . . .

JILONG WAS cramped at the edge of its wide harbor and bore signs of its port heritage in the dingy little massage parlors up and down the narrow streets near the waterfront. Though it was sunny, mist blanketed the road like a fine shroud as it skirted the harbor. The truck ground up a steep graded hill.

We pulled up to an open garage storefront that seemed vaguely abandoned, a stark light shining far back in the airless interior, though I couldn't quite see inside. The street was dark; the rest of the block seemed uninhabited.

I cut the engine, but Little P did not get out. He sat silently, the smooth plane of his face like a thin, treacherous wall. He looked like our father; he had the long, blunt nose and high forehead, the small white teeth. Odd to think that a stranger now inhabited those features. His hands clenched unconsciously on his knees.

He got out of the cab and went into the garage. I followed. The shop was dim and full of wood shavings, and a pair of garish red lights burned on a little altar near a couple of sawhorses. At the back of the room, white, ghostly planks of cedar and oak were piled against the wall like an inert army, unattended: coffins.

"Little P?" I whispered and heard *Little P Little P Little P* whispering back. The altar lights flickered.

Little P came out from the back of the shop with the proprietor in tow, a rough, thick man with a kind of oily pompadour and a finger missing from his right hand. He followed my brother closely and seemed to be wheedling or whining. Their low, muttered Chinese came through, half-understood, as if filtered.

"Next week," Little P was saying. "Next week. To Hong Kong."

The man murmured.

"Yes, myself," said Little P, impatient. "At the Chungking. *Wo yige ren qu.*"

His friend seemed skeptical, dug a finger in his ear, muttered: *"Ni yige ren, queding ma?"*

"I said alone, *duibudui?*" Little P's voice had dropped to a quiet, pleasant register. *"You wenti ma?"*

The man flicked his eyes at me distrustfully.

"I'll wait outside," I told Little P. I wanted to get out of the shop anyway; the caskets pressed in on me at gruesome angles. Half-finished coffins were balanced on sawhorses in the center of the workshop, leaned up against the side walls. I had strange, fleeting impressions of bodies in them and thought of broken glass, a torn fingernail lying in the dirt.

In the glove compartment, I found Little P's cigarettes and lit one.

"Why is it so quiet?" I asked Little P. He had come out of the garage looking more grim and distracted.

"What?"

"This street. There's no one on it."

"Of course not." He jabbed his thumb at the coffin maker's. "With this shit nearby?"

"Why not?"

"No one wants to live on a street with a coffin maker."

"Bad luck?"

"Fraud, raids. Sometimes they kidnap a body for ransom."

"Then why . . ." The question was on the tip of my tongue, but I couldn't ask it; he wouldn't tell me anyway.

"I know a guy in Taipei," said Little P briefly, as if he'd heard me. He went around to the driver's side of the cab and got his wallet and knife. "A stonemason, does tombstones. On his own right now, but he wants to network with other vendors. I'm picking up some casket samples for him."

It was a good story; I could almost believe it, except I knew that Little P was capable of telling the worst story with the unembarrassed calm of truth. *No consequences,* he had said, *if you're not afraid to lose.*

It would take a while for all the samples to be loaded, he told me. We walked into town and had a snack at an open stall: oyster pancakes and rice, with thin soup and a bowl of little dried fish that tasted like salted crackers. Clouds had moved in. Little P ate mechanically. It struck me, as I watched him, that I had not seen him enjoy a meal since I had arrived; I had not, in fact, seen him smile or laugh except in scorn or defense.

We finished eating, paid, went out into the narrow streets to kill time. The bright tinkling of pachinko machines followed us, glimpses of a little temple courtyard full of garland vendors and incense, the white gardenias like confetti.

"You think about my offer any more?" he asked as we came to the warehouses near the docks.

"My passport, you mean."

"Mmhn."

"I've thought. I still don't know."

He looked out over the gray water. "What's to think about? You could get out of this cock-loving hellhole tomorrow and go home. Just like that."

"You don't like it here," I said, surprised. It had never occurred to me before. "All these years I thought . . . I assumed . . . you were happy here."

He stiffened. "Maybe happiness isn't the goal," he said. "Maybe happiness is no fucking good to me."

"What is the goal, then?" I asked. A coldness grazed my spine, like a foot across my grave. *Happiness!* I could hear my mother saying. *If all you want is happiness!* It was like coming upon your name in someone else's correspondence—the sense of two people communing behind your back. Perhaps, in the end, Little P had been closer to my mother than I had been; perhaps he understood her better than I ever would have. A ship sounded its doleful note. We were out along the military side of the harbor now, the water choppy, fathomless.

"Knowledge," said Little P. "Experience." He stood dangerously, deliberately at the edge of the dock.

"Come away from there."

"You wouldn't understand."

"You keep saying that. How can I understand what you won't explain? Get *away* from there."

"You don't explain something like this," he said. He walked a length of the edge, arms out for balance. "Either you know it or you don't. I cut the cord a long time ago."

"I don't know what the hell you're talking about. Goddamn it, Little P."

Seawater sloshed his ankles. He wavered dangerously.

"I used to steal from the register," he said. "At the Remada."

"What? When?"

"When do you think? Two hundred, three hundred bucks a pop."

I stopped chasing alongside. "But . . . why? We always gave you money."

"Why, why." Irritated, he spat into the water. "It wasn't for the money."

"Then for what?"

He struggled internally, his face at once contorted and beatific. Then gave up. "Fuck it. I said you wouldn't understand."

I let him drift down the waterfront, away from me. How quickly one could go from love to murder. A few hours ago I'd thought he was doomed, castrated, bleeding somewhere and alone; now I wished . . . what? Not that he was dead, but that he had never been.

Later, as if he had read my thoughts: "You ever think what it's like to die?"

It was dark; rain drummed on the hood, showed in the headlights of the truck as I drove. A sheen of reflected light off Little P's glasses gave him an eyeless look, the road traveling up his lenses like a scroll of film. The caskets bumped in the truck bed.

"No." The question unnerved me. "Heaven and hell, I suppose. Angels and devils."

"Not death: dying. I mean the process."

"Quit it."

"A gunshot, for example. People say it's like burning."

"Shut *up,* Little P!"

A set of flares showed on the shoulder of the road up ahead. In my distress, I swerved the truck too sharply; we fishtailed, brakes shrieking, before the tires regained their purchase. The purse strap was rubbing my neck raw. I tore it off and tossed it to Little P.

"What the hell is this, anyway?" he said.

I tried to think of a good phrasing. "Ashes?"

"Ashes."

"You know."

"Jesus Christ. I thought you found her a place. You carry her *around?*"

I didn't answer.

"You poor fuck." He stared down at the purse. "For Christ's sake, she's *dead.* Go home. Let me take care of it."

I reached over with one hand and grabbed the purse.

"There's something called memory," I said. "There's something called dignity, even if she doesn't know it anymore. It has to be considered."

"There's something called selfishness," he said. "There's something called pride. You don't believe in life after death any more than me. You really think her burial makes a difference to anyone but you? It's for your own goddamned pride you're doing this— nobody but you."

"What would you know about love anyway?" I shouted. "What would you know about loyalty, or even decency?"

His eyes revealed a flash of murderous white.

"You sanctimonious bastard," he said harshly. "What do you know about anything? I told you, I had reasons! You think I've spent all these years away without giving her a thought? You don't know shit. Give me those!" He lunged at me.

The truck veered as I fought him off, clipping him in the jaw with my shoulder. The tires rutted on the shoulder. Horns blared, headlights blinding from both directions.

"Little P!"

Suddenly he desisted. Up ahead, the red and blue lights of a police cruiser whirled. He slid down in his seat.

"What is it?" he murmured.

"What? I don't know! A ticket?" The cruiser was pulled over to the side of the road, behind a truck rather like ours, the blue flatbed with a tarp over the top. The cop shone a flashlight over the truck's gate, which had not been opened.

When a few kilometers had passed, Little P sat up dazedly.

"Was it a ticket?"

"I don't know. Something. A truck pulled over."

We had come to the outskirts of the city now. Little P was quiet. His thin profile reminded me of a blade against the window. He made a half motion to touch the ashes, drew back, and I saw the glint of a tear on his face.

"I did love her," he said. "But it all got fucked up somehow. I would've come home if it were different. I stayed away for her sake. So don't say I didn't love her. Even though it doesn't fucking matter, now."

CHAPTER 16

Atticus's scandal regarding the opposition candidate broke the next day. I read about it in the English dailies over a breakfast of cornflakes and watery-tasting milk. Zhang's offense was a confusing amalgam of larceny and perversion: he had arranged to receive kickbacks from a nuclear power plant he had pushed for, and he had hired a prostitute and asked her to tie him up and urinate on him, then skipped out on the bill. It was unclear how these two bits of information were related, if at all, and I thought Atticus and his cohorts had done rather badly in this instance; the disparate charges weakened one another and made them look like a hit job. *The China Post,* allied with the Nationalists, angrily denounced the stories as lies. I scraped up the silt at the bottom of my bowl and thought of Atticus, of the weird, strident passion that had possessed him when he had spoken of China, and of his father. It was not beyond him to make up a story.

"It's not a story," said Angel. We were thronging through the crowd near the Presidential Building later that day, where Zhang's opponent, Li, was scheduled to speak. Angel had her camera; one of the dailies had hired her as a photojournalist for the event, but for some reason, instead of her usual boots she had chosen to wear a pair of shiny black pumps, which encumbered her vast feet like clams. She limped along quickly, pausing now and then to grab my arm for balance and massage the backs of her heels. "Zhang is a scumbag. When he was running for Senate, he got his henchmen to beat up a radio personality who was bad-mouthing him on the air."

"That doesn't make him a larcenist."

"No, but it indicates character."

"The prostitute is nobody's business but his own."

Angel made a face. "Why are you defending him?"

"I don't know." A man waving the red and blue fields of the Taiwan flag nearly knocked me over as we ducked under his arms. "Vilification makes me nervous. Any kind of intense communal feeling makes me nervous. This thing, for instance." I looked about at the massing faces.

Angel made her way toward the podium, where a bank of photographers waited for the motorcade to arrive. The audience was quite a bit bigger than the one in the memorial park, and more restive, its excitement felt in the tense shifting along its edges. One dry, shriveled woman gripped the handle of her umbrella like a weapon. When the Nationalist Party candidate had lost the presidential election several years ago, Angel noted, a number of old ladies had gone out and smashed the windshields of parked cars in angry response, the force of pride unstinting even now that their eyes were weakened and blue.

The start time for the rally came and went with no sign of Li.

The coordinator played the same music track over and over again as the wind flagged, picked up, flagged again. The sky looked diffident, and the noisemakers ceased except in isolated bursts, which sounded, in the quiet, like sarcasm. I glanced at my watch; I had promised to meet Grace at noon. Thirty minutes, forty. I slipped up to the podium and motioned to Angel.

"I have to go," I told her.

"You're *leav*ing? *Now?*" Her face fell. She socked me in the shoulder again, slapped me about the shoulders and head. "He hasn't even *got* here yet."

"Quit it." I ducked and caught her wrists. "You can tell me about it later."

She patted my cheek, hard. "Fine. Go then, Casanova. What're you waiting for, smooches?" She planted one on my upper lip, or would have, except I was turning away; her lips brushed my ear.

As I left the grounds, I heard a low rumbling like the first intimations of an earthquake. I stopped, turned. The sound swelled, a river rushing up through the registers, wild, inexorable, erupting in a roar and shout. Chants; the loud gunshot crackle of a microphone being swung around. Hundreds of heads turned in new attention. A young woman hanging off a barricade screamed, wept. Li had arrived at last.

"RABBIT, YOU see?" Grace pointed up at the sky, tracing the billow of a cloud.

"Don't see it," I murmured, eyes half-closed.

"Ear *neibian*. Nose *neibian*."

We drifted slowly on the current, the tepid water washing gently against our paddleboat. The day was warm, with an underlying crispness—too lovely for an English lesson. Grace had suggested lunch and paddleboats at Xindian. The river was wide, its steep embankments glutted with colorful restaurants and cafés. Children's voices floated across the water, the tinkling of bells—sounds of safety, innocence. The anxieties of the last few weeks faded, evaporating in the sun.

"A do not like come here," Grace was saying. "I think he do not like the children."

I opened my eyes with a sigh, idyll broken. "But you said he works as a kindergarten teacher."

"Yes." Grace nodded. "Is very strange. *Tade xin hen shen.*"

I dipped my hand in the water. I doubted A's heart was particularly deep. Muscular, perhaps.

"Do you love him?" It sounded too blunt. I had vowed to keep my envy in check.

She smiled, modest, continuing to look up at the piled clouds, but the smile appeared distressed. "I hope," she murmured.

"You aren't sure?"

"No, no. My meaning is, I hope *he* to love *me*."

"That wasn't my question." I struggled to sit up in my seat.

She glanced back toward shore, uneasy. "We must to go back soon."

"We have the boat for another hour."

She wouldn't look at me.

"Come on, Grace. Is it so hard to know?"

"Please," she said, suddenly on the verge of tears.

"You have the right to want something yourself too." Perhaps she couldn't understand me. "You know what I mean by 'right'?"

"The right. The right." A flash of sudden fury showed in her gentle face, shocking me. It disappeared instantly, but the vestiges of it remained in her voice. "A too, he say 'the right' many times also. 'I have right to go here.' 'I have right to do this.' I know what means 'the right.' But I have not the right. You do not know."

Tears spilled down her cheeks; she turned away from me. The curve of her neck trembled, proud, miserable. I felt worse than if she had slapped me.

"I'm sorry, Grace."

The tremble dissolved into hard, silent sobbing that shook her like a brutal hand. Bewildered, I slid over and put my arms around her. She put her hands to her temples, digging her nails in a little, as if to wipe out a memory, or a vision, but she would not say what this private image was.

Gradually she calmed down, leaning into me. I looked down at her, the soft, dark hair, the surprising flash of strength despite her pale beauty, and thought, *Could I?* To venture out again into the possibility of love, which I'd thought was gone forever—hope and desolation made the sunlight suddenly cold. Even as I shivered, Grace turned her face upward, cheeks still wet. Her eyes darkened as we looked at each other—a glimpse of uncertainty, of surprise perhaps, but not of repugnance or doubt. We were drifting close to shore, but the sounds of voices and bells receded as I wiped her tears away with my thumb, close and tender.

Then, before our lips touched, the paddleboat drifted from under the footbridge, and out of the corner of my eye, I saw a dark figure on the arcade above the waterfront, framed by bright awnings, staring down at us. Instantly I pulled away from Grace.

"Emerson?"

The man moved to the wide suspended footbridge and leaned on the rail, spitting into the water.

"He *wants* me to see," I said. "God. Dear God."

Grace shook my arm. "What happen?"

"Poison."

"*Duyao?*" She scanned the bridge anxiously. "*Shenma yisi?* What poison?"

"Nothing. Let's get back to shore." The lovely peace of the afternoon had been shattered; the voices from the riverbank now sounded isolated, separate and forlorn. I pedaled grimly. "Don't look at the bridge."

But I looked back myself. Poison lifted a finger in recognition— pointing, wordless, at Grace.

"THEY SHOT him," said Angel. We had arranged for tea at a *pao mo cha* house later that evening, at an open-air café, with carved tables and railings, and an arched wooden doorway framing an unspectacular view of the Zhong Xiao subway station. The ubiquitous television was running another news broadcast, and she watched it distractedly, chewing her thumbnail. She held her camera close in her lap, like an animal, and I thought she was referring to the photographers at the rally.

"No, with a *bullet,*" she said. "With a gun. Someone shot Li as he was arriving." She indicated the television screen, where footage of the shooting was being replayed. The candidate smiled and waved, then the moment of impact; his body convulsed dreadfully.

"My God. Is he all right?"

"The bullet shattered his shoulder. They think he's okay. But he's in the hospital."

She had ordered a green tea milk shake, which sat untouched in front of her.

I was still shaken from my encounter on the river. "Good news, then," I said, vague. "Relatively? But you're still upset."

She looked over at me wonderingly, like a zombie, or a doe-eyed fawn.

"I couldn't get a good place in the lineup at the podium," she said.

"I'm sure your editor will understand."

"That's not what I mean. I couldn't get Li, so I was taking pictures of the *crowd*."

She handed me the camera.

The LCD screen was tiny but clear. She had magnified the corner of a frame to show the blocky, pixilated outline of a silver Vespa near the edge of the crowd, a little apart. The rider wore a black mirrored helmet. No different from the helmets on the street every day. But there was something familiar about the way he wore it, and the upright posture: thin, polite, correct. The faint but unmistakable detail of a gun showed in his hand.

I looked at it for some time, then put the camera down.

"No," I told Angel. The same dazed apprehension that gave her the look of a sleepwalker was beginning to claim me.

"It could be him."

"Why would he shoot his own candidate?" I asked. "And the gun?" My shock was so great that the basic logistics of the act overwhelmed me; they appeared as vast and insurmountable as the idea of Atticus—quiet, courtly Atticus; my friend—as an assassin. I wouldn't believe it. But I remembered the helmets lined up on the console, the gun, and my chest felt cold, as if it harbored a secret knowledge that was closer to the truth.

"What should we do?" I asked Angel.

She shook her head. "I gave the photos to the *Times* already. Just not the ones with Atticus."

I looked at the camera as Angel picked it up again. *You know what to do*. But I could not quite say it. A vague fear gathered around the idea, like cloth pinched tight and tighter around a drawn knot. Atticus knew something about Little P. He would be asked about the shooting only, of course, but in custody, under duress, what would he disclose? I didn't know. But if I did not know, I didn't want anyone else to know, either. I had my finger close to the vein, I thought; eventually I would uncover everything, whatever there was to know. Until then, keep quiet, keep low.

"Erase them."

"But I don't—"

"*Erase* them!"

It was the work of a moment to empty out the images. The LCD screen went dark.

I should have felt relieved, but I didn't; I felt only lingering distress and the burden of being complicit, which lay like intimacy between Angel and me. Tentative, she touched my hand under the table, held it.

"What do we do now?" she asked.

CHAPTER 17

WHATEVER RESPITE HAD BEEN PROMISED by the mild weather ended abruptly. It rained for the next several days without stint, a typhoon that flooded the streets and rotted the wild undergrowth tangled in the yard. Angel didn't call; I did not want to call Atticus. Grace was not home. I tried to dial Little P, but each time I picked up the phone, I saw the bloody mess wrapped in newspaper, and nausea curdled my stomach. The rain beat down.

Around ten o'clock on the second night of rain, I got up to empty the buckets under the leaks in the roof. As I put on my raincoat, I heard the gate outside slam, and the streetlight in the half-boarded window flickered, as if shapes had crossed it. I put down the buckets and peered out.

Two figures shifted in the darkness near the door. *Thieves,* I thought instantly and felt for the ashes. I seized a broomstick for defense. But then a knock sounded, rapid and peremptory.

It was raining so hard that it could have been anyone standing there, framed in the crack of the door as I put my eye to it. Then I smelled candy and knew who it was.

"What do you want?" I asked, training my flashlight on him.

Poison squinted and put up a hand; I was reminded of a possum on a back fence, hissing in the glare of a headlight.

"Open," he said.

"Tell me what you want first."

He grinned nastily. "You want I break the door?"

I didn't doubt that he would do it. Reluctantly, I opened the door, broomstick held tense and ready. He strolled in, dripping, sucking his teeth as if he had just polished off a meal. Uncle shambled after him, silent and hooded.

Poison shoved back his hood and took a slow turn around the living room, hands in pockets. The house was still junky, mildewed, but I had put up some pictures: Grace smiling, flashing a V for victory sign; Angel with her camera; an old photo of my mother; a picture from the Sanchong Bridge, where the sunset had spilled onto the river in oily splendor. It shocked me slightly, seeing those pictures from an outsider's standpoint: I seemed to have . . . a kind of life.

"This your home," said Poison, with scorn.

"What do you want?" I asked again.

"Is not what I want. Is what *you* want."

Uncle barked harshly and banged his hands on the makeshift table. Poison muttered to him, and he subsided, glowering. I had not seen Uncle since the spa. His presence seemed a bad omen, an escalation of sorts, as if he had come to survey the work he had ordered, to see it done properly.

"The Mid-Autumn Festival is still ten days away."

"I know when is *zhong qiu jie,*" he said, irritated. "Who tell you when is the *zhong qiu jie* firstly, guy? I not come for money."

"Then why?"

Poison surveyed my picture wall coolly, pausing at Grace.

"I am the honorable guy," he said. "I have say already not touch Xiao P. You not to worry." He licked his thumb and rubbed a smudge from the glass.

I went cold. "What do you mean?" I looked at Uncle, who stared blankly back. "Why not?"

Poison waved Grace's picture at me. "Very beautiful. But all woman is cheap, is whore, *shibushi?* Little money, little fun, is all love to them. How much you pay for her?"

Casually he dashed Grace's picture to the floor, hooked Angel's frame with a finger. "This one, too." He pursed his lips. "Little whore. You pay little whore little money? For less size?" He let the photo drop.

I picked up a bamboo rod and swung it at Poison's head. He caught it in one hand, tore it from my grip, whipped it like a sword at my face. I ducked; the rod smashed the whiskey bottle on the table instead.

He'd been half-smiling, like a satisfied cat, but now the smile had disappeared, and he looked nasty and deranged, inhabited by a theatricality bolstered by many episodes of *The Sopranos*—inert fantasy more dangerous than calculation or intelligence. Uncle brayed. Poison's hand twitched, then stilled. Scowling, he flung the rod across the room.

"Ten oh-oh-oh," he said. "And I do not touch the whores."

His voice held a double note, a threat beneath the threat. With unchecked violence, he grabbed my arm and flung me against the wall. His face was only inches from mine; I saw his lip tremble with rage as he grabbed my groin and twisted, pinched. I understood; it was not just Grace or Angel he was after. I was the collateral too.

"You," he said, pinching harder. "You not forget my present? *Cojones*. You remember."

"Fuck off," I said through my teeth. "I need more time." My heart pounded, though not for fear of my cousin. *I need more time:* it sounded like a line from a movie—a lie. It wasn't time I needed. It was will. If I really wanted to, I felt, I could find a way to get the money. Why couldn't I just pay the ransom and get it over with? "Is what *you* want"—Poison had come so unwittingly close to the truth. Little P, my only demon, and my only kin.

Poison's cell phone rang, a little hip-hop melody against the thunderous rain. His eyes flickered. Reluctantly he let go of my crotch and picked up—*"Wei?"*—disappearing into the back bedroom.

Uncle, still standing near the door, groaned suddenly. His legs shook.

"Here," I said, halfheartedly pushing a chair over. His red-rimmed eyes looked me over with reptilian cold, but I couldn't just let the man collapse on my floor. He seized the back of the chair and leaned on it. Still his legs shook.

"For God's sake." I went over and hefted him into the chair, wrenching his arm crudely. Uncle muttered and tensed, as if to shake me off.

"Fine, okay." I backed off. "Makes no difference to me, you bastard. You could shove off right here. You were supposed to help my brother, not drag him under." I lowered my voice and bent down close, even though he would never understand me, nor would Poison.

"What've you done for him that he owes you so much?" I hissed. "Or is it something you've done *to* him? Whatever it is, I'll nail you for it, if I have to spend the rest of my life here. I'll nail you, I swear."

The dull eyes followed me without signs of comprehension, but somewhere, far back, a light of some kind shone. His mouth wobbled as if to speak.

All at once I couldn't stand it. I gripped his wet lapels and shook him. "*Ni shuo!* Speak, you asshole! *Ni shuo!*"

He moaned in alarm, looking toward the doorway of the bedroom.

At once I dropped him, ashamed. The ashes sat quietly by the dim battery-powered lamp, near Uncle's elbow: brother and sister, one dead, one only half-alive. I stood back and tried to breathe evenly. Where the hell was Poison? I started toward the back room.

Uncle's hand descended on my wrist in a vise grip. Startled, I looked at him and saw that the light I had suspected in his wasted face had come forward at last. But it was not, as I had thought, the light of a knowingness or intelligence. I recognized it instantly. It was fear. He was trembling with effort as he looked up at me and laid a tremoring finger on my sleeve.

"You," said Uncle, in a guttural, forced English that terrified me. He had something small and hard gripped clumsily between

his halting fingers, and he raised it slowly, hand shaking. "Xiao P,"
he said, again with frightening clarity. "You."

Poison came back into the room. The object dropped noiselessly
on the floor as Uncle sank back into the chair.

"You give me the pain," said Poison. "But I am the nice guy. I
am the generous guy. I look. I see. I think maybe you not to lie,
duibudui? The rich guy, the American, he not live *here*. In *this*. So I
give the discount. Nine thousands. I leave the girls alone. Only
you."

He unwrapped a peppermint. "We watch you, assholes. You not
to forget. Nine thousand. *Zhong qiu jie*. No funny stuffs."

He popped the candy in his mouth and cracked it with his mo-
lars. That faint clacking was the last I heard of them as he and Uncle
disappeared into the storm.

When they were gone, I dropped to my knees to retrieve what
Uncle had dropped. A plastic vial, empty, no markings.

THE ROXY glimmered like a lighthouse across the flooded gutters
of Jinshan Road. I sloshed toward it with a sense of drowning as a
fresh gust of wind whipped down the street. The rain had let up
momentarily. A cab sloshed by, headlights doused, trolling for a
double fare.

The bar was almost deserted. Lights blazed, and instead of music, there was only the ICRT broadcast of the weather conditions,
warning people to stay indoors. Among the few patrons, I did not
see Grace.

"Dammit."

The lights blinked and dimmed briefly. The wind rose, and I

thought of Poison, waiting in the dark outside Grace's building, or slipping up behind her on the street, muffling her cries with a gag and the threat of pain.

Heads turned as I stumbled against a table, my legs suddenly weak, vision blurred by the horror of possibilities. My mind whirled. The radio seemed to blare: ". . . high winds up to one hundred kilometers per hour, the storm coming off the South China Sea. Officials have said nearly seventy people are stranded in the southern part of the island following . . ."

Then, like a voice out of a storm, I heard a thick American voice say: "Let me guess what you had for dinner."

A stood several feet from me, holding a glass of milky whey protein and regarding me with a dull expression of judgment and pity.

"High fat content," he said. "McDonald's? KFC?" He gestured at my hand, which was clutching the back of a chair. "Fat blunts your optimal NO performance. Less blood flow."

"Where's Grace? I need to talk to her."

He furrowed his brow. "She's not here."

"Where is she?"

Again the brow furrowed. "At home, I guess," he said finally.

I grabbed his arm, startling him. "Where's home?"

"Hey, careful." He pulled his arm away and inspected it briefly. That plodding self-regard was like an impenetrable wall.

I tried again. "Please, this is important," I said, speaking slowly. "She may be in some danger, and I can't get her on the phone. If you could just give me her address."

He looked at me with a flicker of life, then laughed. "Aw, no," he said, wagging his finger in my face. "Not falling for that. You think I'm stupid?"

"I am not trying to *trick* you. Come *on*."

"No way, man." He laughed again and searched my face for signs of levity. Seeing none, he sobered up a little.

"Suppose I give you her info," he said. He didn't go on, but the language of extortion had become familiar to me.

"How much?" I asked.

"It's not money, exactly."

"How *much*?"

"I'm not trying to bribe you."

He looked toward the back of the bar furtively. Then he made a motion for me to follow.

We passed through the back door into a narrow corridor, then a run-down shop that had been abandoned. The long mirrors on the walls had been smashed; a red canister for money burning lay drunkenly on its side, and the ashes of a recent offering stirred among the glass shards. Rain came lashing through the broken windows. There was no electricity; a few meager candles, some high-beam flashlights were the only sources of light. A group of shadows had gathered in a corner cleared of glass and ashes. Cigarette tips burned like embers.

A flashlight beam swung around as we approached. I shielded my eyes with a hand.

"In or out," someone called. "Not gonna wait forever."

"In!" A turned to me. "Spare a thousand *kuai*?"

I gritted my teeth as I handed it over.

"Grace," I reminded him, but he hushed me up vaguely, some new excitement charging the air.

A kind of makeshift arena of loose bricks had been set up on the floor. In the center, two long, translucent scorpions skittered about grotesquely, illuminated by the beam of a flashlight. The creatures clung together in a static, vibrating effort, then were separated with the aid of tongs. After a tense moment, the handlers pushed the sharp end of a stick at each of them so that they scuttled at each other again with renewed savagery, tails arched in fury. One pinned the other, tail drawn to inject the poison, but was thrown off and pinned in turn, thin, brittle legs waving in an agony of brute will. The handlers separated them.

"Last round!"

The scorpions went at each other again. The smaller of the two grappled desperately with its comrade, its back bent almost double with the effort, but it was weakening. The other flipped it over, pinned it, and inserted its long poisoned sheath between the plates of its prey. The smaller body heaved and flexed; the legs guttered and went still.

"Fuck," someone muttered, while another laughed. "Pay it right here, gentlemen!"

"My God."

In the flickering candlelight, A was sweating, an odd, smeared look of shock and arousal on his face. He gulped. "Every time I see it, it just fucking blows my mind. All that power. The way he just pins him, slides it in—"

"The address."

"What? Oh, yeah." He wandered back toward the door to the Roxy.

As we returned to the bar, a Taiwanese woman came up to A and twined her arms around his neck. Obligingly, he ran his hand down her ass. They kissed roughly.

Trailing the woman behind him, A found a napkin and scrawled Grace's address. "Jinhua Street."

The woman caressed him insistently as he wrote. Older, with a body settling to fat, thick makeup caked around her bright eyes: the kind of prostitute more common in the bars in the Zone, where the old G.I. bars left over from Korea and Vietnam still limped along. I took the napkin, but a violent surge of outrage shook me.

"I don't suppose I should mention your friend here," I said.

He looked at me, genuinely puzzled. "You?"

"*Her,*" I said, indicating the woman with a curt nod. "I never thought much of you, but Grace worships you. She thinks you'll marry her. She's counting on it. She trusts you."

He had been eating nuts from the bar again, but as I spoke, he slowly stopped chewing. A dark flush spread under his skin, and his neck tightened, almost as if he were choking.

"Is she wrong, then? I take it you're not . . . sincere."

He didn't speak. He seemed all at once to be suffering as he gazed at me, the dull film in his eyes dissolving into a pained clarity.

"Don't think I won't tell her," I said and moved toward the door.

I was almost to the entrance when he said, "She doesn't love me."

I looked back. He took a few steps toward me, half-unseeing; his face had undergone a kind of unpleasant transformation, disfigured by anger—not just anger but rage.

"Not love she's after." He rubbed his fingers together in a pantomime of money. "Green card. I can string her along forever as long as she thinks I'm going to take her back home with me."

He giggled, a high, crazed sound.

"Tell you a secret," he went on. "I'm never going back. You couldn't pay me to go back. I'm on a mission. I'm taking back the night. My wife—my ex-wife—she fucked around. She fucked around with my best friend. They hid it from me for five whole years."

"I'm . . . sorry. But that's between you and them. Why punish Grace?"

"You're not listening to me!" he shouted suddenly. "My boy! My little boy! Four years old, looked nothing like me. I taught him to swim. Taught him to catch. I worked my ass off so he wouldn't have to grow up in Meadow Park, with all the other Meadow Park scum. I can't forget. You think you know things. Sometimes you do. Picked him up one day, and I just knew. Didn't feel anything for him. Not anymore."

He sagged, his voice thickened with grief. "When I sat up with him with the flu, he said, 'Daddy, what's time?' My little boy."

The woman stroked his shoulders soothingly, murmuring. He jumped and pulled away from her. He wrapped his arms around himself as if embracing a phantom, feeling up and down his upper arms tenderly in a pantomime of comfort.

"The thing about sluts is, no secrets. Everything out in the open. No one lies and says they love you. No bullshit. You could love a prostie for her truth," he said. "Except that'd ruin the whole setup."

He wiped his face. "If you see Grace before I do, tell her I love her," he said. "Then we can just about call it even. Almost."

He held his hand out to the woman and pushed past me, guiding her with a solicitude and adoration he must have held in reserve for whores, for I couldn't imagine him treating Grace with even half the gentleness.

GRACE'S DOOR was festooned with a faded red cutout of two characters that I could just barely recognize in the greenish light of the corridor: *ru yi,* which she had once laboriously translated for me as "everything as you wish." The brittle paper shook and fell as I banged on the door; it seemed a bad omen. It was one in the morning. The reality of the situation took hold, and my panic suddenly cooled. She would be in bed; her whole family would be in bed. Poison's threats could wait.

But lights had already come on. Grace opened the door, looking startled.

"Something have happen to A?" she asked immediately.

I bit my lip. "No, A is fine. Sorry to barge in like this. Can I come in?"

"*Dangran.* Of course. But you are all wet. I make the tea, *haobuhao?*"

She let me in and took my poncho, hanging it carefully in the entryway, then hurried off to the kitchen. A voice called weakly from the bedroom, and she answered back to assure them that everything was all right. It was not where I had pictured her living, this little, airless apartment full of shoes and dust and rattan furniture with broken weave. Plastic grocery bags were folded carefully on a sideboard, bits of string and rubber bands saved in a jar. A pile of clothing waiting to be hemmed, stockings drip-drying over the kitchen sink.

She brought out a tray of salted plums and a teapot neatly arranged with a little spray of flowers. In the face of her humble economy, and her artless little gesture toward beauty, my errand seemed weak, melodramatic. To worry her without offering a solution would be cruel.

She poured the tea and pushed out a chair for me. If she remembered our moment of romance on the river, she gave no sign of it, neither coyness nor bitterness at how I had pulled away. A didn't deserve her. It would be a favor to her, to disabuse her of her dream. She wore a new necklace, a little jadeite bird on a red string. I reached over and touched it. "That's very pretty."

"Yes." She fingered it too, looking down, and paused, considering. "A give it to me."

I didn't know if that was true, or if it was just a lie she told to keep up appearances. My heart plummeted.

"Listen, Grace." I pulled my chair up closer and took her hands.

I told her. My account was blurred, laborious. I talked in circles, stumbled, repeated myself. The scorpion fight; A; the woman; A's little boy. I recounted a version of the history he had told me, leaving out the bitter impulse toward revenge, but the words seemed dead, disengaged from their real meaning: A; the woman; the scorpion fight; A's little boy.

Grace's gentle expression remained unchanged as I spoke. She said nothing, even when I had finished and was casting about nervously for something more to say. Had she understood me?

Slowly she poured out a cup of tea. Her cheeks had gone a shade paler. She rearranged the plums in their little dish, picked up the pot again, set it down. Picked it up.

In the other room, the voice called again: "Xiao Ru? Xiao Ru?"

"Excuse." She got up. "I come back."

When she returned, she had a young man by the hand—or an old man, it was difficult to tell. The face that peered out at me was wizened, like an old man's, but the body was young.

"My brother," said Grace. "Xiao Xiong."

He was obviously distressed by the disturbance in the night and plucked at her sleeve obsessively. I offered my hand, not knowing what else to do. As he took it, I noticed the fine black down on his arm, like the fur of an animal, and beneath this, withered skin flaking off, leaving sticky, translucent patches through which you could see the throb of his veins. Flesh disintegrating into dust and blood—yet the arms themselves were gawky, adolescent. Next to Grace's peerless perfection, he was a figure of death and disjunction, time out of joint. Distantly, I felt a kind of pain in my hand. He had not let go of it; instead, his grip had tightened, crushing my knuckles like a band of steel. As I tried to pull away, he made a harsh crowing sound at the back of his throat. Grace intervened, speaking urgently, but Xiao Xiong, evidently terrified, shrank away from her, crowing again, and wrenched my wrist around. A sharp pain shot up my arm.

"Xiao Xiong! Xiao Xiong!" Grace pried at his fingers desperately. He let go of my hand, and all at once the two of them were struggling with each other, Xiao Xiong screeching now, flailing at his sister with fear. There was a ripping sound as she broke away from him, and then suddenly the room grew very quiet as she stood, half-exposed, her right shoulder and breast revealed by a long tear in her nightshirt.

Xiao Xiong backed himself toward the living room, like a trapped animal, wailing. With a sob, Grace turned away, clutching the edges of her shirt together.

The shouting had brought an old, silent couple into the room— her parents, I assumed. They stood by, looking at Grace, both resentful and passive, like children.

"Are you all right?" I asked her.

"Excuse," she said faintly. "He is unhappy. It is very late. You wait. *Lai, Baba. Mama.*"

She went with all of them back to the inner rooms, leaving me to settle down shakily on the rattan couch. So this was what her tears had been about, back there in the paddleboat. She worked, I knew, at the cosmetics counter in the expensive Mitsukoshi building; she always came to our English lessons flushed from the perfumed luxury, the chic clientele, the dreamy, confected world of travel and romance made up by soft-focus ads and photos. Round and round she must go, caught between fantasy and truth. Of course she would dream of A, would dream of any path out into the world. I wished now that I had not told her about the prostitute.

When she came back in, she had changed her top and was carrying a piece of paper, which she gave to me as she sat down. In her careful English hand, she had printed a poem:

OSPREY

In harmony the ospreys sing,
On the island in the river.
The modest, virtuous young lady,
For the young man a good mate she.

Here long, there short, is the watercress,
On the left, to the right, tossed about by the current.

The modest, virtuous young lady,
For her he sleepless night spent.
Sought her and found her not,
Thought of her, awake or not.
Missing her, oh! so pensive and anxious;
Toss and turn until dawn.

Here long, there short, is the watercress,
On the left, to the right, she harvests and gathers.

The modest, virtuous young lady,
With lutes, small and large, the young man welcomes her.

Here long, there short, is the watercress,
On the left, to the right, she picks and chooses.
The modest, virtuous young lady,
With bells and drums, the young man rejoices in her
all the way home.

"From the Chinese," she said. "I use the dictionary for translate. You think?"

"It's beautiful."

"I think to give to A." She fingered the pendant on her necklace. "But. You say A . . . not to love me."

"No. Forget what I said, Grace."

"No. You cannot say and then forget."

"You'll find someone better," I said, lamely.

Her head dropped onto my shoulder, soft, light, tentative. It was what I had wanted, had wished for the moment I saw her. I wanted to lift her chin and kiss her, tell her I would help her, take her away. But Poison's insidious threat had changed everything. Now she had to be protected, even if it meant a betrayal of friendship—even if she believed I was abandoning her.

Gently, I kissed her on the forehead and put her away from me.

"You'll find someone else," I said again, and left.

CHAPTER 18

A<small>ND SO,"</small> A<small>NGEL WAS SAYING,</small> "Joe and Andy are sitting in the brush."

"Mm." I pushed a bite of steak across my plate without appetite.

She went on. "They're patrolling the border between Ontario and Michigan, and they're so bored they start playing Twenty Questions. They flip a coin, and Andy calls it. So he sits back and thinks for a while, thinks, thinks, thinks, and finally decides on 'moose cock.' He goes, 'I got one. You'll never guess.' So Joe, he sits back and pushes back his hat and thinks for a while, thinks, thinks, thinks, and finally he says, 'Uh . . . can you eat it?' And Andy thinks for a sec, bites his lip, goes, kinda dreamy-like, 'Yeaahh . . .' And right away Joe goes, 'Is it moose cock?' "

"*Angel.*" I twitched. "Would you stop?"

"It's just a joke," she snapped.

"I'm not in the mood."

"Screw you. Everyone loves that joke."

The whole day had been like this: a little vulgarity, a little irritation, recriminations, and silence. After leaving Grace's apartment around dawn, I had slept a small, fitful sleep, broken by a dream of a little plastic vial being shaken at me. When I opened it, Little P looked up at me from the bottom, battered and bruised. I had closed the cap and thrown him into the sea.

The shame of that dream still clung to me when Angel arrived later. Sick, sore, bleary, I had been dragged from shop to stall, forced to sample a procession of uncomplementary foods over the course of the day: *unagi don* in Gongguan; hot, sweetened *douhua;* greasy fried beef and pepper cakes cooked in an old oil drum on the street. Ruth's Chris Steak House was the last stop on Angel's list of places to review. It was meant to be a treat for both of us, but sadness and guilt remained with me, vestiges of the dream, and of the previous night with Grace, whom I would not see again.

"Bread?"

I shook my head. Vaguely I noted that Angel had dressed up in anticipation of the fancy dinner, her hair twisted into a French knot, her dress gauzy, her plump face made up with surprising skill. I had not told her about Poison's newest threat, which seemed empty now, theatrical.

The waiter shifted and coughed in an excess of attentive service. The luxury of the leather chairs and good wine seemed wrong somehow. I picked up my wineglass; in the distorted surface of merlot I saw my mother looking back at me again, old and worn and haunted by her sons.

A glow like a pilot light flickered up eerily behind the elegant paper partition. It drifted slowly out from behind the screen and floated across the murky dining room at a slow, measured pace. Between the half bottle of wine I'd consumed and the dimness, I had the brief, crazed impression that I was seeing my mother at last in her final form: light, cosmic light, warm, but with a detached, formal grace that kept me from reaching out to hold her, and burning my fingers on the flame.

Then I saw more clearly that it was a cake, a huge white cake with piped rosettes and candles stuck unevenly all over the frosted surface. The waiter balanced it carefully to our table and placed it in front of me with a flourish as Angel began a quavery solo—"Happy birthday to you"—and sang the whole thing through in a brave, thin a cappella.

I looked down in bewilderment. The cake, with all its crinolines and puffs of bloppy frosting, had been decorated by an amateur hand.

"What—?"

Angel whipped out a brown paper envelope and presented it to me across the table. Dubious, I broke the flap with a finger. A little brown booklet embossed with gold fell out. I turned it over and flipped open the front cover.

The laminated first page showed a head shot of me in black and white. Angel had snapped the picture on the street and cropped it down to size. The face was familiar enough—me looking straight into the camera, a little windblown, mouth slightly open in protest. But the information was all wrong. Name: Jorge Santa Ana. Citizenship: Philippines. I fingered the facts dumbly, not quite understanding. Angel nudged the cake toward me.

"But my birthday was in July."

"No way! Let me see." She leaned over, put her finger on the page, on the birth date line: October 1, 1976. I would be twenty-eight.

"You're free now." Anxiety edged her voice as she scanned my face for gratitude, delight. "You can go anywhere you want again." She hesitated when I didn't respond. "I know it's not perfect. I couldn't get my hands on a U.S. passport. Philippines is easier."

Silent, I flipped through the document, page after blank page.

"Emerson, you never look at me," Angel burst out.

The candles, unheeded, were burning down to a soft, melty mass. She had finished off her steak, but in the myopic light she still looked hungry.

"You never look at me that *way*." She sniffed. "When I . . . the fact is, I like you. You must know that."

"But Angel," I said, at a loss. I put down the passport. "I just . . . I never thought about it."

Even as I said it, my mind worked backward over the weeks: the high heels, the makeup, the phone calls. She had come with me to the ossuary; put me up in her bed; given me money, the cake, now the passport. There was something blind at work, if I had missed all the signs, or chalked them up to mere friendship. No, not blind. I had simply not wanted to see.

She threw down her napkin and left. The waiter's eyes popped as I went after her, leaving the enormous bill behind. His shouts dwindled as I chased Angel down the dim, elegant stretch of Min-quan.

Hobbled by her shoes, she could not get very far. Abruptly, she veered into a side alley, ran a short length, stopped, ran, stopped.

Her shoulders trembled with an effort not to cry, or perhaps she was crying already, I could not tell. A broken streetlight popped and sparked, then went out. Her face was turned to a wall. I stood some paces behind her, looking at the curve of her back.

"I'm sorry. There's no excuse."

She picked at a chip of paint, which came off in her hand.

I came closer, hesitant. "What can I do?"

In answer, she whirled around and pressed her mouth fiercely against mine, arms wrapped around me like a vise, willing me to passion. I stirred but did not put my arms around her; I could not.

She withdrew, hurt, humiliated.

"I'm too old for you, Angel," I said gently—but that wasn't it, not exactly. Her dress had slipped a little off her shoulder; the makeup had softened the shine on her nose. She looked, in the darkness, like a vision of a future self: beautiful, witty, generous; her judgments tempered by the memory of impetuousness in her youth. The revelation saddened me, for the dress was pretty, but I missed the army fatigues and combat boots, the way her jaw hardened when she was set on some preposterous idea; missed her foul mouth, her calling me "boyee."

"You're my best friend," I said. "My only real friend. But you deserve to be with someone who loves you from the start. Not some middle-aged sack like me."

"Who said anything about love?" she said unexpectedly. "I'm not asking you to love me." She wiped her nose on her wrist and turned to me, defiant. "Not at the start. But maybe you would after a while? Couldn't you? Could you really not fall in love with me?"

"Angel," I said and put my arm around her—a mistake, because she took this to mean submission and turned her wet face against my neck. Her hand came up to cup my jaw in a clumsy motion of tenderness and affection. I pushed it away.

"I can't," I said. The proximity made me dizzy. *That's all it is, Emerson. That's all it is.* "Not like this. Not without it being right."

"What's 'right'?" she asked.

"I don't know!" I said, suddenly angry. "I just don't want to do it in some shoddy, sordid little way! Not the first time!"

She was staring at me now. "You mean . . ."

I clamped my mouth shut and spoke through my teeth. "Nobody puts a premium on loyalty anymore. On promises," I said tightly. "If I won't . . . go home with you . . . you should be grateful that I'm man enough to say no from the beginning."

"And I'm not man enough to say no? You make me sound like some pathetic little whore!"

"I wasn't referring to—"

"Screw you!" she shouted. "I don't *need* your patriarchal oppression! And I don't need your charity. Go to hell, you bastard—you and your criminal-ass brother."

"What?" I snatched at her. "What about my brother?"

But she had fled, tripping down the alley.

I looked after her. Rain began to fall, little smatterings at first, then beating a steady tattoo on the tin roofs. Automatically I pulled the ashes closer, but the gesture seemed to be just that—a gesture.

Angel's mention of Little P had alarmed me, but for once I was too tired to consider the prospect of immediate danger. It was the older, deeper, more lasting vein of trouble she had called up that tugged at me now—not urgent but pushed down, repressed, muffled for so long that it had the force of an underground tap. Incense burned in a little shop nearby; the smell of consecration, of devotion. J, standing at the balcony of the apartment I had rented, overlooking the Charles. I had stopped sending money home to my mother just so I could afford that little, light-filled bower for the two of us. She had been happy, or so I'd believed. She hung pictures, painted the walls, tended her dusky autumn garden on the balcony, calling to me to come, help her with the late tomatoes she coaxed from the vine. Perhaps it had been only a kind of fiction to her, a return to old, innocent childhood impressions of home that, twice divorced, she already knew were not to last. I refused to share a bed, always putting her off and putting her off—that too taken from the page of childhood for her: love without sex. I never made a move, afraid to spoil the majesty of anticipation with the fact itself. My mother called, cried, said she would cut me off, but her tears and threats were like distant explosions, unable to penetrate the idyll. Eventually the calls stopped altogether.

I could have lived like that forever, suspended in the sweetness of time and hope, but not J. I could still see clearly the gray, chipped paint of the front door that afternoon, putting my key in the lock—strange what insignificant details disillusionment would hold on to. Candles in the living room, a trail of smoke, a glass of wine. In the bedroom, a kind of domestic tableau: J in her robe, the man murmuring to her. Worse, somehow, than catching them in the act, for the scene had an intimacy about it, a closeness that stung.

"Do you love him?" I asked when he was gone.

"For God's sake." Both prayerful and biting at once. "Did you hear a word I just said? Love, love." She yanked the sheet from the bed and threw it to the ground. "It's all I ever hear from you. What does that have to do with anything? I don't even know what you mean when you say love."

I reached out, grabbed her arm, kissed her roughly.

"Ow. *Stop* it! Not like this."

"You said there was no right time."

"I'm trying to *help* you."

I laughed.

"Fine." Her green eyes blazing. "All right. If this is what you want."

Into the living room and onto the couch, stripping off my shirt. The atmosphere was bright and harsh, without any of the mystery I had always imagined. My touch betrayed me: anxious, hesitant. The shock of contact, her warmth beneath her robe. Instinctively I put out a hand, as if to ward off a blow, but she would not stop. A kiss, ungentle, with a brutishness tinged with a taste of stale wine. Her robe came off. Skin, damp, the wet-tipped push of her heavy breasts; the smell of moist soil, a shiver, the white light of the Remada bathroom, looking down at my mother's head. Her hand pressed me, broad, flat strokes, and all at once the harshness and images and dreadful pleasure swam together, too fast.

"Wait!" I begged, trying to push her away. But it was too late. A jolt of dark, agonized bliss—and then it was over.

"Already?" The voice was taunting, but tears, inexplicable, ran down her cheeks.

"You see?" Almost gently. "That's all it is, Emerson. That's all love is."

Rain battened down my collar. I had reached the bright, luminous arcade of Ren Ai Road and ducked under the portico of the Citizen Hotel. As I shook water from my jacket, the passport fell out of the pocket in the lining. I picked it up.

Brown, instead of blue. Jorge Santa Ana, from the Philippines. He would be twenty-eight years old today. I knew it was only temporary, but somehow the document had its own kind of power, quite apart from the reality. However much I knew that I was Emerson Chang, in an official capacity I was Jorge Santa Ana, and that little bit of confirmation stole from me, made me a little less Emerson, a little more Jorge. How easy it would be, in fact, to switch nations, to switch alliances. I had, after all, cut my mother off all those years ago, without a second thought, and for what? For a fantasy of J, a false bliss, a future that was only a chimera, dissolving the moment I put my hand to it.

I riffled through the blank, unfamiliar pages of the booklet again, the tanned, treated paper instead of solid blue laminate. I had thought I would be an American all my life, but when I looked closely, I found I had no objective reason to believe this. America was a contract, based on reason, not blood—and a contract of the will could be broken more easily. Perhaps that was why my mother had never been comfortable in America. She put great store in dynasties, in the pedigrees. She had, I realized now, a great fear of the void—of disorder and mess, of broken lines, of darkness, of individual destinies that in their wanderings destroyed the immortality of the whole. America, in its best days, smashed that immortality, cut its memory short and diluted it with the waves of new immigrants, year after year. At its shining best, it kept itself immortal not through the shadow of threat or empire but through a kind of republic of the spirit. My mother could never understand. She had not believed in heaven, not in any way that other people did. Immortality was only in me, and in Little P; it was only our fidelity to her that would keep her alive in any meaningful sense. I saw Little P in my dream, broken, beaten at the bottom of that vial, and knew that I couldn't let him go.

CHAPTER 19

After wandering under the ashy streetlights for a few hours, I hailed a cab to Tongan Street. The streets looked deserted, loose garbage tumbling in the gutters, the convenience stores like remote white beacons in the chaotic dark.

I had not come here since that first visit to Little P, back in August, in the innocence of early grief and late summer. The apartment building was darkened, and the messy, angry red graffito on the doors had faded and tarnished so that it seemed to be an ancient word, a rune whose meaning had long since been forgotten. I did not ring Little P's bell but instead went up the way I had that first time. At his door, I knocked, and the sound reverberated through the hall and the apartment beyond.

"Little P?"

I knocked, rested my hand on the doorknob. Somehow I knew, instinctively, that he was not there. The locks were not locked. Slowly I turned the latch and let the door swing in.

The place was empty. The trash, the makeshift furniture, even the cracked mirror on the wall—gone, and the smell of antiseptic hung in the air, as if to erase all traces, not only of Little P but of any human touch. The light, when I flicked it on, was cold, blue, unyielding. Wind rattled the windows.

In the kitchenette, I opened the drawers and cabinets slowly, one by one, knowing what I would find: nothing, and nothing.

The screen door to the tiny balcony flapped. Mechanically I went outside to close it, looking down at the shadowed street whipped by the wind as I wrapped my coat around the ashes to keep them warm. The red lights of the Buddhist temple burned ghoulishly in the street below, the open entryway glowing like fire in a cave.

The wind picked up suddenly, rustled the trash bags in the corner of the porch. Something light and hard rolled against my foot. I bent down to retrieve it.

It was a vial, a little plastic vial identical to the one Uncle had fumbled and dropped. Fear rose again—fear, confusion. Was it drugs after all? That was too easy an answer to be right. Then I remembered Uncle's look of lucidity and terror. No. Whatever the vials were, they were a secret beyond any conventional drug cartel.

I tucked the vial in my pocket and left, not bothering to close the door behind me. Back down in the street, I hurried toward Roosevelt Road.

THE PALACE beckoned, just across the busy six-lane dividing the long walled courtyard of Longshan Temple from the Wanhua district. From the outskirts, and in the buzzing light from McDonald's and the ancient streetlamps, the neighborhood seemed more than usually dingy, the dark, craggy buildings like the walls of a canyon, the road a crevasse down which I skittered with a peculiar dread. Quiet for a Saturday night, dirt scudding along in the gutters, skinny, misshapen alley cats darting in the shadows. I stopped directly across the street from the karaoke, looking up at the poor, stained façade. Strange how deserted the Palace was, always.

A sudden arc of light: a truck turned the corner at the end of the street, came barreling through, turned again. As it passed, I saw, suddenly, a glimpse of a shape reflected in the dark glass doors of the Palace—brief, huddled, staring out from behind a stack of Shaoxing wine boxes behind me.

I whirled around. She tried to duck away but was not fast enough, and instead crouched like a cornered cat. The notched lip: the girl from Uncle's—the one Little P had called Poison's girl. Her legs were bare and scratched, her skinny frame hidden by a stiff, cheap new dress. She didn't recognize me, of course, only stared in mute terror, holding a plastic bag to her chest as if for warmth.

I raised my hand uncertainly in greeting. Instantly she bolted across the street, disappearing into the alley next to the Palace.

"Wait!"

But she was already gone.

I stood paralyzed for a few moments, uncertain whether to follow. The doors to the KTV opened, and I had to draw back farther into the shadows, for it was Little P who stepped out. He looked carefully up and down the street, put on his sunglasses, dug in the pocket of a black overnight bag slung over his shoulder. When he lit a cigarette, I cursed inwardly; I would never find the girl again now.

At last he ground the smoke out, wheeled his scooter into the road, left. As soon as he was out of sight, I ran around the corner where the girl had gone.

I found myself in an alley that dead-ended in a concrete wall. She could not have gone very far; she could not have doubled back without me seeing her. I looked around, bewildered. She could be inside the Palace now, but then how could she have gotten in? There was no back exit, no fire escape, very few windows—no windows near the ground at all. I walked up and down the length of the building.

A stack of corrugated tin rose several feet on a wooden flat. Someone extremely agile could jump from the top of it to the balconies of the adjoining apartments, and from there to a second-story window. The window did, in fact, appear to be broken.

With difficulty, I clambered onto the flat and hopped up and down, trying unsuccessfully to gain a handhold on the nearest grille. It seemed impossible; she could not have gone this route. The tin sheets made so much noise that I was afraid someone might call the police. The ashes twisted about my waist on their thin cord, binding me. At one point I had a firm grip, but a tearing pain in my right shoulder forced me to let go, and I dropped back onto the flat, panting.

With dreadful precision, I jumped up and caught the rails again, swinging my legs heavily forward for momentum. Again my shoulder pulled, but this time the pain was endurable. I hung there for a moment like a sack of grain, then struggled wildly, pulling myself upward until my toes gained a hold on the metal. My weight bent the rails slightly; the balcony screeched and groaned. It was not the most subtle of break-ins, especially since I was now looking full-face into various apartments as I sidled, awkward, from balcony to balcony, trying to reach the broken window. A little boy observed me stolidly from behind a screen door as I passed by. On the next balcony, a washing machine slopped warm, soapy water all over the floor. Almost there. The window was wider than I had thought, but the frame still held shards of glass like a mouthful of jagged teeth. After some hesitation, I wrapped my hand in my handkerchief and gingerly grasped the side frame. A moment of panic as I let go of the balcony grille. Then I was inside.

It seemed to be a storage room. Cardboard file boxes and plastic tubs leaned up against the walls. There were more of the torn-out banquettes jammed in here at angles, along with a few low tables of the kind that stood in the karaoke rooms, and boxes in which mirrored balls were nested among their electrical wiring like large bejeweled eggs. I recognized, as my eyes adjusted, the dismantled lid of a coffin, which was propped in the far corner like the dim outline of a tomb.

The coffin itself lay on the floor behind a row of broken TVs. The light reflecting through the window was veiled, dim. I picked my way around the furniture, banging my shins once or twice. Somebody might have heard me, but it didn't matter. The closer I got to the heart of the matter, the less I cared for caution. I stood over the casket, assaulted by a dizzying sense of claustrophobia that surged violently and then passed.

The interior was empty, but the coffin had been sealed and then unsealed at some point. There were holes in the top-facing surface as well as bent nails strewn about the floor. A splinter caught in my palm as I ran my hand along the top edge of the casket, trying to think: Atticus saying, "Principle!"; Officer Hu and his gun; the stonemason; Little P, his lean, wolfish face full of anger and remote misery: "You wouldn't understand."

My fingers had been automatically tracing a kind of Braille cut in the side of the casket, near the lid: rows of dots hammered out with the smallest of nail tips in the thick-hewn wood. The dots were the size of ants, close-set and decorative, I supposed, running the length of the coffin. I pulled my hand away.

I went out into the hallway, checking it cautiously first, but the Palace was not open yet, and the second floor wasn't for customer use anyway. The fluorescent tubing had gone out in all but two fix-tures, which buzzed and trembled with a greenish light. There was a smell of paper and incense, and of something organic or fecal—close, sour-sweet, like a humid pasture in summer.

I crept along, keeping close to the wall. The floor was eerily silent, and my shoes squeaked so loudly that I took them off and continued in my stocking feet. My moment of recklessness was over. I didn't want to know about Little P's misdeeds anymore; I just wanted to get out of the Palace uninjured and undetected. There was nothing incriminating to be seen here anyway. The doors were all closed and locked, the transom windows covered over with yellowed newspaper.

As I rounded the next corner, the elevator suddenly came to life. The doors slid open on my floor. A soft voice, a man's, muttered lowly, and then the brisk sound of footsteps approached. I fled noiselessly down the corridor. The voice grew louder.

It was Big One; he seemed to be hectoring someone, alternately coaxing and demanding. He kept saying, very pointedly, *"Ni,"* meaning "you," and I supposed he was on the phone. I had no time to consider, however, because he kept approaching. I tried the doorknobs desperately: locked, locked. One was unlocked. I slipped into the room and shut the door just as he rounded the corner.

In the dark, I pressed myself up against the wall and listened. His tone was a queer mix of coyness and threat.

I waited until the footsteps disappeared. The unwashed smell I had noticed in the hallway was stronger in here, and gradually I became aware that I was not alone. The air was too warm; it had a quality of breath. Something bumped softly against the back wall. My hand found the light switch; the overhead bulb flickered on.

They stared back at me, four or five of them: girls of about fourteen or sixteen, huddled together on a cot in the corner. They were dark and skinny, and stared dumbly at me, blinking in the sudden exposure. Bare-legged, they pulled their skirts down instinctively, veins showing like contusions on their skin. One of them had been tatting in the dark, a length of dirty lace across her lap. The harsh gray-green light revealed the stark room without mercy: two cots, some boxes for clothing; that was all. The floor was bare, and the walls hadn't been finished. Peels of paint came off the surface like sores. The girl with the tatting spoke up.

"I don't understand," I whispered. She was speaking some kind of dialect. I think I spoke in English; I was so shocked that I didn't know. She repeated herself and then, in a terrible, primitive gesture, pointed into her mouth to signify food.

I turned out the light again; it didn't seem callous, it seemed the only thing to do. Darkness resettled; I went back out into the hallway, closing the door softly behind me. Dazed, I wandered down the hall, not caring that I was in plain view.

Bits of song rang intermittently through the corridor. Big One had occupied a room at the end of the hall, leaving the door ajar, like a boast. He had turned on the disco ball so that the room was full of points of lights in soft, dreamy rotation and was seated on the black banquette, holding a microphone in one hand and singing along with the lyric prompts in a lusty tenor.

The girl I had followed in from the street was draped across his lap limply. Big One's fingers made little wet circles along her inner thigh. Her thin dress had been torn off; her body was like a child's, thin and flexible, and her face was flat and unemotional as she lay humiliatingly sprawled against Big One's bulk.

The song ended. Big One sighed, momentarily sated, then grasped the girl by the arm. She began to struggle, her face still silent and affectless. Big One slapped her and grunted in slippery, intimate Hokkien. He stood up and pinned her to the banquette, one fat thigh between her legs. He fumbled with his zipper. Again, he spoke, the harsh sound of threat and seduction together.

She made a hard, bitter sound. Big One laughed, twisted his hand in her hair, and pulled it hard. She cried out, flailing. He stroked her throat tenderly with both thumbs and muttered some kind of expletive, gasping as he rubbed himself against her. Suddenly he pushed her roughly onto her side and barked a command: Roll over. *"Bie jiao."* Don't scream.

Obedient, she put her head down on the banquette and rolled

over. She saw me in the doorway over Big One's shoulder, I think. Her expression did not change. The disco ball made its soft, mitigating rounds as the next song began. Strains of the melody followed me down the hall, back out the window.

PART 3

CHAPTER 20

NEXT WEEK, Little P had said. *Hong Kong. Chungking.* These three facts, dimly recalled from that eerie trip to Jilong, took slow root in my mind. *Next week. Hong Kong. Next week.*

I arrived in Hong Kong on Thursday evening, blinking in the sudden dazzle of Chek Lap Kok, the white, glassed-in hangar filled with late orange sun. Kowloon Bay glistened, a sheet of wrinkled silk, as the Airport Express sped toward the metropolis. The sky looked like fire.

I closed my eyes, but the impression of flames remained. Flames, prayers, money for ghosts. Longshan Temple, where I had gone to burn an offering for my mother only a week ago. The darkened portals of the temple had led directly into the cavernous apse, the idols of the deities arrayed, smoke-lidded and pensive, on a dais before rows and rows of tables. The murmurous quiet of supplication, the punctuating clatter of wooden bones being thrown. In the back: a fire in an enormous kiln, banked on all sides by mountains of gray ash, while behind the temple, a pyre cordoned by a low stone wall burned duskily with paper prayers submitted for the dead.

My eyes flew open. The Airport Express shuddered along its track, and the numbness that had gripped me ever since the discovery at last dissolved. Disgust welled up; I put a handkerchief to my mouth, retching. The purse of ashes sagged beside my carryall. I kicked it under the seat, suddenly enraged. My mother—her blind loyalty to Little P was worth nothing, would change nothing. I had been prepared to accept anything: drugs; embezzlement; arms smuggling; even, perhaps, murder. But this—it wasn't even mere prostitution. I knew instinctively that the girls I'd seen were just the surface of it; a malevolent shadow moved behind them, and I was afraid.

As I sat, a cold rill of sweat ringing my neck, an old beggar with a tray came shuffling down the aisle. He touched my shoulder, spilling his pathetic wares into my lap: a single pen, a package of nuts, a dirty silk scarf. I shook my head. He insisted, pawing at my arm. I got up, gathered my things, and moved to a seat in the next car. I felt horrible doing it, but I couldn't bear his presence. It wasn't his dirt that was repellent, or his rank smell. It was the importunate, half-formed sounds he made as he pushed his merchandise. They reminded me of that hoarse voice in the back room, asking for food, for help. I had no idea what to say.

LITTLE P had not mentioned a time for his arrival at Chungking Mansions, which meant that I would have to position myself in the lobby and wait for him to appear. This plan, conceived in innocence, was immediately crushed as I stood in the garish neon-lit maw of the Chungking entrance that evening and watched helplessly while throngs of foreigners pushed through the open arcade. Not a hotel so much as a marketplace, a mall, and a city of itinerants. Money changers sat resolute and forbidding behind their bulletproof glass and cages; a Sikh with a rifle dozed catlike and watchful. I waited for an hour, studying the restless crush of residents intently. Indians, Pakistanis—men of the subcontinent shuffling around in pairs, mostly, and some strung-out backpackers, a crush of indistinct locals buying pirated software. The Sikh was getting suspicious. His eyes flicked at me from time to time, and he held his clips more prominently in view. I stood my ground. Another half hour passed. I would never find Little P this way.

But as I was about to leave, I caught a flash of metal rounding the corner to the elevators. Keeping an eye warily on the rifle, I edged toward it. I don't know how I knew it was Little P; something in the heart recognizes its own.

I'd hesitated for only a moment, but it was enough for him to slip into the elevators, for the sallow doors to slide shut and the ancient cables and cogs to churn upward, slowly. Eighth floor. I skirted a group of nuns and darted into the other car.

The burnt-out corridor smelled of cardamom and rot. A pipe had burst somewhere, and wet footprints ran in all directions across the tiles. Odd voices from behind an apartment door, which swung open in a burst of chatter to reveal a full restaurant with brocaded tablecloths and wine and candles, like a mirage in the desert. Then the door fell to, and in the restored dimness, I saw again the flash of metal, down at the end of the long hall.

Slipping a little, I followed it, footsteps squeaking. He did not look back, but he began, imperceptibly, to walk faster, with a hunted gait. I hazarded after him without trying to conceal myself. I was through with that. Atticus was right. Caution, fear—they diminished you, shriveled you. If there was a darkness to behold, I wanted to know it; I wanted to look into my brother's face and see it fully once and for all. Perhaps then I could begin to build the bond again: banish the darkness, take him home. I slipped in a puddle and fell heavily against the wall. Still without turning, he broke into a swift, silent run, darting through an exit and down the stairs. I struggled up. I could not lose him.

"Little P!" I shouted. The cry redounded senselessly in the piss-smelling stairwell. He did not look up, only flew down the steps. "It's me! It's Emerson!"

He might have gotten away, but the door on the ground floor was locked. I could hear him jimmying the knob frantically as I limped down the last flight. Cornered, perhaps at last he would talk.

"I only want to know . . ." I said. Then stopped, for the man cowering against the door was not my brother. He was older, more devolved, more debased; his eyes shone with an addict's dreadful misery and desire, and he whimpered as I stood before him.

The stairwell door suddenly opened from the other side, and the junkie fled past a couple of Indian men, who brushed by me without looking; they did not want to involve themselves. The door closed.

In the stillness, a great exhaustion came over me. Even if the man had been Little P, what would I have done? I could not even imagine anymore. Somehow my brother had made the future into something blank and terrible, resistant to all efforts at love, or thoughts of possibility.

I caught a sound above me on the concrete stair—not loud but stealthy, deliberate. Quickly I flattened myself against the door, mind whirling. Only Atticus knew where I had gone. A soft muffle of footsteps trying to conceal themselves in the bare chamber.

A silhouette appeared at the top of the stairs, dark, plain, oddly retiring.

"Who is it?" I whispered.

Silence.

"Who are you?"

She came forward, a shadow separating out from shadows.

My legs began to tremble. I sank down on the urine-stained floor and pressed my fist to my breastbone, trying to breathe.

"Angel."

"Don't get mad," she began, standing over me.

"How the hell . . . ?"

She blushed.

"You followed one me."

"The whole way."

Her mouth primmed up in silent defense. Planting her heel on the ground, she cocked her head skeptically and stared me down. "So. Are you going to buy me a drink or what?"

I HAD not seen her since that dismal steak dinner, and it was clear, from her pointed silence, that she had not yet forgiven me.

"So what did you come for, anyway, if you're so pissed?" I asked finally. We were in Lan Kwai Fong, the cobblestone walks packed with revelers and colored lights, the clinking of ice in highballs.

Angel forged ahead, tight-lipped, her steps clipped and angry as I trotted after her. "What makes you think—" but then the rest of her words were swallowed up by a burst of laughter from the open windows of a pub.

"What?"

She whirled around. "I *know*!"

"Know what?"

"About your brother!"

I grabbed her arm as she turned away. "What do you know?"

She twisted out of my grasp and fled down the street.

Stumbling, I followed her into a dark churchyard surrounded by a thick hedge. Water trickled somewhere; white statuary peered eyelessly from the hushed steeple.

"Angel!" I hissed.

She was scrunched in a nook of the hedge, sitting on a wooden bench. One boot was off, and she was rubbing a twisted ankle. I planted my foot at the end of the bench. The seat jumped violently, jarring her.

"Just what do you know about Little P?"

She sniffed. "That he should be in jail."

"Prostitution is legal in Taipei," I said, defensive.

"Yeah, but smuggling's not."

When I didn't say anything, she looked up again. "*Human* smuggling, Emerson. Those girls . . . they're not local. They look like they're from the mainland. Sold, most likely. Or else someone lied to them to get them to come."

I sat down on the edge of the bench.

"I thought you knew," she said, suddenly frightened.

I pressed my hand to my breastbone, wanting to loosen the bond about my chest. "I didn't know the girls were illegal."

"What did you think?" said Angel skeptically. "That they were just staying in those horrible little rooms for fun?"

"I don't know what I thought," I said. "I didn't think." Rather, I didn't want to know. I thought of my brother: when he was little, he had gone through a phase in which he could not sleep unless his pillows were arranged in a certain way. I would look in on him after closing up the office and find him in his hot, close room, sleeping hard and serious in that little-boy way, arms flung up over his head in an expression of trust. "Will you fix it?" he would ask, coming to my room with his broken transistor and hopping up on the bed. There was the way he always sat too close as I took the radio apart, curious and rapt. How could I connect those memories with the degradation in the back rooms of the Palace?

"How do you know about this, anyway?" I asked Angel.

She chewed a nail.

"Good God, have you done anything but follow me in the last week?"

"I wasn't spying," she said. "I was . . . You pissed me off, you bastard."

She calmed down. "It's not important. Anyway." She pulled her camera out of her bag. "I followed you to the Palace. There's an easier way to get in, you know. Through the basement of the building next door." She fiddled with the camera, which blinked on with the sound of chimes. Then she handed it to me.

The shots had been taken at night, from outside the Palace, under the sodium-looking lights of the alley. The exposure was bad, but you could see clearly enough the Palace signage, and the outline of two men. From that distance I couldn't tell who they were; they might have been Poison and Big One, or they might have been Uncle or Little P or any of the clerks they kept at the desk. They carried a large block between them.

"Coffins," said Angel. "They've been transporting them in coffins from Jilong down to Taipei. They bring them across the strait at night, I think."

The shots of the Palace disappeared; the next was a close-up of the coffin I had seen dismantled in the upstairs room. The tiny Braille markings I had felt in the wood were holes, airholes. Why had she documented it so thoroughly? I fast-forwarded through the rest of the frames unthinkingly.

"Why haven't you gone to the police?" I said, suddenly hoarse.

She frowned and tucked a lanky piece of hair behind her ear.

"I don't know." She glanced at me, then away. "Because he's your brother. I thought . . . if you wanted me to hide these . . . just until you can get him out of it."

Angel, I don't love you, I wanted to say—just so she would remember, and perhaps protect herself. Pity and gratitude throbbed in equal amounts, giving me a headache that seemed to encompass more than just anxiety for Little P. I shook my head to clear it.

"I have to talk to him," I said. "I can't understand how he got mixed up in all this." I plucked at the grass. Shame swelled in me. "If it's just money, he has an out. My mother left him the motel."

"Is your uncle threatening him?"

The old man, with his menacing bulk; the shuffling; the as-
phyxiated breath; the snorting and labor it took to keep him alive.
No, perhaps he didn't do the threatening himself, but he had Poison and Big One and his other minions to do it for him. Then I
remembered his visit to my house, the strange flash of fear, the little
plastic vial, which still rattled hollowly around in my pocket. It
made no sense. But if Little P was under pressure, we would get
him out somehow. I would get him out.

"It was brave of you to come," I said suddenly, looking down at
Angel. She didn't look up. I put my hand over hers and squeezed it
once. She waited. When nothing happened, she gently pulled her
hand away.

ANGEL, IT turned out, had done a good amount of snooping.
Along with the pictures, she had managed to trunk-track Little P's
phone calls with a CTEK cable pilfered from the electronics market. Through the static, she had heard him murmuring about a
meeting—seven o'clock, Friday—though the place was not clear,
nor was she certain whether it was 7:00 A.M. or 7:00 P.M. I would
have to stake out the Mansions at both times.

No sign of Little P in the lobby on Friday morning, though I arrived two hours early and stayed until almost ten o'clock. The
room I had rented in Wan Chai was bleak and stuffy when I returned, discouraged; I called Angel, but she was nowhere to be
found.

That evening, however, I had not made it halfway to the Wan
Chai station when I noticed her hanging back behind me, trying, I
suppose, to follow. I ignored her; she knew everything already.

Shadowing me through a transfer at Central, she nearly stepped on my heel, but I allowed her to think she was doing relatively well, until I boarded a car that was almost unoccupied. She drew up short. Then, coolly, she walked to the opposite end of the car and sat down. The absurdity lasted three stations.

"You might as well come over here and sit," I said finally. "You're not fooling anyone."

Shamefaced, she got up and walked over to me. We rode in silence for another stop.

As we approached the Mansions, I began to lag.

"What are you doing?" asked Angel, frowning.

"I don't know what to say to him," I said. My palms were sweating. "He's not a little boy anymore."

"Look, boyo. First, you're going to tell him you know about the girls. Then, you're going to tell him we have proof. You don't have to blame him; tell him we know he's just Uncle's henchman, and that he won't be implicated if he gets out now and leaves—goes back to the U.S. or somewhere, doesn't matter where. It's the goddamn timing that's important. Give him, I don't know, a week. A month."

"You should be making the demands," I said dully. "I don't have the stomach for it."

"This is for *him,* you idiot, for his own good. Sooner or later he's going to be caught if he keeps on."

"And what if he doesn't listen to me? What if he calls my bluff?"

"What bluff? We're not bluffing. If he doesn't get out, he'll be reported too."

"I'm not reporting my own brother," I said, appalled.

Angel looked at me.

"It's abhorrent, what they're doing," she said, very quiet, and I knew she would not be swayed. "They're *prisoners*. They're being held like animals. I should have gone to the police with these right away," she said, biting her lip.

"*No*. Please. I know it's wrong, I *know*. But I can't turn him in. There's something not right about all this. He's just . . . confused. Or else he's being pressured somehow. If I can just get him to—"

She grabbed my arm and gestured. A figure had come out onto the sidewalk; in the flare of a match, Little P's thin face lit up, then died out. It was too dark for him to identify me, and he seemed disinclined to look around in any case. I raised my hand weakly and said, "Uh . . . ," the way one signals a waiter, but still he didn't see me. He moved off down the street.

"Shh," said Angel. She signaled for me to follow.

In the rain, people appeared indistinct, vague shapes moving behind a scrim. Little P followed the jagged back street for a few blocks, then turned on Nathan Road and headed toward the harbor. He walked purposefully and fast, through the throngs wrapped in plastic ponchos, then darted across the street, holding a newspaper over his head, disappearing into the crowd farther ahead.

"There he is," said Angel, pointing. A cab nearly ran her over as she dashed out into the road.

We followed him all the way to the Promenade, where across the darkened harbor, the Bank of China rose like a prism from the gray sea. The crowd was sparse here; we hung back and watched, in case

Little P should turn his head and spot us. A bedraggled seagull huddled beneath a bench, letting out a plaintive scree now and then as the waves splashed the guardrails. If he was aware of being watched, Little P did not show it. He crossed the wide plaza around the clock tower and went into the ferry building.

"Hurry," said Angel, beginning to run.

But when we reached the terminal, Little P was not there. A ferry to Central was pulling away from the pier. It seemed impossible that he could have gotten on. All the same, we watched it with despair.

"Shit," breathed Angel.

"Do we take the next one?"

She shook her head. "I don't think there is a next one. We don't even know he's on there, anyway."

The terminal was wide and open; I looked around wildly. "Where else would he be? Behind the fucking trash can?"

"Don't swear at me," she said, angry. "There's all kinds of levels to this place. You haven't even *looked*."

"Fine." I tore my hair. "Let's get going."

We made a cautious sweep of the lower level. The concourse was empty and quiet, rain drumming softly on the high windows, until some passengers from the departed ferry filtered in, coming down the ramp from the upper levels: a woman with a shopping bag, two or three men in dark suits and shirts. One of the men, greased and heavyset, was having problems with a cuff, which flapped about as he fumbled with the button. We passed him as he paused to wipe his nose with the back of his thumb. There was a cut across his knuckles.

"Wait," I said, halting.

"What?"

I watched the men as they put up their umbrellas and went out into the rain. Then I turned around and went up the ramp, walking quickly. Then running.

"Hey!" Angel protested, but I was too far ahead to listen. An ungrounded fear slowed my heartbeat; it was like stop-time, sounds and colors illuminated with painful clarity. I ran down the concourse. The corridor split off four ways at the end, and I stopped.

A man came out of the bathroom at the end of the south-facing corridor. I watched him approach, a figure in a shabby black suit, small and neat—too neat, like a false alibi. He glanced at me as he passed by, a look he tried to pass off as bored, incurious. But his eyes locked on mine a moment too long. A single drop of blood stained his white cuff.

"Hey!" I shouted. He began to trot. "Hey!"

He ran, sprinting along the north corridor. I started after him, but in a few yards I gave him up and went back in the direction he had come from. Angel was too far behind. This time, I thought. This time I knew what I would find.

In the dingy yellow-tiled bathroom, someone had left the tap running. I stepped inside; a leak in the ceiling had covered the floor with rain. Red had bloomed in the water, into tendrils that dissolved and turned the water a violent pink. Little P was lying facedown in one of the stalls.

"Little P?" I turned him over. His face had been smashed, and his left hand was bloody and contused.

"Little P?" I gathered him up and lifted his torso across my lap, cradling him clumsily.

"Emerson?" Angel splashed through the puddles.

"He's all right," I said. It sounded queer and weak in the echoing chamber, like a prayer rather than an assertion. "He's all right. Go find someone. Find someone."

She lingered, distraught.

"Run!" I yelled.

CHAPTER 21

HIS ARM WASN'T BROKEN, just fractured. His nose and left eye were swollen and purpled. Though he looked bad, his injuries were minor. I had brought him back to his room at the Mansions at dawn, so doped up on painkillers that he clung to me as I lowered him to his bed.

"You're okay. You'll be fine," I murmured. He didn't argue. I thought he was asleep until I tried to get up. Then suddenly his grip on my shoulder tightened and he said, harshly, in my ear, "Meet me tonight."

I thought he was hallucinating, still caught in whatever transaction had gone on before they knocked him out. "It's over, Little P. It's me."

He laughed. "I know," he said. "I know who you are."

His gaze seemed to go right through me: cowardice, fear, the arrogance of my heart. He did, indeed, know who I was; he was perhaps the only person who had ever known me, darkness and all. I might have prevented all this: given him the will, paid Poison. I touched his injured arm, not exactly meaning to hurt him, and he cried out. The Percocet was starting to wear off.

"Meet me tonight at the Admiralty," he said through clenched teeth. "Nine o'clock. You want knowledge? You want to know?"

I gave him a couple of Percocet and a glass of water from the disgusting little basin in the corner of the room. He swallowed the pills dry and slipped back down onto the bed.

"Are you going to be all right here?" I asked. "No one's going to . . . find you?"

"No," he said. He coughed, retching a little. "Even if they did, what do I care?"

A roach made its desperate way up the dirty pane of window, through which the autumn sky showed bleakly, white and gray.

"Nine o'clock," he repeated. He turned his face to the wall.

IT WAS still early when we arrived at the Admiralty. The entrance was low and wide and muffled with a heavy black curtain, and yellowed placards taped to the window declared "Most Beautiful Girls!" and "Your Fantasy!" Ambient music spilled out into the street, where a number of pale foreigners wandered separately.

"Well, this is the place," I said, resigned. Without revealing too much detail, I had tried to dissuade Angel from coming along, but she wanted a little titillation, a drink.

"Only the British would name a strip club The Admiralty," she said, digging in her purse for the cover charge. "How is that erotic to anybody?"

The stout matron at the door turned out to be the bouncer and cashier both, and as she took our money, she rattled off a little spiel that was meant to be sexy and suggestive ("You look for fun tonigh', huh? Our girl lot of fun") but lost something in the bored, dry transaction of money for sex, especially when she and Angel scuffled over the amount of change owed. Inside, the bar flanked the sides of a short catwalk illuminated by blue lights, with a pole at either end, and every once in a while a girl in a bikini and plastic high heels would clamber onstage and do an indifferent little dance. Mostly, though, the dancers sat around the inside of the bar munching sandwiches and drinking Cokes. The place was not very crowded, which gave it an intimate air of soiled hopes.

I scanned the bar but didn't see Little P yet. Still, I felt anxious as we took seats and ordered drinks. Immediately one of the hostesses came over smilingly and tried to strike up a conversation. She was very small, less than five feet even in high heels, and wore a G-string with bits of tinsel sewn around the waistband and a tiny gilded bra. Her eyes were smudged with black pencil, and her skin had been dusted with glitter. She toed the floor, then came up very close and said, "You wann buy me drink?" focusing her attentions on me.

"I don't know," I said.

"Oh, buy her a drink," said Angel, who was very interested in the bar. "Give her something for all that effort." She was referring to the heels.

The drink was a thick, greenish blue liqueur that came in a cracked four-ounce glass. The matron gave it to me on a wrinkled paper napkin and said, "T'ree hundred."

"For that?" It was about forty dollars U.S. The girl looked at me patiently, expectant. I dug through my wallet: not enough.

"Angel—"

"I've got fifty."

Together, we presented the girl with the glass. The little prostitute looked dubiously from Angel to me and furrowed her brow, plainly distressed about where her responsibility lay. At last she drew up a stool, placing herself firmly between us. You had to admire her sense of fair play.

"Where are you from?" asked Angel determinedly: the notebook had come out. The girl was not very young at all, it turned out; she was thirty-eight, a fact that she stated simply, without coyness, dangling a loose heel carelessly like a little girl.

I glanced over at the door. A few men had come in, none of them Little P. Where was he? I swallowed a mouthful of gin without tasting it. Annoyingly, the girl had turned her attention to me again. She stroked my neck with feathery touches like gnats and put her arm around my neck, trying to perch on my knee.

"No thank you," I said, disengaging her arms with difficulty. Angel tittered.

"I would expect you at least to be outraged at this—all of it," I told her.

"Come on, Emerson," she said, giggling. "She's got three kids at home."

"Just what I need," I snapped. "A thirty-eight-year-old mother of three sitting on my lap."

A new bump-and-grind had started up over the sound system. The little hostess was into it, swinging her hips and caressing my chest, straddle-grinding me with professional abandon.

"*No,*" I said firmly, muffled by her breasts, her taut brown body pressing close at my face. She ran her hands through her long dark hair and draped it deliriously over us like a curtain. "No," I repeated. I tried to claw my way out of the hair. "No."

Piqued, she unstraddled me and moved off in a huff. The musky dark of her skin was replaced by the sight of Little P across the bar, watching me.

He was alone. He had not hired anyone to come and sit with him. This made me obscurely happy, for it seemed to speak of integrity, despite any other evidence to the contrary. I went over to him in the corner.

"How are you feeling?" I asked.

"Not much," he said. His glass of gin was half-empty. "Not much of anything."

"No wonder," I said, moving his glass away. "You're going to kill yourself one of these days, or get yourself killed." His eye and his nose had swelled up greenish yellow, and he was unsteady, limp, speaking sluggishly, though his meanings were clear enough. "Who did this to you?"

"A man named Wei Li," he said thickly. He looked at me through his slitted eye. He was determined to be candid, I saw, but I was so far outside the sphere of his life that his candor was of no help to me.

"Is he the one who ships the girls over?" I said. "Or is he someone else?"

His head jerked up slightly. But if he was shaken, he was too hardened to show it for long.

"Neither," he said, angry. "How did you know?"

"I figured it out," I said, thinking of the little girl's face as Big One heaved above her. "I saw it. I wish I hadn't. I wish I didn't know anything about you."

"I told you to go home," he said.

"Did you really think I would do that?"

I had the will in my pocket, worn and tattered by now. I took it out and threw it down on the table.

"It's the will," I said as he flicked his eyes at me.

He frowned. "Why the hell is it . . . ?"

"I've had it with me. I lied to you about the lawyer. I admit it, all right? And I'm not proud of it. But I wanted something from you."

As he leaned forward to take the envelope, I grabbed it back and held it beyond his reach.

"And I still want something from you."

He watched me, the first flare of greed and surprise quenched by caution, suspicion. "What?"

"I don't like you," I said. "I might as well say it. But it's my obligation to love you. I doubt I could stop even if I tried. So you *listen* to me." I pulled my chair closer.

"I've got pictures," I said quietly. Angel was watching us; I avoided looking in her direction. "I've got pictures of the girls. I've got pictures of you smuggling the girls in. I'm holding off on reporting Uncle until we get you out of this. You've got a month."

I slid the envelope back toward him. "I want you to put the sale of the Remada in motion. Sell it, and get out of here. Get rid of any documentation that links you to the Palace. You can deposit any checks in an account under my name if you think they'll be trying to track you down. I'll help you any way I can. I just want you to start over, Little P. Take the money and start over."

He looked at me mazily, concentrating very hard. Suddenly he laughed, an ugly, abrasive sound. "And where am I supposed to go?" he asked.

"Anywhere! Bali! South America! Wherever you want. Just start over."

But he was already shaking his head. He didn't say anything immediately, only motioned for another drink from the bartender. I didn't stop him. I told myself I didn't care if he drank himself to death—if his heart slowed, growing colder and then stopping altogether. It was what he wanted, apparently. Sex, exploitation—he preferred these things to the chance my mother was offering him through the inheritance.

"You remember when I ran away? That day?" he asked suddenly.

"Sort of," I said, impatient. Some of the old bitterness returned as I recalled the morning he left. My mother had run alongside the cab knocking frantically at the windows as he disappeared.

"I used to dream about that day," said Little P. "Still dream about it. Her face all bloated with tears. She was knocking and knocking on the window."

It was an unexpected admission; I had thought he'd forgotten about the way she doted on him.

"I've been trying to explain it to you ever since you got here," he said. "I know what you think. You think I'm a punk-ass loser who fucked you and Mother ten times over. But when I left, I had good intentions. I was stupid, but I was never a complete prick. I just wanted to touch the world. I wanted to know what there was to be afraid of. You and her—the world was always out to get you. Felt like living in permanent lockdown, permanent fear. I still have nightmares I'm being chased through the motel. Round and round, room after room. When I turn around, though—isn't anyone there. But *I'm still afraid*. You understand me? *That's* the legacy she left behind. Terror. Weakness." He flapped the envelope in my face. "This is the least she owes me."

He drank off a finger of gin and put the glass down abruptly. His lip jerked with that incessant tic. It occurred to me that I had seen Little P drink before but had never seen him drunk.

"So I went to China, and that was a head job. The school was a front. I had no income from day one."

"You sent us letters about your students for a whole year."

"Fake," he said. "The 'school' took my filing fee and disappeared. The office I paid at was gone when I went back for work the next day. All the furniture was still there, no people. I latched on to some other foreigners and traveled with them for a while. It was okay. No, that's a lie; it wasn't okay. But I wanted to learn, and I learned. You want to know what degradation is?" He laughed. It sounded like he was choking. "The most twisted, deformed, mutilated man with no arms or legs, lying in the middle of a busy street and nobody stopping, nobody blinking an eye. A five-year-old kid with a baby begging on a train platform and having a crippled woman in a chair push her down, slap her for moving in on her turf." He shrugged. "And that's just the tip of the volcano in a place like that. I got out as soon as I could. Went to Taiwan."

He rattled the ice in his glass and signaled for another.

"I thought Uncle could help me without involving you and

Mom. I went to see him totally unannounced, and he gave me a job. He sponsored me for a work visa. He let me stay with him until I made enough to move out on my own. He was good to me. He was good to everyone," he said. "That was part of the problem."

He shook out a cigarette. One of the dancers came up and lit it for him, which he barely acknowledged with a wave.

"For a long time I didn't know exactly what the Palace did. I mean, I knew it was a karaoke bar, with girls, but the girls were legitimate. The economy was better back then. Uncle and his family weren't lucky enough to invest a lot when the index shot up. But everyone was feeling the rush of the boom, and when I got there, the Palace was swinging. So I never had any reason to think about the business at all.

"Later on, stuff tapered off—not drastically, but enough so that we ended up short one year. Nothing to worry about. If it was just Uncle acting alone, the Palace wouldn't have changed. But Poison complained. He thought it was the hostesses bleeding us; they got good contracts, fucking Coco Chanel wages. But they were hard to deal with: bitchy, picky. The Palace was high-class then. Uncle wanted to be fair.

"So Poison's idea was to bring in girls from the mainland. He had friends in Fujian who were willing to round up girls from the countryside. Poor as dirt, happy to work for less. Mainland cunts fetch a higher price than local ones anyway. Uncle agreed. He didn't want to, but the Palace was hurting now. He had to do something.

"I didn't understand all of this at the time. My Chinese was still a baby's, and no one really talked to me anyway." His face flushed, and he made an unconscious fist. "But they made that mistake of assuming I was stupid because I couldn't speak. That's why they chose me to take the cutter out to meet the boats in the strait; they thought I wouldn't understand what I was doing. And you know what? The *wangdan* were right. I didn't understand. Not at first."

He put a hand to his eye, touching it blindly.

"It was one night," he said, halting. "Near dawn, more like. Done the same run a hundred times now, but I was more nervous this time. The Fujian boat was really late; I could see them steaming toward me through the fog, and I thought . . . I thought it would be risky to try to get back to shore; I knew the coast guard's beat. But I didn't say anything. I just loaded them on and headed back.

"It was going to be a beautiful day. It's shitty that I remember thinking that, but it's true. It was so quiet on the water, and the mist was rising. I look at those Chinese landscape paintings sometimes, the ones with the mist and the mountains and water, and I know exactly what kind of peace they're trying to show. There isn't anything like it anywhere else in the world. It was summer. I even remember a seabird coming straight down from the sky.

"But then I saw the patrol. They were pretty far off. Too far off for them to get a good look, but I could tell they were making a direct line. They were coming right for me. No way I could get back to shore without being intercepted; I'd waited too long. So I panicked. Don't even remember what I thought. Just—threw them off."

"The . . . girls?"

"I threw them off. I picked them up and threw them overboard. One of them, I remember, was grabbing at me with these warped fingers. But she'd painted them, you know—her nails. They had this sparkly pink polish on them, like she thought she was going to be married or something. Stupid cunt." His voice broke, then smoothed. "They were tied up, their legs and arms. It didn't matter. They couldn't swim anyway, they were from inland somewhere, some dirt farm. The way they looked at me—like animals dying. Without understanding a single fucking thing."

The girl in the back room, with her haunted, feral eyes. A blackness surged up in my chest. But I had not fully understood. "So they . . . What did they do?"

He looked at me with contempt, or pity, the rims of his eyes red with the alcohol. "They drowned, you asshole."

I could not speak. I gripped the ashes hard beneath my arm and was glad for once that my mother had not lived long enough to see Little P again. One side of his mangled face glistened in the weird blue light, but I wasn't sure if he was crying. I concentrated on his thin white scar, the old one on his cheek; it seemed the only lingering mark of the brother I knew.

"But why didn't you just leave Taiwan then? You had no obligations to the Palace."

"It was . . . for Uncle's sake."

"I don't believe you," I said flatly. "You really must think I'm some kind of asshole, with a lie like that. You're no Boy Scout. You have no fucking loyalty. You'd sell your own mother." I waved the will, then slammed it down on the table.

"I don't give a shit what you believe," he said, but I caught a look of fear in his face. "It's the truth."

"Let's just say it is, for the sake of argument. You still have no obligation to keep working there."

"You *are* an asshole." His sloe eyes blazed, scornful. "These girls earn more in one day than they'd earn in a month in China! They get breakfast, lunch, dinner, and a new outfit every three months. Hot showers, and we let them earn their way back to the mainland after five years. You may not like it," he said, cold. "It doesn't fit with the rules of the decent little Shangri-la you carry around with you. But that's how things work. That's how you get it on."

"So this is *what*? A public *ser*vice?" I shouted, feeling sick. He had reached the point of drunkenness where he was no longer exposing anything true; it was sheer ugliness and twisted logic. "You think you're some kind of *savior*?"

I went on in lowered tones. "You're not stupid. I know you know what's what. So what's the *real* reason you keep on?"

He went silent, staring down into his glass. I felt him slipping away, and knew therefore that I had hit upon a truth.

He propped his head up painfully on his good arm. I was having a hard time breathing.

"Get out of this, Little P," I said softly.

"I can't." He shrugged off my hand.

"What about the pictures?"

"What about them?"

"Don't make me choose."

"You've already chose," he said. "Haven't you? You've already made up your mind. Nothing I say or do will change that. Am I right?"

Stiffly, he got to his feet and glanced around the Admiralty with distaste.

"Well," he said. "See you."

I didn't even notice until later that he'd taken the will.

CHAPTER 22

U NCONSCIOUSLY, I think, I was counting on Angel, counting on her desire to be loved, but she was not in the end as
conveniently smitten as I'd hoped she would be.

"I was wrong," she said the minute we were through customs.

She had been silent the entire flight from Hong Kong, eating
her crackers and sipping a Coke with unaccustomed pensiveness.
I'd watched her, apprehensive, as her jaw began to jut forward like
a barometer of thought: a decision was being made. Now she
turned to me abruptly in the concourse.

"I can't believe I even considered it." Her face had blanched, her
lips white and trembling.

"What are you talking about?"

She wiped her eyes and gathered up her bags with grim deter-
mination. "I'm going to the police."

"No!" I dogged her, desperate—ashamed too, but I could not do otherwise, whatever she might think. "*Please,* Angel! Just a week. I'm begging you. A favor."

Outraged, she turned on me. "A favor? And what have you ever done to deserve it?"

"I was honest with you."

"My *dentist* is honest with me," she said. "But I wouldn't cover up murder for him." She regarded me in a way that shriveled my soul, as if I were a stranger, and repellent. "So take your honest, pious ass and shove it. You won't make me an accessory to rape."

No argument could be made against her; there was no argument except that of blood, and Little P was not her brother. I watched her disappear into the crowd.

My phone rang insistently.

"*Wei?*" I said dully. "*Wei?*"

ATTICUS WAS dozing when I arrived at the hospital, head nodding in sleepy assent over a book, his fingers still vaguely pressed to the page, as if he had been in the middle of a discovery when he drifted off. He looked small and gnarled in the clean institutional bed, and I was shocked by the transformation of his face, which was hollow and gray, the features drawn together as if by a taut string. He had collapsed at home a few nights ago; no medical explanation had been proffered, only nerves, exhaustion, overwork. Asleep, he seemed broken. I stood at the window and watched a thin breeze stir up the grit in the gutters.

When I turned back, Atticus was watching me. He had closed the book and sat with his hands folded across the cover. "So," he said faintly. "You are back from your trip."

I nodded. Tentatively I came closer to the bed.

"You don't need to say," he said. "I see that Xiao P has already said."

"I offered him a way out," I said, "but he won't take it. It's like he's . . . joined a cult or something." Atticus stirred beneath his sheet, fingers plucking at one another restlessly. "Those girls. Those poor girls."

"The girls then, or the girls now?" said Atticus.

"You knew about the girls he killed?" I was startled— unreasonably so, for of course he would know. Everyone at the Palace had known. But for Atticus to know, and do nothing about it . . .

"And you never went to the police."

He reached for his tea. I put the cup ungently in his hand.

"I am not a vigilante," he said. "It is not my business to make things in the world fair."

"They were *murdered*," I said. It was the first time I had said it aloud. I thought of a body sinking silently down through a dark, shadowed canyon of cold water.

"I am weak, I have admit to you already," Atticus was saying. "I have warned you many times."

"Weakness doesn't even *begin* to describe it," I said. Tears ran down my face.

Atticus sighed, winced. "I will tell you something, Xiao Chang," he said quietly, "and you do not need to repeat this to any- one else, *haobuhao?* A talk between friends."

I made a noncommittal noise. He looked at me, a note of plead- ing in his eyes, then went on.

"I have report on the Palace before."

"You . . . When?" I stared.

"A few years ago, when I have just come back from the States. When I was braver." He was silent; he seemed for a moment transported to darkness. Lines of pain, perhaps of despair or shame, creased his face.

"And?"

He looked down at the coverlet. "And. And nothing. And I come home from work one night, and there is a man in the alley who says he is a friend to my sister. And I invite him upstairs, and when I close the door, he attacks me, and break my legs. Both legs. With a pipe."

His voice shook, regained its poise.

"And then I do not remember. And he hit me in the head, and I am unconscious. And he drives me out to Tainan, and he leaves me there, in the country. In the field."

He began to tremble, sweating, and moved his head violently in a gesture of escape. "And there is your 'and,' Xiao Chang."

"Atticus." My stomach had clenched into a tight fist, aching. "Why didn't you ever say so?"

"I do not wish to recall," he said. "I wish to forget, as much as possible."

He closed his eyes for a moment, as if swallowing something painful.

"But then you went back to work there. After they tried to kill you."

He shook his head. "It will not seem rational, I know. But after my legs heal, after I am out of work for so long, no one else will hire me. I depend on the money. I am an old man; I have spent my life in other countries. In France, in the U.S. So there is no pension. I have built nothing up. And I cannot live without some extravagance. I cannot live without some luxury. The Palace"—he shuddered slightly—"they know this. They know I am safe now. They know I will never talk. They know I am their—the French say *larbin*. You understand *larbin*? Their servant, their slave, *mais plus vulgaire . . .*"

"Their bitch."

"Yes. They know I will not talk. And I am useful to them." He smiled, sickly. "It is the way the business works. The way *this country* works. Reporting would do no good, *duibudui*? The problem is deeper. What is needed," he said, "what is needed is a new order. A new world."

I sat back, all anger dissipated. What good would it do, making a sick old man suffer again the horrors of an event, the horrors of conscience? It wouldn't change anything about Little P.

Atticus winced, his face blanching briefly with pain, and I sprang up.

"No, no." He gestured for me to sit down again. "I am all right."

He composed himself, lying back tiredly against his pillows. After a moment, he said, "So what will you do?"

"I don't know," I said. Something occurred to me. "You told Poison where I lived."

He grimaced. "I ask for your forgiveness. They have their ways to convince, you know. You will forgive weakness in an old man."

I shook my head; it was such a small thing now. "It doesn't matter anymore."

Then I frowned, preyed upon by a new concern. "If I go to the police," I asked, "will you . . . be implicated too?"

He smiled broadly. "Don't worry about that," he said. "I do not care too much about my well-being anymore. It may not matter, very soon."

He sounded as if he were consigning himself to death, or predicting it. The clock on the wall ticked louder.

I put my hand on the bed.

"It was you, wasn't it? The shooting at the rally."

He regarded me impassively, retreating behind his veneer of silent wisdom. It was impossible to know him; there was a barrier beyond which I could not reach.

"I do not deny," he said at last. "I do not confirm."

"But why, Atticus? You worked for him. You answered his phones. You drove his campaign truck. He was *your* candidate."

His hand plucked the coverlet, agitated. He was silent.

"I am not admitting anything," he said finally. "But with a gun, one does not always aim to kill." He hesitated. "There was a report, the night before the rally, that the party was threatening voters in Wanhua. Not so unusual, I know. But just because it is common does not mean it is acceptable. The KMT are rotten—all gangsters, you know this, all corrupt. They care nothing for the power we have built, or try to build. But after so many incidents, the KMT still have credibility somehow! You know the president, his wife?"

"She's in a wheelchair."

"Because the KMT ordered a hit on her husband. By mistake they hit his wife instead. They ran her over with a truck."

"You don't know that, Atticus." That had never been proved.

"I *know*. I know who did it. They can cover up. They can play dirty all they want, but I *know*." He panted painfully, his skin damp and musty with the odor of age. I had touched again that curious sorrow, the grief that ate him up at the thought of his little island country. It was patriotism at its loyal best—and what had it come to? He wiped his eyes with the back of his hand.

"So on the day of the rally, I did not think so much. I knew what I had to do. If the KMT is going to be dirty, I am going to be dirty too. I did not tell Li what I am going to do; I do not want him implicated if things go wrong. I thought, If the people see this good man cut down, they will think it is the KMT's doing."

"And vote for him instead of Zhang."

"What is needed," he said again, with bitterness, "is a new order. I am only calling on their sense of right. I am only making it clear to them what the Kuomintang is doing all along. I am reminding them of the KMT's sins. Is this what they want for their government? For their country? You see this?"

He shook a page of newsprint that had been folded beneath his book.

"From this week. It says Taiwan was refused entry into the WHO, for diplomatic reasons. Meaning, for fear of offending China."

He moved his head restlessly and threw down the paper. "There is no moral fiber in the world. This is the WHO, the World Health Organization. Not the UN. Not a military alliance. Not even an economic treaty. It is about disease, about dying. It should not be about politics. China prefers that we die rather than let us go. Other countries, they prefer that we die rather than risk offending China."

He fell back, exhausted. "I am only telling the truth."

"You said you weren't a vigilante. And Li lost the election anyway."

"It is the *effort* to learn the truth that matters, not only the result." His hands shook with rage. "What I failed to do for those girls, I may still do for my country. I may still redeem myself."

"That's . . . They're not the same thing, Atticus."

"Sometimes things take too long on their own." He closed his eyes, shook his head. He was growing hazy, confused. "The KMT would have us return to China, eventually."

"Maybe that's what people want."

His eyes flew open. "People want that because they are getting rich off business in Shanghai, in Beijing," he said angrily. "They just want stability to keep on making the money, money, money!" He spat out the word. "It blinds them to what is important."

"And what's that?" I asked softly, worried, for he had turned livid and looked feverish.

"Pride," he said. "Autonomy. Memory. It didn't work," he said hopelessly, and tears spilled down his cheeks. He turned his head away. "Everything I did, it was no help."

He uncurled a hand beseechingly.

"Maybe people haven't forgotten them," I said. "Maybe they've forgiven the past. Maybe they just want to move on."

"Never." He clenched his fist and put it beneath the covers. The feverish look had passed; now he seemed only tired and spent. He closed his eyes again and didn't open them. I thought he was asleep, and I was about to get up and go away quietly when he murmured, "Emerson?"

"I'm still here."

He looked at me, a little fuzzy. It was hard to tell what he saw, for though he was looking at me, he was focused on something quite far away.

"I am getting older," he said. "I am already old. I told you before: I always thought I would see true independence in my lifetime. But it is not so certain now. How long do I have? A year? Two years? Five? Maybe not even so much.

"I want to tell you a secret," he said. "Sometimes I think it does not matter what happens to this country, as long as there is a resolution: either we are part of China or we are not. It is the uncertainty that will kill us, you know. Never to know where we will be in fifteen years, or ten years, or five. Why should we bother to build a freedom, or love, or business, if it will just be taken away?"

He passed a hand wearily over his eyes and felt for his tea. I took the mug into the hallway and poured out the cold tea in the drinking fountain. When I came back, Atticus had dropped off; he had taken his painkillers before I'd arrived. I filled the mug with fresh water and placed it next to the bed. He was really asleep this time, not just dozing, and his face was drawn again, no longer animated by the thought of principle.

A young man came into the room. If he was surprised to see me, he made no sign of it; he was too intent on Atticus to pay me any attention. He removed the book on the coverlet and placed a plastic pitcher of water on the bedside stand, then wiped Atticus's face with a wet cloth. Atticus muttered; his hand came up unconsciously and clutched the man's wrist with tenderness. In a little while, he slept.

I was standing by the window and happened to be glancing down at the street when the air outside suddenly constricted, seeming to breathe in. There was a moment of silence, and then the breath was released in a slow chord that mounted steadily until it reached a note of doleful, jaded warning. I had forgotten about the air-raid drill. The siren was sounded only once a year, an annual reminder of the tenuousness of the sunlit peace in the unsentimental streets below. I peered down at the sidewalk. The desolation was eerie at noontime: no people, and no cars along the thoroughfare. The only sign of life was a lean stray cat prowling along the perimeter of the park boundary across the street. I was glad Atticus was asleep. The ghostly voice, so plaintively raised, served only to confirm his particular despair.

DAWN OUTLINED the mountains in clear blood red the next day, the Mid-Autumn Festival at last. Poison had been shunted to the back of my mind, but with the deadline came a renewed apprehension. Another storm was gathering over the strait, and the massing front cast a queer, glossy twilight even at noon. All day I felt that I moved behind a wall of thick tinted glass.

Around four o'clock, after a desperate, fruitless search for Angel, I came home drained—too tired, in fact, to notice the little lick of fire in the bedroom, wavering hesitantly in the dark. Then the light approached. Angel's face swam up in the flicker, like a tense, unhappy ghost.

"I didn't know where I should go," she began.

Her nose quivered; I'd brought home takeout from the eatery down the street and had been cracking open the box when she came out. Meekly, she ate two of my dumplings with her fingers and looked over at me. "Can I stay here for a while?"

I turned away. "What's wrong with your grandparents' place?"

"It's for them that I left."

Despite myself, her urgency hit its mark.

"What is it?" I asked.

She swallowed. "I went to the police. Yesterday."

"And?" The word was choked; I didn't want to know.

"I'm . . . not sure."

"Are they going to arrest Uncle?"

"I don't know."

She walked up and down the room, twisting her fingers anxiously.

"Something weird is happening," she said. "I went down to the precinct this morning to talk to the officer, but when I got there, they said there was no history of my report. The disk I left there, with the images, my statement—there's no record of them anywhere."

"No proof?"

"There's proof. It's still on my memory key." She jangled the stick at me, distracted. "That's not the problem. Last night I was home alone. I fell asleep watching TV, you know? I must've slept too long, because when I woke up it was already dark, and everyone else was out at dinner. I was too lazy to get up and turn on the lights, so I was just lying there when I heard something at the window. Like a scraping, or clicking, but really soft. I thought it was just an animal or something, but it went on for like a few minutes, so I got up and pulled up the shade.

"There was a face out there, Emerson. He dropped down so fast I didn't get a good look, but he was there. He was trying to cut the outside grille. He thought I wasn't home."

"You don't know they were targeting you," I said. I ate a dumpling; it tasted like cardboard. "There are lots of break-ins."

"Not where I live." She stopped pacing and looked at me. "You can't cover for him forever," she said. Her voice rose as I ignored her, dumping out the bagged soup into two chipped bowls. "I can't just forget."

"I am not turning my brother in," I said. The statement had the ring of a carefully constructed conviction, when in fact I had not known what I believed until this moment. "You do what you want, but I won't be a party to it."

"I thought you were my friend," she said. "I thought you were a good person."

"Well, you were wrong."

Her mouth quivered. I lowered my gaze to the table, where the spread seemed suddenly cheap and impoverished. For Little P, for my mother, I couldn't let it go, even if I should lose all face before my best friend. She rubbed her eyes, leaving dark smudges under them. She looked very young and very tired.

"Sit down," I told her. I pushed the take-out container over to her. "Finish this. Then go take a nap. You can have the bed."

"What about—"

"We won't talk about it now. You look exhausted."

She began eating, face still streaked with tears.

"You know I didn't mean it, about being your friend," I said. "Of course I'm still your friend—if you still want me. But you're a better person than I am. I can't see past my brother. You do what you think is right." I squeezed her hand.

After dinner, she went straight to bed. I washed her dishes, then sat at the kitchen table trying to read. High winds from the approaching storm had knocked power out momentarily, though the rain hadn't come yet, and candlelight wavered over the page like water. I went into the bedroom to check on Angel; she had thrown the covers off and was sleeping with her arms flung over her head, breathing quick and anxious. I covered her again and went back out into the dining room.

My bottle of Jim Beam was dry. The wind whistled in the rain gutters, high and lonely. I thought of the night Uncle and Poison had paid me a visit. My money was still locked safely away in my account. Angel's disk, her report, our proof—surely it would reach the right desk somehow, surely someone would take up our tip, and when they did, when the police busted the Palace, the mah-jongg debt would be erased, and Little P would be safe, from Poison at least, if not from the harshness of the truth and the law. I clutched at the fact of his physical safety like a drowning man at a straw. It was not enough.

Outside, the front gate clanged loudly. In its wake, I became aware of a sudden soft scritching, like nails scrabbling at glass. The noise stopped, then started up again, more deliberate, accompanied by a thin metal jangling.

The only weapon I had was a rusted hammer. I picked it up and opened the door quietly.

The sounds were fainter out here, but I paused and listened very carefully. They seemed to be coming from the side yard, in the thicket of azaleas covering the bedroom window. I tightened my grip on the hammer and crept around the corner. Again, the scritching stopped.

"Come out!" I hissed. "You want your money, you come out and get it, you fucker."

The bushes tossed and waved in the wind, but no one emerged.

I was sick of feeling hunted, sick of groveling, begging, bargaining. I marched up to the thicket and ripped aside the branches, hammer tensed and ready. Then I froze.

It was an owl, a small one with deep, hooded eyes that blazed at me in the weak light from the street. One claw was caught in a length of rusted chain dangling from the branches. As I reached in to untangle it, the bird beat its wings and let out a thin, raucous cry.

Once freed, it fluttered to the top of the fence and looked back at me. Dreamily, I moved to the front gate to watch it. I had the odd feeling that the bird was leading me somewhere, that I should follow it. Its dark silhouette darted down the street, to a wall topped with broken glass. The creature reminded me oddly of my father: an impression of sternness; stillness; the silence of pride. It had been years since I'd thought of him. He had died too long ago, his mark upon his sons overlaid by the imprint of my mother. It occurred to me, following the bird's jagged course in the dim light, that this had been his home. He had passed through these streets without any sense of strangeness: thinking of love, maybe, thinking of exams, schoolwork, what to eat for dinner. He would not have learned English yet; Little P and I were not even ideas in his mind. If—through some wrinkle in time—I were to meet that young man now, the fact of communication would stand in the way. Crude gestures, pictures drawn on the ground—those would be our common tongue, the most primitive of languages, as if we were strangers, or brutes. The owl, opening out its wings, caught a gust of wind and disappeared into the dark night sky.

Smoke drifted through the alleys as I turned back toward home. Thin and gauzy and smelling of gas—a fire in one of the eateries along the main avenue, though it didn't smell like a grease fire. Neighbors had gathered on the sidewalks, looking up and down the block through the gathering white air. A cat wailed. An old man in his undershirt turned a sightless eye toward me; somehow I could hear the burning of his cigarette. I began to run.

Behind the rotting fence of my courtyard, the house was burning, a violent yellow flame in the front window, which had already been shattered by the heat. The frame stood broken and silhouetted against the blaze, and the fire was burning hard enough that it seemed viscous, the thick roiling of the flames like mercury, like oil and water. A piece of the frame broke and fell into the yard, and the hedge went up with bright, crackling alacrity while the house roared. Far off, there was a siren.

"Angel!" I yelled through the fence. The fire cut a neat swath through the undergrowth. I ran to the gate and tore it open.

A neighbor grabbed my arm. *"Ni bu yao jinqu,"* he said. You can't go in there. Wait, sir. Wait . . . But I pulled free and charged ahead.

"Angel! Angel!" The flames from the window bit the edge of the roof, curling the tin back upon itself with a dreadful shrieking. Inside, glass crashed like a breaking board, the tinkling like a chime.

The south side of the house was still quiet and dark, waiting for the coming destruction. Coughing, I ran around the side yard to the back.

"Angel!"

I thought I heard a weak voice calling from the kitchen, but as I rounded the corner, a hand, impossibly large, loomed up in my side vision, and the voice dropped to black as my sight inverted and fell away. Pain filled my head slowly, and I thought I heard myself say, "Where did you go?" But I couldn't be sure, and whatever the meaning was, was lost.

CHAPTER 23

A LIGHT JIBBERED, GIGGLED, GLOWED, then became a silver static that jumped into focus now and then, a dull talking head with stock prices running top to bottom along the sidebar.

"*Xiuli,*" shouted Big One, waving his tiny *paocha* cup in the air. Fix it!

"I can't fix it! *You* fix it," said Poison. He punched the television. The picture jumped, then settled back into snow. He pulled off the wilted antenna and threw it to the ground. "*Ni ma de!*"

One side of my face felt hot and poisoned as I raised my head from the floor. The first thing I felt for was my mother, who, miraculously, was still there, though the cord had left a rope burn on my neck and had frayed at the join. Everything else lay behind a matted screen. With some painful squinting, I made out a pair of odd white, egglike spots on the floor, an arm's length away, and contemplated these for a while. Upon concentrated inspection, they turned into my glasses, bent and cracked beyond repair. I reached out blindly and put them on. The room jumped into semiclarity threaded with lines, like a picture in a broken frame.

I was in some kind of basement or garage, without windows, and with white tube lights exposed and humming on the ceiling. The floor was bare concrete, and the walls were pitted and daubed with plaster. The closeness of the air made me drowsy, and there was the inevitable smell of incense and exhaust. The banquettes, pushed at random angles against the walls, told me that we were somewhere in the Palace. Big One had pulled a crate up next to him and was dousing his teapot with boiled water in a shallow stone bowl. A couple of other men sat at a card table near the door, looking bored. One of them handled his piece awkwardly, spinning it around his right index finger.

"Put that away," said Poison, cuffing him. The man put the gun down on a crate, and I saw that an assortment of weapons had been laid out there, knives mostly, also a heavy joist with a nail. I wondered if the joist had come from my house, and if that was what they had used to knock me out.

A faint nausea rolled up from my stomach and tightened my throat. I turned my head to the right. Angel was lying slack and bloodied next to me, her cheek pressed into the ground.

"Angel?" I whispered. We were not tied up; I inched closer and touched her hair. "Angel?"

She groaned quietly. I looked over at the thugs. They were still occupied with the television reception. "Are you all right?"

Then she was awake. She raised herself painfully and gasped, lifting her left hand, which was grayish and swollen. She had been cut across the scalp; dark rivulets had dried on her skin.

"We have to get you to a doctor," I said.

"I'm all right," she said. She cradled her wrist and looked around the miserable little room. "The photos," she said suddenly. "The photos."

"It's too late to think about that now," I whispered.

"I have them . . ." she began, but Poison, alerted by one of the other men, saw that we had come to and interrupted us with a bang of the joist.

"No talk!" he shouted.

"You can have your fucking money!" I shouted. He blinked, startled. "Tell him," I said to Angel. She relayed the message tremblingly. There was silence in the room, then a burst of laughter. Big One rubbed his feet together in amusement as he emptied the spent tea leaves into another bowl, and the man at the table began spinning the gun again. Poison smoothed his hair back and sneered.

"He says he knows," said Angel. "He says he'll get it from you one way or another. But this isn't about the money."

"Then what's it about?"

Poison shook his head and grinned.

"I don't know what he just said," said Angel.

"I want to see my brother," I said, trying to get up. Immediately Poison hissed at me, brandishing the two-by-four.

"*Sit down.*"

"I want to see my brother."

Swiftly he crossed the room and advanced on me. The nail in the board was rusty.

"*Sit down.*"

I sat. After a moment of tenseness, Poison smiled and sauntered back to the television.

We waited. The minutes crept by, as uniform and indistinguishable as ants along a baseboard.

"I'm thirsty." Angel had crawled over. "What's happening?"

"I don't know." I looked at my cousins. Poison had managed to fix the reception so that the newscast held steady, though the screen was split between bottom and top, and he had settled back with a magazine, thumbing the pages industriously like a schoolboy. Big One was asleep. The others were eating something—it smelled like curry and rice—out of foam boxes. "If I could somehow get hold of Little P, maybe he could do something. Get us out . . ."

"I have to use the bathroom."

"Can't you wait?"

"I don't think so."

Angel stood up. Instantly the men sprang to their feet; Poison brandished his magazine.

"*Wo dei qu xishoujian,*" she said haughtily, even fastidiously. The thugs looked at one another; this was not a provision they had prepared for. They rubbed their necks and shuffled their feet. Poison cursed.

Finally, they sent one of the younger, anonymous men out through the side door with her. He carried a knife, but he did not look at all certain about how to use it, and I hoped that Angel would make an escape. Minutes ticked by. The television went blank again. Poison pounded it with his fist.

But eventually they came back in again. Angel had cleaned herself up; her face was raw and pale, and her wet hair stuck to her scalp.

She waited until Poison had readjusted the television and the others had settled down in their former positions before she crawled over to me.

"It's not locked," she said in a low voice.

"What isn't?" I looked at the main door, which was heavily guarded by the four men.

"The side door," she whispered. "I pushed the lock when I came in. If we can just make it over there . . ."

She was distracted by sudden activity around the card table. The men were standing up, clearing the table, and collecting their knives and joists and guns. Poison had been talking on his phone, but now he snapped it shut and took up a little snub-nosed revolver. Big One turned off the TV. Startled, Angel and I froze.

There was a long silence as the thugs stood about. They seemed to be waiting for something. Poison kept eyeing the entrance, and at last I heard a quiet step in the hall. It approached modestly, without any hurry or hesitation. When it stopped, there was a tapping at the door.

Little P stepped inside, shutting the door quietly behind him. He gave me a long, straight look as he entered, as if nothing had ever happened between us, and I stood up, weak and relieved. He spoke to the men, who stood back; Poison made a little argument that I couldn't hear or understand, but finally he stood back as well, muttering.

Little P stood facing us, though he did not come any farther into the room. His injuries had healed a bit since Hong Kong; the only permanent mark would be a kind of line across his upper lip. He looked smaller somehow, more condensed, as if everything that was inessential had been boiled down since I'd last seen him, and what I saw now was my brother in full truth.

We regarded each other silently for a while. Finally I raised my hand.

"Hello, Little P," I said faintly.

"Hello." It must have started raining at last; he wore a dark trench coat, and his head was sleek and wet, though his shoes were spotless. He tucked his hands into his voluminous pockets and came a few feet closer.

"How've you been?" I asked after a moment.

He considered me. "You really want to know?"

"No. Yes. No."

"Good," he said. "No more lies, right? No more bullshit. From here on out, just the truth between us."

"There isn't any more truth to tell, Little P."

Angel had stood up next to me, holding my arm involuntarily, but Little P didn't even glance at her. There was a deep, unfocused look in his eyes, eerily calm; the eyes seemed to flicker over me searchingly, without coming to any conclusions. He took another step.

"You're right," he said. "Maybe the problem is too much truth. I wish you hadn't told me about those pictures," he said.

"I wanted to help you."

"It makes everything so hard."

"It's not hard at all," I said. "Leave. Get out. Do you think I want you to be caught? I wouldn't do that to you."

He shook his head.

"It's not that simple." He lifted his chin at Angel. "She's still got the originals."

I felt a little sick. "How do you know that?"

"Officer Hu gets his cut," he said. "We expect at least some protection."

"He stole the report," I said. "He took the disk."

He inclined his head noncommittally.

"Okay," I said. My chest was being clamped by an inexorable hand; I struggled for breath. "All right. All the better. Bought you extra time. Run now. Come with me. Get out of here while you still can. I'll help you sell the Remada. You can live off the deposit. Anything. Just get out."

"No. I can't leave."

"I don't understand!" I shouted. "I don't understand! What have they ever done for you here that you owe them your loyalty? Have they ever given you a second thought?" I pointed wildly in Poison's direction. "He was going to kill you, you know that? Because of a debt I owed. For eight thousand bucks, he would've knocked you off. Is that family to you? Is that devotion?"

"You poor fuck," he said. "Do you really believe Uncle's the puppet master? You really think he's running this place, in his condition?"

"With Poison. With Big One."

"Those assholes?" He cocked his head. "Don't insult me. No more lying to yourself."

He took another step. "It's me," he said simply. "It's always been my show. All those cocklovers"—he indicated the men ringed silently around the room—"they answer to me. Those girls upstairs, they brought them here on my order."

"But Uncle—"

"Uncle," he said, almost scornful. "Screw Uncle. I used to respect the man, you know? A real leader. But his weakness is conscience. Conscience and age. He's got no fire anymore. If he did, I wouldn't have to keep him down. I wouldn't have had to take over at all."

"Keep him down?"

He tucked his hands deeper in his pockets and shrugged. "His stroke. It was never the kind to turn him into a vegetable."

Darkness encroached as my hand closed over the vial in my pocket. Trembling, I brought it out. Little P regarded it with a level gaze, unsurprised.

"Zolpidem," he said. "It slows the nerves. Inhibits reaction."

"But why?" I whispered. "Why?"

"The man runs a whorehouse for seven years. All of a sudden he gets religion or something and says he wants to close? No fucking way," he said. He blew a bit of betel nut out of his mouth. "He was going to run it into the ground. Somebody had to do something."

The tic at his mouth had stilled for once. "I could've taken him out a long time ago. But he's more useful alive. We need someone to hang it on if it ever goes down."

He took another step. "What I said to you in Hong Kong. After those girls drowned. I stopped writing to you then. Stopped calling home. You have no fucking idea what it's like, what pictures go through your head. Year after year." Another step. Getting close enough now that I could see the faint white line of that old scar, that old wound from childhood. "I robbed; I cheated; I lied; I killed. Exile is the punishment. No court in the world could do worse. I cut everything inside of me out. There's nothing left in here," he said, knocking on his breastbone. "Nothing but the fact of what I did. I cut myself off from any kind of grace. If the Palace goes under, I'll be damned for nothing."

He shifted. The tic threatened to return, but he fought it down.

"So let it be for something," he said. "Let it be a mark that I was here. Any kind of mark is better than none. Grace," he said. "Immortality. You have to earn it. I wish you hadn't told me about those photos. But I'm the *laoban,* now. As boss, I have obligation."

The lack of article seemed to signal something broken, or failing. From the pocket of his coat, he withdrew a small revolver.

"No!" cried Angel. "Don't! I'll give you the pictures! Right here! Right here!"

"Angel, *don't!*"

But she took the memory key from her pocket and threw it. Without thinking, I dodged forward, trying to intercept it. A flash of white phosphorescence blinded me before the report shattered the air. Angel screamed.

I dropped to the ground. Little P's face intent and murderous as he loomed over me, put his foot over the key, aimed. A shout, enraged, as Angel threw him off balance. Again the flash, the splintering shot.

On my hands and knees behind the embankment of banquettes, memory key in hand. Angel was close behind. Bullets rained on the booths, pitting the back wall. We ducked and crawled toward the side door. Gun smoke and concrete powder rose dreamily in the air.

Through it, above the vinyl seat backs, I could see Little P advancing like a specter on a battlefield, sighting along the muzzle, expression obscured. No time to say a last good-bye before he disappeared, swallowed up by a foreign land, with its foreign code of honor.

Another flash. Angel shrieked, stumbled. Her shout was enough to jolt me out of numbness. I caught her up, throwing her arm around my neck, and we ran.

CHAPTER 24

N"*IMEN YAO QU NALI?*" asked the cabbie. Water rose in the streets. The storm had hit sometime in the night, the rain now weak but steady. Shaken, we didn't answer; where was there to go now? A crowd of brutish faces had converged on the cab window as I slammed the door shut and locked it, desperately. I would never get that image out of my mind. Angel gasped a little; she had been hit, her arm grazed by a bullet. Blood bloomed on her sleeve.

"*Huochezhan. Baituo ni kuai yidian,*" she told the cabbie weakly.

"You need a doctor," I said. "We can't get on a train."

"We can't stay in the city. Look." She glanced back through the window. A couple of pinpoints of light showed on the street behind us, gaining speed. Of course; they would follow us—hunt us until nothing, no trace of the degradation in that back room, existed anymore.

"Where will we go?"

"Wherever we can."

At the station, she instructed the cabbie to go around back, among the empty buses and delivery trucks. In the graveyard of loading bays, we skirted the building and ducked into the cavern of an open dock. The taxi drove off. A few seconds later a couple of scooters swung around and paused, idling. Waiting. From this distance one couldn't make them out clearly. The lights above the door of the loading bay flashed a warning; the door would close.

"Go," said Angel quietly. We scrambled down.

Inside the ticket hall, the placards on the enormous timetable shifted at intervals like blinking eyes. We scanned the board: the train to Hualien would leave in two minutes. Angel hung back, looking white and drawn. I took her hand and coaxed her down the stairs to the platforms—"Just a little farther. Just a little more. Just a little more, and then you can rest"—even though I didn't believe it myself. There was no peace to be found, not anymore. Little P had killed it. Another casualty of his.

Underground, the station and its grim tracks had a nightmarish glare. The train waited. At the end of the silent car, Angel and I huddled, watching the platform: nothing. The band about my chest loosened a little. Perhaps we had earned a little respite, a little bit of rest.

Suddenly the door separating our car from the next opened. Big One grinned, wielding a knife, his gums dark and bloody red. He seized me in a headlock and dragged me, gagging, silent, toward the end of the car. I seized the back of a seat and held on, resisting. He dug his blade into my knuckles, tightened his choke hold. I let go.

But he had not counted on Angel. Through the roar of blood in my ears, I heard her shout, saw her lunge at us with the fire extinguisher. A light, heady poison filled my lungs as she pulled the pin. Big One coughed, gasped, his hold loosening but not letting go.

"Emerson!" Angel dragged at my legs.

Blind, Big One flung open the exit door at the end of the car, choking, still dragging me. One foot balanced on the metal joint connecting the cars, he tensed, ready to spring to the platform, but just then the train shuddered and began to move. For a horrible moment, as he slipped, I thought I too would be pulled under in his killing grip, to be ground up beneath the train along with him. Then he shrieked, let go, falling to the murky tracks as the engine picked up speed.

Angel grabbed my arms and hauled me back into the car. The doors closed implacably. I saw, with a flood of fear and sickness, figures rushing the platform as we pulled out of the station. Only the underlings, I thought, not Little P himself—but the wound had not gone deep enough yet, and I couldn't help but look for him.

AT HUALIEN, we were swarmed by taxi drivers the moment we exited the station. The rain had abated, but a jagged breath of fog obscured the peaks of the mountains in the distance, and the sky had lightened by only a degree, into a tumescent shade of pearl. The town was like an afterthought, clustered around the rails, small and ragged, tattered pennants flying from the turret of a castle façade, as if we had come to the ends of the earth and found the remains of a carnival. We would head up to the mountains. Angel plodded on gamely behind me as we walked, looking for a car rental.

"Angel?"

Silence. When I turned around, she was slumped up against the grille of a shuttered shop, holding her arm.

"Sit down." Gently, I eased her down onto the sidewalk.

"Go," she murmured, her lips gray. "They'll be here soon. On the next train."

"No. They know you know. It's not safe for you."

She closed her eyes. Despairing, I looked around; a dingy Cosmed sign glowed down the street.

"Wait," I begged her. "Wait."

I bought two rolls of gauze and some cotton batting and propped her up, babbling nonsense as I ripped away her sleeve and applied peroxide, swabbing at the ragged edges of the wound: ". . . when you get back home . . . a job at the *Times* . . . no more of these silly reviews . . . you'll do what you're meant to . . . when you get back home . . ."

"Emerson." She winced as I tightened the gauze about her arm.

"Yes?"

"Look."

Some distance down, a few shadows crossed the mouth of the alley. Even from here, there was a malevolence in the air. Angel shivered. We were half-hidden in a doorwell, but the cover would not last. I dragged Angel to her feet.

"Can you walk?"

She nodded faintly.

"All right." I checked the street; the shadows had disappeared. "Just a little farther."

We walked as if in a dream. A fog was moving in; bells and whistles from the pachinko parlors echoed gaily through it, like the clanging of a lost buoy.

"Where are we going?" said Angel mazily.

"There was a rental, a car and bike rental up by the Cosmed—"
I pulled up short. "Ssh."

Someone had paused at the intersection ahead of us. A bank of
fog drew in, let out; still, I could not see his features. Tentatively I
took a step backward. The man seemed to make a movement toward us, sniffing. Again I backed up. Someone had been burning
money in the rain. My foot hit the edge of the metal canister and
sent it sprawling, clanging like an alarm.

"Come on!"

Half-running, half-dragging, Angel stumbled on my heels.
Ahead, the mouth of a darkened video arcade beckoned. A black
light filled the interior. Angel's face showed up stark and luminous
as we ducked blindly through the maze of battered consoles.

At the back of the arcade, we stopped, panting, to listen. Voices
carried in the dim ether, calling out "Dance!" and "Fire in the
hole!" The arcade was long and low, video gunshot echoing softly
in the rafters. We crouched down and waited. Minutes passed. My
back cramped. It might have been merely a local out there . . .
There was no proof that the men were Little P's . . .

I began straightening up, feeling duped, when Angel grabbed
my arm. Footsteps approached, fleet and searching, then the smell
of cherry candies. A neon blue light flashed, and Poison's shadow
was thrown up on the back wall.

Angel gestured. There was a large black booth in the corner,
mounted on a platform with heavy black drapes drawn over its
entrance. It might work, or we might be trapping ourselves; I
counted on Poison's general stupidity.

Noiseless, we climbed up and drew the drapes over us. The interior smelled of heat and vinyl. A dim red bulb showed an exact replica of an old Chevy, the kind my parents had once had—bench seat, lap belts, enormous steering wheel—except a projection screen hung down where the windshield should be. Huddled below the dashboard, tired, afraid, I had a kind of hallucination: I was eight years old again . . . my father was still alive . . . and my mother . . . I counted the swags of phone lines in the window as we drove . . .

I don't know how long we waited. Outside, the dreamlike voices went on, calling "Fight! Fight! Fight!" but the drapes mostly muffled any outside sound. Time ticked. I had never really believed that blood would betray its own. But he had meant it; my brother would kill me if he could.

"I have obligation," he said, and when I turned in wonderment to look at him, he fired, sending the bullet into the back wall. I reached out and touched the place where the lead had entered. He fired again. Was it only wishful thinking, or had he hesitated—thrown his aim? Hope rose. Perhaps some blood feeling still lived in him.

"Let go," said Angel.

I startled awake.

She pulled her arm away. I had been gripping it hard to stanch the blood. "Let go. I think it's better now. I think he's gone."

Stiffly, we climbed up onto the seats. I rested a hand on the steering wheel.

"We have to get moving," she said, but didn't move. It was too difficult, just now, to think of leaving the quiet, muffled peace for the storm.

Suddenly, the platform bucked.

"Emerson," said Angel queerly. The platform bucked again.

Slowly, the dim bulb died out, leaving us in the dark. For a moment nothing happened.

Then a picture flickered up on the screen. The film was dated, scratchy and discolored, but it was clear enough. We seemed to be driving slowly down a street, down a wide avenue lined with houses and sidewalk and lawn. A dream of an American avenue on a summer's day, the sun glinting in coins on the windshield. Two lines of trees made a canopy over the blacktop, the wind tossing the leaves.

Sun dappled the asphalt as we made a wide arc onto another street of broad-leafed trees and picket fences. The speakers were broken; children played noiselessly in the street. A woman in a neat dress and toque walked along the sidewalk, greeted the milkman, walked on past the neat cape houses with their trim lawns, and flowers blanched and washed out by the acids eating away the film. Main Street, with its stone-laid town hall and drugstore with a new striped blind. My heart ached at the brightness of the vision. The wheel spun of its own accord beneath my hand. My childhood had been the motel and the tenants, I-80 and the cargo trains running less than a mile away. These dreamlike trees and boulevards, sunlight and fences—they had never been a part of my experience. Where, then, did the longing come from? As if somehow, somewhere, a memory of home had been injected into me like a virus, false, foreign, and without a cure.

"Look," whispered Angel, reaching for my hand. We were approaching the highway. A little fan in the corner whirred; the platform creaked and tilted to give us the illusion of banking on a curve. The road dipped, swelled. We were going faster. The white painted lines seemed to skim off the screen and fly toward us, and

I let go of the wheel, which turned without me. Up ahead, the highway crested; the peak loomed before us. We were going fast now. At the top, I closed my eyes and waited, breath suspended, for the road to drop away.

THE ROAD to Tianxiang led first across a drab flatland dotted with quarry works, then up through Taroko Gorge along ledges blasted from marble. Daylight was dying, the dark storm clouds funneling off over the sea. Angel kept her head turned, looking out her window.

"If something happens," she said after a while, "tell my parents that I love them."

"I don't know your parents," I said. "You'll tell them yourself."

She looked at me, and I knew she was hoping for more—an admission, a lie; a cheap exchange of words that would never hold weight when the trouble was over. I cared for her—but that was all. She waited. I concentrated on the road.

After a while, she turned back to the window. She was crying, I think. For the first time, doubt ran below my conviction, like a hint of a stain. Perhaps Little P was right. The desire for purity— in love, in life—had ruled me to the exclusion of everything, both love and life. To deny Angel comfort, even if it were a lie—that amounted to a kind of cruelty. But it was too late for me; I didn't know how to do any differently.

We continued on, kilometer after kilometer in the growing dusk. Angel made us pull off at the rest stop shakily erected on a wide, flat outcropping of cliff, and while she was in the bathroom I walked to the edge of the cliff and looked over: far below, a river cut like a chalk line through the gray stone. Angel came out; she had rebandaged her arm by herself, and her face looked gray and pinched as she got back in the car.

We went on in silence, until all at once Angel pulled herself upright. "There's a car behind us," she said.

I glanced in the rearview mirror. Through the heavy mantle of mist, I could see a dark shape some distance away, without headlights.

"There's only the one road," I said. "Of course there's someone behind us."

"But it's been behind us since we left Hualien. It should have passed us at the rest stop."

I tried to look more closely. The tires slipped onto the shoulder.

"That can't be the same car," I said, but a cold rill passed through me. Without exactly meaning to, I pressed on the gas, inching the speedometer up. The car behind us kept pace. Angel faced forward.

"Don't stop at Tianxiang," she said. "Follow my directions." She scrabbled in the glove compartment for a map. "If we can make it as far as— Emerson!"

The car behind us had swerved into the lane of oncoming traffic; now it began edging up beside me.

"Is he crazy?" cried Angel. Again my tires slipped onto the shoulder of the road. A jolt; a shriek of steel on steel. "He's trying to push us off!"

I rounded a curve. The enemy pulled back as a car rounding the bend in the opposite direction blared its horn, but once the straightaway resumed, he inched up again. Another jolt. We braced ourselves. Sparks flew; a smell of burning as we clashed again. Our rental stuttered, coughed, ground on. We were coming up on the resort at the top of the canyon; the lights of a hotel glimmered into view. The other car had almost pulled even. If I turned, I could have seen his face.

"Hold on." I jammed my foot on the gas. We shot past the pursuer. I thought we might lose him around the approaching bend. Then an explosion of lights, glass, pain.

"MOTHER?" THE word splintered the dark. Jigsaw angles loomed, neither up nor down. "Mother?"

Bits of glass sparkled all around me like translucent stars. I put out a hand to find the ashes, encountered nothing. A sense of suffocation encroached, drawing its hand over my face. Blindly, I kicked and fought, drowning.

"Ssh. Emerson. It's me."

The paleness spoke urgently. As if from a great distance, I recognized her.

Angel took her hand from my mouth. "Are you all right?"

"What happened?"

"We flipped over. Are you hurt?"

I moved my head. Pain shot weakly through my neck and side, but I seemed, miraculously, whole.

"Thank God. We have to get out. Now."

Little P. The gun. Memory came back like a flood of cold water. With difficulty, she unhooked my seat belt.

"Get out on this side," she whispered, kicking splinters of glass from the back window. "Away from the road."

We were out and halfway down the embankment when I stopped.

"The ashes! They're still in the car!" I turned back.

"Leave them!" whispered Angel.

I ignored her.

"Emerson!"—despairing, but she did not stop me.

In the mess of shattered glass and smoke, I found the purse beneath the front seat and gathered it to me with a cold apprehension of temporary grace. If I had lost her; if I had left her there in the dark . . .

Headlights blazed down on the wreckage suddenly. A figure moved against the backlight; a shout went up.

"Run!" screamed Angel.

I slung the purse strap over my shoulder and hurtled after her. Another shout went up behind us.

Slipping, sliding, we went down over the lower embankment. I whipped my cheek on a branch and fell, jarring my shoulder, fell again. The brambles bit at me; I tore myself loose and looked for Angel, who was some distance ahead. The full moon was just rising above the gorge, and by its gathering light I could see her and the brushy, clay-dark terrain that went down and down, all the way to the bottom of the canyon. The brush dropped off, and I could hear the river running mightily below us in the white dark.

"There's a bridge," gasped Angel as I caught up to her. "There's a footbridge down here if I can find it again."

There was a crashing in the bushes above us, a faint halloo. We ran, Angel faltering, while my breath caught in my side. The sound of the river became clearer, if not louder, and all at once the path turned sharply and we were facing an old bridge, frayed rope and rough boards.

"Here!" called Angel. She flew ahead, turned. "Hurry!"

I hung back. Not an ordinary bridge; a relic from another era, made of sisal rope and wood. Some of the planks were already missing, some wearing away. Through the gaps I could see the faint white phosphorescence of the river below. The wind caught the ropes and lifted them, setting the bridge swaying over the chasm. I sank to my knees, gripping the rope rails shakily.

"Don't think about it!" Angel yelled. "Don't look down! Just keep going, one foot at a time! Keep going!"

I put one foot on the first plank, followed by the other. Immediately the wind tossed the bridge violently, and I sank to my knees again, whimpering. *Get up,* I ordered myself. *Get up.*

I raised myself again and continued, agonizingly slow. The rope fibers came off in my hands as I gripped them, and the rotted wood creaked and splintered underfoot. The whitecaps of the river were directly below me now; I looked down and saw them roiling. It must have been half a mile down, black as pitch, and still I could hear the roaring of it. Now there was a darkness. My legs buckled and would not move. I clutched the rope.

Angel was almost at the other end, shouting, "That's it, Emerson, you're almost there, keep going, keep going." I had to find a way to tell her to go on, hurry, without me.

The bridge shuddered and rocked. Someone had reached the foot of the bridge and was making his way toward me, slow but relentless. Sunk down on the rotting footboards, I froze and watched him come with a feeling of fatality. Though there was moonlight,

I could not see his face; he seemed a figure of blank malice—dark, shadowed, foreign, and absolutely unknowable. I twisted my hand tightly in the ropes and moved a few inches toward the opposite shore, my breath rattling, eyes fixed on the approaching fate.

He had picked his way easily over the most treacherous parts of the bridge. Now he paused to gather himself and, with a fury and swiftness that stopped my heart, charged toward me, the faceless blank intent and savage.

A crack, and then he vanished, one of the planks split, falling away.

Angel shrieked. "Emerson!"

Huddled against the ropes, I stumbled forward, the bridge swinging tautly underfoot. I was almost there.

A scraping, a screech of wood giving way. I fell, caught at the remaining plank, and dangled there, legs suspended horribly above the roaring void.

"*Emerson! Emerson!*" Angel's face appeared above me, a face viewed from underwater as you drown.

I twisted, kicked, trying to pull myself back up. Angel shrieked anew; she seemed to be pointing at something farther down the bridge.

"Goddamn it, Angel! Help me!"

Then I saw: my pursuer. He too had caught himself before falling, and hung helpless, gripping the ropes and footboards. For a split second we stared at each other, bound together in horror at the darkness below.

I swung a leg up, hooked it over the rope railing. The other figure shouted, struggled. *Help me*—was that what he was saying?

Save me—was that it? Strange how the words meant nothing to me, not anymore. I cared nothing about mercy, about love, about forgiveness. I only cared to live.

Without warning, the wind lifted the bridge and shook it, howling. My hands slipped. I shrieked as I swung upside down over the river, dangling by one leg. The water rushed overhead now, the patterns of white and dark like the bottom of the sea. Then my enemy— The wind had shaken him loose, and with horror I watched him fall away, spread-eagled, oddly silent. He had so far to fall that he seemed not to be falling at all but flying, released, like a soul wafted gently into the black. Coins tumbled from my pockets.

Angel was edging out onto the bridge sideways, trying to reach me. "Give me your hand!" she shouted.

But just then I felt the ashes slipping; the cord had caught and ripped on a nail. Wildly I grabbed at the purse as the cord unraveled, slipped from my neck. A couple of threads held; the purse dangled, a momentary reprieve, precarious, brief. I groped for the cord.

"Emerson! You have to give me your other hand!" Angel's face strained above me, white and terrified.

Then the threads snapped. The purse disappeared, end over end, winking once at me before the chasm closed up behind her.

I laughed, I think—or was it crying? Angel was screaming at me, "Give me your hand!"

A great wind caught the bridge again, lifting it up and dropping it, and in the danger of being suspended over the void, there was, too, a curious sense of being free.

CHAPTER 25

"DOES IT HURT?" asked Angel. Hesitantly, her fingers traced the blue contusions on my arms and sides.

"No," I said, and it was true. The cuts and bruises, the discolored rope burn—none of it hurt, or at least the pain was distant, as if my body lay far below me while I looked on, both doctor and patient, author and man. I watched Angel's hands remotely in the harsh fluorescent light: tenderness, and caution. Still, I felt nothing. I caught her hand.

"You're tired," I said. "I'm all right. You sleep. It's time to go to bed."

She dabbed the last of the peroxide on my cuts and went into the bathroom, shutting the door.

Water ran in the sink, a civilized sound. I looked around. The Catholic hostel had taken us in without question, bloodied and stunned as we were. And just like that, all traces of the trauma were beginning to fade. The room was clean, spartan: two hard twin beds, an institutional towel, a tattered copy of the Bible. I slipped under the sheets and turned the pillow. A haven for travelers—safe and warm now, but some part of me could not believe in the safety of things anymore. Images I had never seen before kept swarming me like legions of a dark army: a glass of water, shattered violently on the floor; a fire blown out; a clean bed broken by the blast and annihilation of a bomb. The figure dangling from that bridge, begging "Help me"—I had turned my back on him. I had let him die. If love could fail—if it could not protect its citizens from death and forgetting—what chance did objects have?

Angel came out of the bathroom and turned off the light. The clock ticked. Angel stirred once and then was silent. I was glad she could sleep; she had been through enough.

But as I lay awake, the darkness seemed to expand and grow colder. I turned over. I saw the body in the ravine; Little P and his gun; Atticus in his hospital gown; my mother; the white, disingenuous figure of the Buddha on the hilltop, his finger pointed enigmatically up. I turned over again: the body in the ravine; Little P and his gun; Atticus in his helmet; my mother . . .

"Angel?" I said, and, simultaneously, "Emerson?" came from the other bed.

I couldn't see anything as I crossed the room and slid under the covers, but it was all right; it was enough to touch someone tenderly in the anonymous gray, to feel curiosity and compassion in the press of a lip, a mouth. She was crying. In the dark, I fumbled, touching clumsily upon her face and her breast at the same time, so that ever afterward the taste of salt and the hard, hollow sense of pleasure would be linked. Regions I could never name before came clear to me now, humid or dark or musky: the wet, dark portals of some cavern in the sea. It would have been a lie to say that I loved her—but a lie was better than nothing now. Better, perhaps, than love itself. I held her, looking down at her lovely, honest face with sadness and a new humility. In the slit of moonlight through the blinds, her eyes widened with pleasure and astonishment, and I thought, *It is what it is; this is all*. Eventually you learned to play along with the world—to play in tune, and thus make its harmonics resonate, on and on. Adapting, surviving. Living: that was the only kind of immortality there was.

But then all thoughts grew scrambled as I moved awkwardly, faster. At the bright precipice of pleasure, I felt a great heave of vertigo, suspended above the canyon again. In the moment before gravity gathered to pull me downward, something else fell away from me, small but final, flashing like a coin. Inevitably, I let it go, although at the last moment I cried out; I think I said "No!"

Then the world inverted itself, soundless, and when the vertigo cleared, there was just the ticking of the clock again, and the clean white beds. Angel's hand was twisted in my hair. I rested my head on her shoulder and slept. When I dreamt this time, it was about nothing—about a wide, flat road.

IN THE morning, a stripped white sun shone in through the plain blind. I awoke early. Sometime during the night, I had disengaged Angel's arms from around me, and she had withdrawn to the other side of the bed, the sheet pulled up around her waist. Her mouth was open, and she had one hand pressed tightly against her chest, as if she had been hurt or was protecting something in the hollow of her breasts. I leaned over to touch her cheek, but my hand hesitated, passing over her shoulders and neck, and in the end I didn't touch her at all. Was she safe, now? Was I? Little P was gone. Without him, would Poison continue to chase us? I thought of the girls in their airless rooms, trapped and sallow; I thought of the ones he had murdered. No trial for them, no justice.

Hurriedly, I got up and showered, threw on my damp clothes. The sun was almost up now, the small light outside the window strange, yellow, moody but clear. Before I put on my shoes, I went over to the bed again and covered Angel up. I sat looking at her for a moment. I wouldn't take her with me. Better for her to think I'd abandoned her, though my heart broke a little to imagine it. But otherwise she would follow me back to the city, and the danger would begin for her all over again.

I fished the memory key out of my suit pocket, where I had buttoned it in tightly, securely, like a treasure. Indeed, it was the only treasure I had left. In its little green casing, it shone like the future.

Carefully, I put it away, buttoned it up again. It would be lonely, perhaps impossible, to topple the Palace without Angel. They would want the source of the photos, and I would never implicate her. Regardless, I would bring the Palace down: with pictures, with publicity—with a gun, if I had to. But there would be no evasion of the truth this time, no innocence. If my family's only legacy was wrought in evil, I would tear it down.

Out on the shoulder of the road, the sun was emerging from behind the mist, brightening and darkening. I checked the sky, which moved above me with the threat of solemnity and grace. A bird sang two high notes in the black slate landscape. The road was a gray, flat plain, unwritten, like the road in my dream. Unencumbered, I felt a strange lightness of being. My mother was gone, and my father was gone, now my brother too. But somehow the terms of extinction were not what I'd thought they would be.

The bird sang its two notes again and suddenly winged west like a shot across the sky. I turned and followed it as best I could, down the road, walking slowly at first. Then I trotted. Then I began to run. Fast, hard, breathless—for a new day was breaking. I couldn't let it get away.

ACKNOWLEDGMENTS

My deepest gratitude to the following:

To the Taiwan National Endowment for Culture and the Arts, the Fulbright Program, and the Massachusetts Cultural Council for financial support; to Dr. Wu and the folks at the Foundation for Scholarly Exchange in Taipei; to Wendy Lesser for her encouragement and good advice; and to Jin Auh and David Rogers for their tireless enthusiasm and thoughtful editing.

To Ha Nguyen, Amy Lin, Shing-Shing and Anching Lin, and to the Platt family for their love, patience, and friendship.

Most of all, to Stephen Platt, who never lets me forget what I can do.